BLÀS

ROOTS IN THE SOIL

C C HUTTON

BLÀTHS

COPYRIGHT

In memory of my amazing aunt, Agnes Murray, without whom I would never have been able to read, let alone write

FOREWORD

Fàilte/welcome to my fictional community of Blàs set in the spectacular North Highlands of Scotland. Just a wee note before we start. I've included notes at the end of the book on things I thought might interest you. A little about blackenings, foraging and the Dandie Dinmont terrier for example. A recipe for the chocolate, Mela Blàs, can be found there too. If you feel you would have liked me to include more, drop me a line and let me know. I would love to hear from you. Blàs Three should be out next year. I'm working on a title for it now. It will have a sea element. Thank you for allowing me to share Blàs, its people, customs and stories with you.

Ceitidh xx

1

"I'm glad we decided to do this together. I was fed up racing you to the patch," said Auntie Lottie.

Our hands were the colour purple, not with the cold but with the deep autumn hue from the bramble juice. Somehow, Auntie Lottie and I had never quite returned to our previous relationship of almost niece and pretend aunt. Not blood relatives, we had awarded each other these family titles unconsciously when my mum had died. Auntie Lottie had been, after all, one of Mum's best friends.

The fact that we had worked together on many language courses throughout the Highlands over the past year, had helped us move our friendship onto a more equal footing. We had established ourselves as quite a partnership in the Gaelic world. I wondered, at times, whether this was how an agent or manager would feel, as I once more booked and arranged courses around Auntie Lottie's availability.

"Well, it looks like someone else has been using our patch. Or maybe it is just a bad year. There don't seem to be as many as usual."

For as far back as I could remember this area has been full of long, sharp thorns protecting the juicy brambles from people like us. The yield had always been reasonably good, even when we were both picking separately.

"Maybe it is finally growing too old. Perhaps, we should look for another area." We stopped as one, heads tilted, listening.

"Did you hear that?" Auntie Lottie asked. Branches were cracking underfoot, and the sound of children's voices could be heard. It only took a few moments before we recognised the English accents. These children were either tourists or, if I wasn't mistaken, the Smiths, a new family who had recently moved to the community. The bairns emerged from the trees into the clearing and stopped in confusion.

"What are you doing in our den?" Fawn stood with her hands on her hips, looking accusingly toward Auntie Lottie and myself.

"Yep, you are way too old to be playing in the woods, you should leave it to the children." Stag placed himself directly behind his sister.

"Don't be rude, what would Dad say? Sorry, we just came here to play." Swallow, their older sister materialised behind her siblings.

"No, this is our place! We found it, so they should move. We are not leaving." The twins swung round to face their sister.

"Just ignore them. They thought they had found a new den. Do these woods belong to you then?" Swallow looked around, ignoring the twins as they glared at her. Before we could respond, more bashing and thrashing could be heard as their brother, Lark, threw himself clear of a tangle of branches.

"Told ya I would find you all. And I stopped and had a feast on these berries too. Oh… morning." Blood trickled down his cheek from a cut courtesy of the bushes he had scrambled through. His dark hair was full of leaves and branches, while his clothes were dishevelled and ripped in places. He ran a hand over the top of his head, picking out foliage nonchalantly, while throwing a disappointed look toward his siblings when he registered there were adults in the woods. Like countless other children before them, they had obviously felt these woods belonged to them alone.

Even though they had only been in the village a short time, they had made their presence felt. The twins had mostly been allowed to roam about unsupervised when not in school. Swallow and Lark could be found with the established group of children who ranged together far-and-wide around the area. The Smith children in general were a tight little group of their own – the older siblings looking after their younger ones. The woods would have called to them as they had to generations before them. A natural playpark, a place to leave home and adults behind, to live out adventures from their imagination and try out new things without adult supervision. Coilltean Sìthiche, as this wood was known locally, was not owned by the village. No one remembered who legally possessed this piece of land. It was assumed one of the many absentee landlords who held great swathes of the Highlands must be the rightful owner. No one knew for sure, and as long as they didn't interfere with our lives, our foraging or our fun, then we didn't really care who techni-cally owned them.

"These woods belong to the fairies." Auntie Lottie spread her arms wide. "So be careful. Never come here on your own or at night… or we may never see you again. They will swap you for their own folk."

Swallow and Lark smirked as the twins squirmed.

"Are there really fairies. I mean real live ones, not the made-up ones in books?" Stag's eyes were staring around the clearing.

"Don't be so soft." Lark ruffled his younger brother's hair affectionately. "She's just making it up to stop you coming in here on your own at night. Do you think I would be seen dead in here if there were fairies? I would never live it down – me and fairy people, that's not happening,"

"Lark is right. There are no fairies here."

Fawn and Stag looked at their brother and sister, then at

Auntie Lottie who nodded and smiled at them. Two totally confused children. She was loving this.

"Do you know what these woods are called? I bet you don't?"

"Don't tell us," said Lark scornfully. "Let me guess… Fairy Woods. It is, isn't it? It has to be Fairy Woods."

"Well, you are more or less right. It's called Coilltean Sìthiche – that's sheeich; it's Gaelic for Fairy Woods. They've been here since the beginning of time. So be careful. Don't fall down any rabbit holes and stay away from any tunnels they might lead you down. Some of them go all the way down to the fairy kingdom. We're off to make some fairy wine. Enjoy your brambles." I followed Auntie Lottie out of the clearing and back into the cover of the cool trees. At least two pairs of wide blue eyes watched us depart as we became swallowed up in the shadows.

"Those poor bairns. You'll have been given them nightmares. You'll have their father coming to your door, asking you to apologise." I turned toward home.

"Rap, not a bit of it. He just lets them wander aimlessly. You forget, Stroma, they are not from around here. They don't know the danger hidden under all that foliage. You were brought up to respect the dangers, even if you didn't know it at the time. If this stops them getting into bother, well that would be just fine. But I have a feeling we may well be pulling them out of some misadventure before long. They can't be left to run wild without any supervision when they are completely unaware of how dangerous it can be here."

"Well, I hope you're right, Auntie Lottie. But from what I've seen of the twins, at least, you may have just whetted their appetites for an adventure."

We left the woods behind as the afternoon drew to a close, and shadows began deepening. I hadn't really considered the dangers the woods posed for the unsuspecting, until Auntie Lottie had mentioned it. As we had grown up, we had, through trial and error, and under the watchful eye of the community become aware – almost without being conscious – of the hazards around and about.

Many pitfalls were waiting to trip up the unsuspecting in the countryside. Some we all chose to ignore, like McPhail's Hill with its horrendous machinery at the bottom waiting to impale you after a sledge run. Others nobody ignored – like the changeable weather that could take you unawares, and which peat bogs hid dangerous depths. I hoped Auntie Lottie's tactics would work, but only time would tell.

Months. It felt like I hadn't spoken to anyone for months. In actual fact, it was just a few days, but the wind and rain had harassed and hassled everyone in doors. People who ventured out raced around bent-up, shoulders hunched. No friendly faces could be seen as scarves were pulled up with hats rammed down. We resembled masked alien beings, without faces. Lashes blinked away water that beat and battered into hoods. Eyes took the full force of the brisk wind and rain.

Five days of this continual torrent, and at last the wind had dropped allowing us to stand tall. Rain still fell, but it was the light mountain drizzle that soaks everything in a nice considerate manner. Doors opened, and the inhabitants started to emerge and congregate in huddles to pass the time of day. Now it was news that poured down and seeped through the community.

I had watched Maureen swiz around in her wheelchair since eerie first light, avoiding as many deep puddles as possible. Old Tam, and his rather smelly but faithful ancient sheepdog Shep, had been one of the few who had continued to venture out during the stormy days. Neither one seemed to have noticed the lashing wind and rain. They had plied their way to their port of call, the local shop, and back every morning like the loyal puffers of bygone years. Steaming their steady course regardless of what the weather could throw at them, providing the only splash of colour among the numerous shades of grey seen throughout the storm.

Old Tam had finally succumbed to wearing a waterproof coat. His usual tweed cap was now held firmly in place by a hood. As the rain had raced down the window panes obscuring and distorting the images outside, a flash of bright orange could be detected chugging past. On Old Tam's port side, the steady roll of a shorter vessel, encased in the same bright orange, could be seen. Old Tam was the only person who could have persuaded Shep into anything that resembled any form of clothing. Morag, Old Tam's granddaughter, had tried, as the summer had turned into autumn, to cajole Old Tam himself into wearing something a bit more weatherproof, but to no avail. Eventually, she had gone for his Achilles heel.

"What about Shep then? He's not getting any younger, the poor old dog. It's not good for his joints to get cold and wet. He needs a bit of help to see out the worst of the weather, and there is no way he is going to let me or anyone else put something sensible on him."

"Eez got a guid thick coat eezsel. Eez does nae need an airy-fairy dug coat. Ee'd look glaikit, eh be that embarrassed tae tak em oot so eh wid. Eez's a dug fae goodness sake. Nae sel-respectin dug wid been seen deid in a coat."

"But grandad, it's not for fashion you are doing this. He's getting old and frail, and so is his once thick hair. Look how he limps about. It's just to give him a bit of protection and keep him warm. He doesn't have to wear it when the weather is dry. No one would see you when it's that bad; no one notices what you have on in that kind of weather. I'm sure you could persuade old Shep if you put a decent coat on too."

It was true, not many of the villagers would have noticed if the rainwear had been a subtle blue or black. But as soon as his son knew he could get his dad into something that would keep him warm and dry, he had gone looking for the best he could get. It had resulted in a fluorescent padded jacket that could have kept a North Pole explorer warm. It probably could have been spotted from there as well. This meant that both Old Tam and Shep could be seen through any kind of weather. We hoped now that if old Shep went on a walkabout on his own, as he appeared to be doing more often, he would be found so much quicker.

I now watched the old man and his dog out the window. Maureen had stopped Old Tam's progress, and both had been deep in conversation for ages. Maureen was nodding as Old Tam pointed back up the road. Old Shep stood or more correctly leant against his side, waiting patiently. Even he knew there was no hurrying these two when they got together. Obviously, they had a piece of juicy gossip to be dissected. I dragged my eyes back to the computer. *Concentrate*, I told myself.

The allure of talking face-to-face with another human being was becoming too strong. The fact that I was considering going out in the rain to listen to what Maureen had to say proved this. An hour longer was all I could do. Even the rain was better than this. Maureen by now would have had her fill of gossip and would be off to disseminate what she had learnt from Old Tam. Grabbing my coat, I swung open the door. Instinctively I ducked, avoiding the walking stick baring down toward me.

"Ah, Stroma, just the person I was looking for. Ellen's, thirty minutes, and bring your notebook." And she was gone. *What now?* I wondered. Had someone got flooded and needed help or, worse, run out of tea? I had been too long inside; I needed to get out, stretch my legs and clear my head before I was fit for any sort of human company.

I made my way down toward the woods. Before I got that far, children's voices could be heard laughing among the sodden trees. The Smith children had become firmly established within the community. Auntie Lottie's attempt at keeping them out of the woods hadn't worked very well. It had become their favourite playground. Fawn and Stag were always being pulled back home by their older brother and sister when hunger took over their need to play. The children could be heard at all times of the day and night running about wild and free.

Mushed-up leaves squelched under my feet. The bright coppers, rusts, and golds smashed into a dirty, muddy brown beneath my boots. Water dripped everywhere, including down my jacket, so I turned for Ellen's home which I knew would be warm and dry.

"Are you looking for fairies too?" Stag's head popped out from the side of a big chestnut tree.

"It's too wet for fairies today. They wouldn't be able to fly – their wings would get too wet." I answered.

"Oh, we didn't fhink of that."

"Should you not be getting back for something to eat? Your dad will be looking for you."

"Nah, he won't. He's too busy. He's off for a confab, he says anyways."

"It's not a confab, you idiot. It's a confaburince wif them others." Fawn appeared beside her brother.

"Well, watch you don't get too wet, and mind it's slippy hereabouts. See you later then." Leaving the woods, I noticed someone had dumped a sign face down in the mud. No doubt Paul of the Sheds would clear it away in the general tidy-up that would happen later.

The familiar smell of homebaking soothed my soul when I entered Ellen's house, instantly evoking happy memories of childhood. I heard familiar voices as I walked toward the kitchen. Paul's low rumble was followed by Auntie Lottie's laughter. What appeared a small gap in conversation was probably Mary having her say in her soft lilt. I opened the door just as Maureen's intense tone took over the proceedings. The smell of coffee and cakes barely covered the wet, musky odour of Old Tam and Shep.

"Ah, here she is at last. Come away in. There is tea in the pot. Right Rap, what was it you were saying?"

Rap was there. That was a new addition I hadn't expected. He had worked his way well into the community if he was now included in this circle. He took up the refrain.

"Well, I just think we should do something. I don't know what my children would do if they couldn't get into the woods. That's why I'm here really. This lady here"—he pointed to Auntie Lottie—"informed me about your meeting, so I thought I should come along and offer my support."

I heard a loud sniff from Maureen. Auntie Lottie appeared to have out-positioned Maureen with regards to integrating herself with the Smith family. As they both knew only too well, the path to more information about these new residents was to befriend them at every turn. Maureen may well have delivered the latest news around the district, but she had lost an opportunity that her rival had grabbed. Auntie Lottie had been the one to invite them into our inner circle.

"Okay, so that's the situation with the woods," Ellen said as if I had been in the meeting from the beginning.

"Excuse me, but why are we talking about the woods?" I helped myself to tea and a slice of lemon sponge cake.

"Oh." Maureen squealed with glee. "I forgot to tell you. I bumped into Old Tam and Shep here this morning, and he confirmed what I had heard."

I obliged her by saying, "And that is?"

"Coilltean Sìthiche, the woods are up for sale." She paused for effect. "Because the owner died."

"That's sad," I dutifully interjected, though in truth, I had no idea who the owner was. "And why is that important?"

"Apparently, it was that old rogue Campbell Fraser who owned them. Remember he died last year? Well, it turns out he owned all that land around Coilltean Sìthiche. Imagine him living in all that poverty in that run-down old croft, and he actually owned all of Coilltean Sìthiche."

"And?"

"Well, his heir, some cousin or other abroad, of course, wants to sell it and get the money. He has no intention of ever visiting Scotland, so he just wants to be rid of it and pocket the money. He obviously has no soul. My mother knew his mother of course. Strange woman – she had no soul either." Of course Maureen was acquainted with the family. She knew everyone within the district. Really she should have been making a fortune drawing up family trees. Instead, over the last few years, Maureen had invested her savings and her gregarious soul into qualifying as a humanist. In her official capacity, she now had access to the records of any new babies in the area, as she could hold naming ceremonies. She also saw the actual records, confirmation in writing of who was related to whom. She knew firsthand who was getting married, and to which family and their family ties. All these connections, relationships and family histories she already knew of course. Now, however, she had all the relevant paperwork and authority to confirm it all. Not merely hearsay, gossip and rumour came out of Maureen's mouth – not anymore. Now she had the power to back it up. Maureen was about to turn her hand to performing funeral services. At least she would have a good grasp of who the deceased was before she officially met the bereaved families. Although there must be a fair few worried what she might divulge about their dearly departed at their funerals.

"Well, what can we do? None of us have the money to buy it. Who would want it anyway? Maybe any new owners will keep it the same. No point in getting all worked up for nothing."

"Now, Stroma, we know you don't like change, but it is highly unlikely the woods will stay the same. But you are right, perhaps we should wait until we know more." Ellen passed the milk to me for my tea while the others speculated among themselves on who might buy Coilltean Sìthiche, and what they would do with it.

I was just wondering why I had been called to attend –

surely, it wasn't just for my company – when Ellen continued. "You may have noticed Mary isn't here tonight."

I had. Her absence was strange. Mary was generally at every meeting held in Ellen's kitchen, regardless of the subject. I hoped she wasn't ill. We were all looking forward to celebrating her eighty-first birthday. She may have been nearly fifty years older than me, but she was no less my friend despite our age gap. Looking around, I realised age had never been an issue to friendships in the community. There sat Ellen, Auntie Lottie and Maureen, all in their fifties, and yet, we were all part of the same friendship group.

"Stroma, Stroma, are you listening? I ran into one of the members of the ceilidh band, and he seemed a bit vague about the party on Saturday."

Well, that explained why Mary wasn't here and I was. Ellen wouldn't have wanted Mary to hear there was a problem with the arrangements for her dance, and since it had been my job to book the band, Ellen wanted me here.

"Ach, I wouldn't worry about that. Mike is the only one who really keeps the others right. I spoke to him yesterday. Everything is fine, they'll turn up."

"Well, if you are sure..." Ellen paused only for a moment. "Going back to the subject of the woods before we finish for the night. I think we should recheck where we stand regarding cash flow and the Development Trust, just in case we need to step in quickly. Stroma, I'm sure you have that all in hand, but maybe take a wee look, and you can update us at the next meeting."

Just like Ellen, covering all possibilities. "Okay," I agreed, "that's no problem. I've still got a couple of cheques to bank yet, but if there is no rush, I can get that done next week."

I may have tempted fate by my lack of urgency, as events were about to overtake us.

3

"*Where is she?*" The collective murmurs drifted up into the hall's refurbished ceiling. Auntie Lottie's voice rose above the crowds.

"I told you they would come. Informed them myself it was a great way to meet everyone." Since her permanent return to Blàs, Auntie Lottie had firmly established her position as bearer of the latest news. Now, she constantly vied with her old school-friend, Maureen, to be the first to filter it around the community. It had taken her only a day to integrate herself with the new family in the village. Helped, no doubt, by our visit to the bramble patch when she met the children. She was then able to follow that up with inviting their dad at Ellen's house. By that time, of course, she knew their family name – the not unusual: Smith. Although to be honest, in Blàs, the name Smith was rather unique. Their first names were far more distinctive. Rap used this as the shortened version of Ralph. Neither was a common name in the area, but then again neither was Swallow, Lark, Fawn or Stag. Auntie Lottie had surmised enough to guess their family situation to an extent, and then she had invited them all to Mary's birthday party at the hall.

Not to be outdone, Maureen had already discovered most of

that important information. Rap and family had not stood a chance. Maureen had made a beeline for their home, producing a honey layered cake as the entrance fee. Rap had been interrogated mercilessly, until sated, Maureen had left, feeling smug and ready to belch her new-found information around the community.

She hadn't thought, however, of inviting them along to the celebrations and, thus, was feeling a bit peeved. Auntie Lottie, on the other hand, had been way more subtle. She had no intention of baking anything to wheedle out the details from the new inhabitants of Rose Cottage. She had gone straight to the source of all indiscretion within the family – five-year-old twins, Fawn and Stag. Desperate to outdo each other, they had filled her with every morsel of information they could think of and left Auntie Lottie to digest it all.

"Rap, come away in; you've already met Ellen. You will have worked out by now that, if you need anything arranged, she is the one to ask. Ellen, this is Rap's eldest, Swallow, then it's Lark. And the twins, Fawn and Stag, you will have heard all about." Maureen was quick to reaffirm her rightful place as town crier and proponent of all local gossip.

Three of the most important women in my life crowded around. Ellen, Maureen and Auntie Lottie had all been in school together along with my mum. A formidable force, apart or together. After my parents had died, they had supported me and my decision to become my younger sister Iona's guardian. I would never have coped without them. However, those days of being responsible for Iona were well past. My mum's friends were now my own. Although they did behave like many blood relatives at times, in that they felt it was their right to interfere in my life. I thanked my stars that I still had close friends of my own age who were not so inclined.

"We brought this as a birthday present. Where is the leading lady? Is she here?" Rap looked around the hall. Mary had never been a slave to the clock, or any other device that could tell her when to be where.

"I wouldn't bother looking too hard, she hasn't made it yet, but if we held up starting the party to wait for her presence, we could still be waiting at midnight. Is that nettle wine you have there?" asked Maureen.

"We made it two years ago, the last batch we all made together. So it should be good. I'm more into nettle beer myself now. Although what with us flitting up here, we didn't make any this year," replied Rap.

"Well, I wouldn't worry about that. There's plenty hereabouts who will have homemade beer of one description or another. If you are lucky, you may get a chance to sample some tonight." Maureen smiled at Rap.

"If it's beer you are after, I know just the man. Paul, Paul, can you come here a moment and bring some of that wicked beer you brought with you?" Auntie Lottie pulled the advantage back and signalled over to Paul MacQuin. He was better known as Paul of the Sheds in the community, due to owning a wide range of sheds, barns and outbuildings in the area. Many males envied him so many places to 'hide away' in, as they saw it.

In reality, Paul needed some of the sheds to store the equipment he used for his many jobs. These ranged from inshore fisherman to providing a variety of rescue services, including those by sea and land. Paul of the Sheds was also famed as an expert brewer, although this wasn't one of his official jobs. No, it was only a hobby, a serious and competitive one, but just a hobby all the same. Or at least that was what he said. As far as anyone could prove, he didn't actually make any money from it. Rumour had it, however, that there were a few hotels and B & Bs around the area that offered 'craft beers' which tasted remarkably like Paul MacQuin's brews. He didn't like the thought of the taxman homing in on his illicit gains, so he was always going to brush away any suggestions that it was himself who produced that beer.

Paul of the Sheds wandered over, beer in hand. The men immediately engaged in conversation around recipes, methods and what was good about homebrewing. Rap was probably relieved to get away from Auntie Lottie and Maureen's constant probing. Dismissed from their conversation, Auntie Lottie turned her attention to the missing birthday guest.

"For goodness sake, Ellen, should we send Stroma off to fetch Mary?" It wasn't every octogenarian who had their personal photographer at their birthday. However, when Ellen's partner Helen had offered to create a record of her birthday, Mary hadn't been about to turn that gift down. "Surely Helen has got enough pictures of her. Really, she should have been here by *now*." I noticed Auntie Lottie wasn't prepared to miss out on any of the celebrations to retrieve the birthday girl herself.

"I'm sure Helen will take just the right amount. You know fine well it will be Mary holding the whole thing up," Ellen replied.

"Can we go to get her too?" Fawn had pulled her brother toward me. "We heard she lives in a cave and is ancient..." Before I could formulate an answer, a buzz of excited voices could be heard from the hallway. The ceilidh band had started to play 'Happy Birthday', as the older generation gathered by the door. Swallow and Lark had removed themselves from our wee grouping and were pushing their way forward to see this 'celebrity' who they had heard so much about. Maureen had strategically placed herself at the head of the queue and wasn't letting anyone pass, never mind how small and nimble they were. Her wheelchair blocked any such moves. She would be the first to finally welcome her friend to her party. Paul had moved off, and I found myself next to Rap.

"So how are you all finding the place then? It's not the warmest time of the year to be moving here. But at least you don't have to contend with the midgies." I was babbling, I knew. It came from a horrible belief that both Maureen and Auntie Lottie would have already informed him that I was single. They had both told me on separate occasions during the day that Rap was a widower and so, in their eyes, available for me. Even Mary had joined in. "Just right for you dear," had been her contribution.

A man with four children in tow was not my idea of a good catch. However, as far as the team of Mary, Maureen and Auntie Lottie was concerned, any new male was a good catch for me. Their ideas and mine did not match in any way or form. It was not that he was repugnant. He was okay if you liked the slightly long-haired, long-limbed, dishevelled look, but I wasn't on the market. Not that they knew that.

"Hard to say, we've only been here a short while. So far so good. Look would you mind if I sort of mingled. I'd like to meet as many people now as I can. Should save on all the visitors we could get… if the last few days are anything to go by. Or at least, that's what Maureen and the other one said."

Ouch! I was so glad Auntie Lottie was too busy speaking to Paul to hear. I felt I should warn him to dismiss Auntie Lottie at his peril, but then, I was fairly sure he would find that out for himself quickly enough.

Mary had finally made it into the hall and had been greeted by many of the community. Music soared around the rafters as the partygoers were invited to dance the 'Dashing White Sergeant'. People good-naturedly grabbed the shyer dancers and led them onto the floor. The dance was enjoyed to the rhythm of a reel and required two groups of three to face each other at the start. Stag and Fawn were scooped up by Auntie Lottie who instructed them on the steps and movements required. Swallow and Lark had looked a bit shocked at first but had agreed to accompany others onto the floor. Only the infirm, the birthday girl and those busy catching up with each other were left behind while the dancers and musicians began their symbiotic relation-ship. After ten minutes of laughter, swirling and stomping, the twin performances came to an end.

Everyone was breathing heavily, the musicians grabbed their

pints – supplied of course by Paul – and the participants collapsed on the chairs spread out along the hall.

A hush developed while Maureen took the floor. She had reluctantly taken on the mantle from Angus, our bard. Although she was more than comfortable spreading 'news' around the area in small intimate groups, she was less happy delivering stories, fables and poems to a larger audience.

❧

"You see, Stroma, I am more a factual kind of person," she said, very straight-faced. "I'm not that creative. I'm okay with the historical parts, but this delivering stories in a dramatic way… well, it's just not me."

Auntie Lottie had sputtered into her tea, Mary had giggled behind hers and wiped a tear from her eye. Maureen had misread this as grief at the thought of Mary's much-loved husband, our bard. "Oh, I am right sorry, Mary. I didn't mean to upset you. Angus was such a talent. Nobody could possibly do his job justice."

"Not to worry, Maureen. I'm happy to know someone has taken it on. It would be so much worse if all his stories had been lost to us."

This had all taken place in Mary's kitchen months ago. Although Maureen's delivery was rather painful to watch, she was still the most suitable to tell our community's stories. Her knowledge of people's family trees and our many traditions was unsurpassed. We could only hope her delivery got better over time.

❧

Maureen stationed her wheelchair in the middle of the hall and wiped her hands on a towel before she delved into a poem at a rate of knots. She finished out of breath, red in the face, and gave an enormous sigh. Maureen had managed to mention Angus briefly within the poem. The only rhythm she had achieved was one reminiscent of a runaway train gaining speed. As to eliciting a peel of laughter at the conclusion… well, it was more a collective gasp of bewilderment. The initial relief the community had felt that someone was willing to take over as bard was diminishing at greater speed with each awkward delivery that Maureen gave. At least now though, Angus could be mentioned with affection instead of sorrow.

"Mum would have loved that." Swallow was standing next to her dad with her arm around his waist. I just stopped myself from saying, *Really? Didn't she like poetry then?* before Maureen joined us. Lark was hovering nearby surrounded by new friends who had warmed to his quick charm. It was easy to see why it hadn't taken him that long to become an accepted member of the children's community.

"Come on, you lot. Let me introduce you to the birthday girl. Here, Mary, look what they brought you." Maureen ushered Rap and his family over toward Mary.

"Happy birthday, Mary. I hope you don't mind us gate-crashing your party. Come on, kids, at least wish her a happy birthday." Rap turned back to his children.

Mumbles of happy birthday could be heard from the eldest two who peered out from under long-fringed, dark hair.

"God, you look really old. How old *are* you?" Two sets of enquiring blue eyes arrowed in on Mary.

"Oh, how nice, nettle wine. I haven't had that in years. My Angus used to make it at the start of summer. He was more into nettle beer come the end. The more the merrier I always say. That is friends and family, not wine and beer." Mary laughed. "Although I can be partial to both."

"Really, are you a hundred? Lark said you were, but I don't believe him. I fink you are older. What age are you?" Stag persisted.

"Now, you know you shouldn't ask a lady her age. But

seeing as it is my birthday, and you could easily read it from my birthday cake over there, I see no harm in telling you." Before Mary had even finished her sentence, the twins ran over to the table to inspect the cake to see for themselves just how ancient Mary was.

A disappointed voice could be heard echoing around the hall.

"But you are only eighty-one. Fhat's not anywhere near a hundred."

"You can still share my cake with me though, can't you? Though you might prefer a chocolate crispy first, and there are loads of tasty things to eat before we cut my cake. Go on, help yourself – you are a growing laddie after all." Mary started to fill a plate to hand to Stag.

This was Mary, the way she had been from as far back as I could remember. Children warmed to her. She had this knack for making each one feel extra special. Nobody could resist her bidding. Once subjected to her considerable charm, it was difficult to say no to any of her requests. Half the grown-up community around Blàs had ended up in all sorts of trouble and schemes by helping her out, myself included.

The band geared up for another chance to encourage the revellers to dance around the hall faster than they could down any more drinks. This hall, we had fundraised for, had replaced the old Victorian icehouse that we had previously used for community events.

We now had warm, children-friendly toilets, no blast of ice-cold air when you left the main room, a mouse-free kitchen and a venue we were all proud of.

An old folks' club was held once a week throughout winter, while soup and sandwich lunches were held all year round. There had been that time too when Auntie Lottie had run her rather peculiar hairdressing salon from the premises. And a few other local weddings had taken place within its walls since Agnes' that first year.

We had no idea, as we once more enjoyed our new hall, how

important it would turn out to be that we had that experience under our belts of coming together as a community to fundraise. When we first formed the Development Trust, it had not only led to our hall being renovated but also to the building of new houses for rent. All that project managing, as it turned out, had only been the practice run.

4

M y phone was ringing. Good. Fine, now I could go back
to sleep... Help! My phone was ringing. I fumbled
about, my eyes still glued shut, until the smooth rectangle fitted
exactly into my palm

"Hmm," my brain and mouth just about managed between
them. My ears became aware of the howling wind and thundering rain assaulting the windows.

"Stroma, thank goodness. Stroma, are you awake? It's the
bairns, Rap's bairns, they are missing." Auntie Lottie's words felt
like a bucket of ice-water had surged over my head and down
my body, instantly waking me from my drunk-like mode.

"What happened, where are they?" Okay, so maybe not quite
as wide awake as I had thought. I had already jumped out of bed
and was doing the one-handed dance around the room.
Attempting to dress, while still holding the phone.

"We are setting up a search party. They have been out all
night. Everyone who can is meeting up at the hall in twenty
minutes. Ellen and Mary are already phoning around for help to
make hot drinks and food for all those taking part. Paul is coor-
dinating, and the police have been informed, but they are too far

away to do much tonight. Oh God, what if it's my fault? Please hurry, Stroma."

A second of stillness before the sound of the weather battered against my window again. *Who would want to be out on a night like this?* The thought trickled through my brain. Those poor children! I hoped they were at least sheltered.

Fifteen minutes later, complete with good walking boots, a high-vis jacket and the rest of the paraphernalia needed for an evening search, I was ready. Warm hat, gloves on, chocolate to keep my energy and mood up and, of course, phone in pocket, I marched up to the meeting point. I tugged at my hat to check my torch was firmly attached. Other figures similarly attired were making their way into the hall. Even in that short distance, it was obvious protective clothing was needed. Driving rain combined with the freezing wind would chill even the best dressed on short journeys.

On entering the hall, I immediately started to boil. Outdoor conditions called for layers of warm, dry clothing, few of which were appropriate for indoors. The search party was slowly melting into the floor in our combined layers. Paul was busy delegating jobs and organising groups. Rap, who normally appeared to walk around in his own world with not a care in the world, had aged at least ten years since I had run into him the day before.

He had laughed good-naturally as he trudged back homeward, laden with yet more bags of provisions. "Bloody kids, I can't keep them in food at the moment. Spend half my time walking backward and forward to this damn shop."

All resemblance of nonchalance had disappeared from his countenance. His hand continued to rub his head back and forth resulting in his hair sticking up on end and highlighting the strain on his face. As he paced, he pleaded with Paul's back to hurry things along.

"What if they have gone fairy hunting? I shouldn't have made up that story." Auntie Lottie whispered in my ear.

"There is no way Swallow or Lark believe in fairies. Don't blame yourself. Look, go and talk to Rap – he looks like he could do with a friend right now. He'll be desperate to get this search started, but you know how long this stage takes. Get him a cup of tea or something."

"Yes, you're right of course. This is not about me or what I said. Of course the other two don't believe; they never would have gone on a fairy hunt. What am I thinking?" Auntie Lottie muttered the latter to herself.

She appeared unusually flustered. Giving her something to do would help control all her considerable nervous energy. In truth, I was barely containing my own fear. Anyone lost on a night like would give us reason to worry, but children... I pushed my concerns down and forced myself to focus on what needed to be done. Adding to the already high levels of anxiety wouldn't help anyone. I turned again to Auntie Lottie,

"Nobody thinks clearly – apart from Paul – at a time like this."

"Yes, you're right. Darling Paul." Auntie Lottie shot him what could only be regarded as an affectionate look. Was there something going on between them that I hadn't, or rather the community at large hadn't, picked up on? Surely not, his reputation as a womaniser was widely known. For that reason alone, Auntie Lottie wouldn't go near him. Maybe she was just grateful he was there taking command.

Eventually, just after 7.00 a.m. when the night was drifting away to allow the light in, we were almost ready to go. Paul had taken the time to speak to Rap, Auntie Lottie, Old Tam and myself about where we had last seen the children, and if we knew what areas of the woods they normally frequented. Rap was unable to remember the names of any of the local bairns his children played with. Thankfully, Karen, one of the primary school teachers and one of my best friends from school, supplied Paul of the Sheds with a few possibilities. Others in the community had come forward with their own information. Everything had been written down to hand over to the police once they arrived.

Areas highlighted on a map showed where the children had been spotted playing. One group of searchers were sent to the beach to check for any sightings. Our groups were given instructions on how to go about a coordinated search of Coilltean Sìthiche. Rap, although relieved to finally see some movement on the search side, was not happy.

"But I've already been down the beach and in the woods. They wouldn't have hidden from me. They are not there. I would have seen them. We've got to find them, Paul. I lost their mum. I can't lose them too. I should have taken better care of them. I shouldn't have let them play on their own. But that's the way we agreed we would raise them. I promised her, you see. I promised her I would let them be free. I promised, and now I've lost them. What am I going to do?" Rap was distraught.

"We'll find them, Rap. The police and will be here in the next few hours. Unfortunately, DJ and his scent dogs are out on another shout. If we haven't found them by the time he returns, then his dogs will. They have never failed us yet. So we have to be careful that we don't destroy any trails. But given your bairn's ages and the time of the year, we can't afford to wait – we have to start now. We've had a phone call from Inbhirasgaidh. They are organising to have their people out too. It's only experienced rescuers I can afford to let into the woods until the police get here. The rest will have to stick to main roads and the beach area far enough away from any swell. We simply can't risk anyone's life." Paul of the Sheds was experienced with dealing with worried relatives and wasn't going to let Rap's obvious fear control the search. He relented enough though to allow Rap to attach himself to our group, mainly because he couldn't trust him not to go tramping off on his own and maybe destroying any clues as to the whereabouts of his children.

We trudged our way up toward the woods. The sound of our marching boots dulled the noise of the wind. It had calmed a little as it often did at break of day, but still the rain fell. I slipped on the wet ground as I fumbled to put on my head torch. Fallen leaves, broken branches and sticks added to the almost icy effect as we took our first steps into the forest. We fanned out when we reached our designated starting point.

A small wire fence had been erected, leaving the villagers in no doubt that things had changed. These woods may have been explored, used and generally loved by the villagers, but we didn't own them. The fence was a statement, an attempt for the new owner to claim his rights to this living wood. Some villagers had already broken and stamped on this barrier to let their feelings be known about who they believed had a right to ramble in Coilltean Sìthiche. *These are our woods*, it declared. They couldn't be shut off from the community simply by fence posts and some wire. As if to confirm this thought, I almost tripped over the 'for sale' sign that had been pulled out once more and trodden into the earth. The warm embrace that I felt every time I put a foot inside this beautiful place was still there despite the worry and the weather. Trees offered some protection from the still biting wind, but the swaying in the top-most branches warned us all that it hadn't given up.

Underfoot had become more treacherous the further in we went as rivers of water flowed along the paths and tracks used by walkers and cyclists alike. Every so many steps, we would all stop, someone would call out the children's names and we would listen. All that was heard back was the rising wind, and as dawn broke, there was a calm before the wind asserted itself once more. Branches, rain and our own blood thumped around our bodies, deafening our ears to the sound of children's voices. After a collective sigh, we gathered our breaths and carried on.

Stick to the job, don't think about how cold, wet and miserable it is, or how long the children could survive in this cold. Don't think the worst, don't even go there. Just keep going, one foot in front of the other. They must be alive; they are resourceful children. I was sure others in the party were having similar thoughts. Swallow and Lark would look out for their siblings, but they were young themselves. *Please, please, let them be okay.*

We leant forward as we trudged uphill. Water droplets sprayed us from the frothing torrent that the river had become. Rocks and stones were slippery from both the rain and the swollen spate. Deafened by the water thundering past, we had to revert to hand signals. Our party was engulfed by the crashing noise, then suddenly, silence. Everything had stopped, a brief interlude, as we turned a corner of a rocky outlet and found some shelter from the clamouring elements.

"If they crossed, they would have had to climb up here first. I think we should push on until we get as far as Sìth-bhrugh. They could be sheltering there."

No one wanted to mention the raging flood we had just passed or the low possibility of the children navigating it safely. It was too upsetting to even contemplate.

"It's a long way for wee ones to be walking," Jill said.

"We don't know how long they have been on the move. I had business in Inbhirasgaidh; the twins were in bed before I even left. I should have known they were up to something by that alone. They never go to be bed without a fight. I did a rough check on them when I got back, but they all seemed asleep, huddled under covers. I didn't want to disturb them so went off to bed myself then checked them again later. The twins normally have legs and arms slung out of their covers, and I need to wrap them up or they will be through to me looking for warmth. But they were all still huddled up. So, I went across to check properly and found they had stuffed their beds with clothes. None of them were there. All four were gone. So, you see, they could have been walking for hours."

"Come on, you heard their dad, we need to push on before we go back and get debriefed and pass it all on to the authorities." Paul of the Sheds strode on along the path, and we turned as one and followed him into the storm again, only now we were sheltered a bit more by the rock formations. The slippery mud was thinner, but the leaves still made it difficult to keep our footing on the track. Incessant rain slowly turned to a light drizzle that calmed and soothed the nerves. Dark grey clouds became silvery tipped, and the prospect of the sun finally breaking through became a welcome possibility.

We tramped on, keeping our eyes and ears open for any sound or sight that might indicate that the children had been this way. Nothing worth noting was found. We needed to turn back soon and find out if it was feasible to get hold of dogs to help. Paul could update the police who would be almost in the village by now, hopefully. We stopped again a little further on. Rap and Jill shouted, and we all waited, listening, hoping with every breath we took that we would hear their voices in return, but nothing came back, not even an echo. We heard nothing. In the end, it turned out it was another sense that would give us what we needed.

"Can you smell that?"

"Yes, it smells like smoke."

"Oh God, the forest isn't on fire, please, my children…" Rap's voice shook.

"Nope, nope, it's not that kind of smoke. If I'm not mistaken, that's bacon I'm smelling." My stomach started to rumble, drowning out anyone else's reply.

"Wait, Rap, wait."

Rap had taken off like a hunting hound, howling back over his shoulder, "That's the one thing Lark can cook. Bacon sandwiches. It's them, it's them, we've found them." Rap suddenly dropped out of sight. His legs unable to keep pace with his need to see his children, he'd fallen head over heels into the cold, wet bracken. We stooped to pick him up on our way past. His hair and clothes were plastered with gungy, brown leaves. No long-term damage was done, but he would have to check for ticks when he got back home. But that was the least of his worries until we could confirm that the breakfast makers were his children. It was hard to believe that anyone else would be camping out on a day like this, although we did get the occasional travelling tinkers.

Following the smell of bacon, we soon spotted our prey. Four sets of shocked eyes locked onto us as we surrounded them. They were safely sheltered under Sìth-bhrugh. Dry and far from hungry. Bags of food could be seen littered around the area. Sleeping bags, clothing and jackets were bundled together on makeshift beds. Pots, plates and cutlery were stacked near a smouldering fire surrounded by a circle of small stones. This was not a case of poor children lost and survival of the fittest. This was a covert, planned operation. This was a mobilisation of troops. This was children taking control.

"Well, at least you know where all that extra food was going." I hoped to reduce the awkwardness of the moment. Rap hadn't noticed, unlike the rest of this so-called rescue party, just how well-organised his family's encampment was. He was too busy cuddling and crying over them to notice much.

"Daddy, Daddy, we slept out." The twins had thrown themselves into his arms and were clambering over him.

"Hi Dad, do you want a bacon sandwich?" Lark didn't look too happy at being found. Swallow was staying a safe distance back. She knew that any danger they could have been in was nothing compared to the trouble that could come their way now. Being the oldest, she would know she was the one most likely to pay any price for their little adventure. Paul, after a quick assessment of how the children were, had radioed in that they all appeared safe and healthy and in no danger, at least not from the elements.

"Bacon sandwiches all round, I think, before we head back," Paul suggested. We sat in a circle and listened to how the events of the night before had unfolded from the children's perspective. Once everyone had had something to eat and a warm drink, Paul quietly informed the children of the dangers they had put themselves in. He outlined the threats within the woods, the river and the elements, and left them without a doubt what could have happened to themselves and any member of the community who had come out to search for them. He said there was a knack to looking after themselves in this environment.

"Get down to the hall on a Tuesday night. There is a class there for youngsters on wood survival skills and the like. We have a ranger come in each week. And I think you should maybe offer to clean everyone's boots as a thank you for looking for you in this awful weather."

"What? But we were okay, we knew what we were doing. Look, our camp is full of food, and we have beds and every-thing,' Lark wailed.

"You don't understand." Fawn started to cry. "We had to come and warn the fairies that someone was buying the woods and they could be 'victed. We can't let that happen, Daddy. You can't let that happen, Daddy, you need to do something."

They loved these woods just as much as anyone who had been born here. Nothing and no one were going to be allowed to knock them down. As soon as the wire and fences had gone up, they had torn them down. By the time the 'for sale' notice had gone up, they had already started storing food, and their plans were well underway. They were going to claim squatters' rights. Lark and Swallow were sure no one could get them removed if they claimed their right to squat in Coilltean Sìthiche itself.

"We're ecot warriors, and no one can get us to move," sniffed Fawn.

"Well, whether you are or not is beside the point. Paul is right. You have to pay back for all the worry you have caused. So yes, you have to clean the muck off the searchers' boots and apologise for all the worry and hassle you caused. I think maybe I'll come with you to these wood survival classes. They sound like a great idea."

"Would you, Dad? Would you? Then we can learn how to defend the woods properly," Lark said.

I didn't think the children had really got the gist of what Paul had been trying to get across, but in the end, they had shown how Blàs and, in particular, these woods had become as much their home as ours. Our little community had not taken long to work its way into their hearts. If nothing else, at least their escapade had shown they were trying to do something practical to help. Hopefully, the adults would be able to bond together too and find a better solution to saving these woods than camping out in them. Only time would tell.

5

"So, all those in favour raise your hands."

Events had moved on at a fast pace since the 'rescue' of the children. Less than a week after they had spent the night out in the cold and wet, Rap and his brood could be seen going door-to-door around the village. They tramped about wrapped up against the cold but determined to get their own way regardless.

"I'll be dammed if these bairns are allowed to think they can get what they want by running away and causing a stir. We can't deny that they have given everyone a boot up the bum, but there is no way they are going tonight. Can you imagine it? Every time they disagree with their dad or the community, they'll be off? Or worse, the other bairns follow suit." Ellen was adamant, and no one was about to argue.

So, banned from the meeting the children were. The adults needn't have worried though – Rap's children were none the worse for their little adventure, but their dad had had a considerable fright. He was determined, at least for now, to know where his children were at all times, and that they paid more attention to what he said. Whether this parental discipline would continue, only time would tell, but at least for the next wee while, the Smith children had tags on their movements. Rap had agreed with Ellen's reasoning, as well as fearing what their next escapade might be if they were allowed a voice at the meeting. He had felt they needed to do something practical, even boring, to help safeguard the forest though. Going around the doors and asking people to come along to support the cause had fitted these boundaries perfectly.

❧

So it was that Swallow, Lark, Stag and Fawn found themselves being 'babysat' by their teacher while their dad attended the meeting about the future of the woods.

I had already spoken with both Karen and Grace about the event during our weekly catch-up, which was fortunate as it was becoming increasingly difficult to keep to our weekly arrangement now both of my old school friends were parents. As such, I had arranged to have their proxy vote if necessary, though thanks to general lack of progress, it was looking highly unlikely that I would need it.

Rumours had been rife about who was interested in the purchase of the woods. As with all scaremongering, comments and complaints were voiced at equal high volume.

"Wild camping, they say. I'll give them wild. We'll be left with all sorts of rubbish scattered around the woods."

"A hunting club, can you imagine? We'd never get in. It would be disastrous when the birds are laying; their young would get scared by the dogs. 'You can't come in, we're having a shoot, too dangerous.' Be awful."

"Whut wid be affy is if thay done th seam as thay done to thon ane near tae Inbhirasgaidh. Looks likh an auld battlefield – tree limbs jist laying aroond gaein grey, raggit stumps stickin up, akers o em. Naething but devastation, brok wir herts, ye ken."

Old Tam bent down and rubbed Shep behind the ears. "Did it no, auld boy? Cannae gae bak thar tae wuak, jist sae sad."

Maureen leant over and whispered into Auntie Lottie's ear. "Oh my, a nudist camp! My, the midgies will have a field day."

Laughter broke out among the crowd. A hush then descended as Paul of the Sheds stood up. He laid out what the woods meant to him and why he thought we should consider the option to buy. Many schemes he knew of could help, and we could always ask for advice without committing ourselves. After Jock shouted out, "Get the folks that were involved in the bid for the community hall set up again?" Paul stressed the importance of the whole community getting behind this project. In the past, it had been left up to Ellen, Maureen, Mary, Auntie Lottie, Paul and me to carry forward any projects. So far, we had set up the Development Trust, renovated our hall, and overseen the building of a new housing development that was rented out to mostly young families and the elderly. The community was happy to see all these developments but reluctant, on the whole, to step forward and help in any official capacity.

"It's all very well coming along and supporting fundraisers. Anyone will tell you that even our beautiful hall here could not have been built without the support of all who came along and put their hands in their pockets in one way or another. But if we are going to take on these woods, we need to know that more of the community will take on the responsibility of the actual committee work. We need new blood and more practical help if we go forward with this. But before we get that far, we need a lot more information. At this stage, the first thing we have to find out is if we, the community, *want* to go forward. Then we can organise for experts to come and visit us. They will let us know what is really involved and where we can get help. So remember now, this vote is just to find out if we want to look into the possibility of owning the woods ourselves. All in favour, raise your hands." Paul sat down as a forest of arms rose in the air. Thunder echoed around the hall as stamping feet emphasised the community's agreement. When the vibrations slowly receded, Paul of the Sheds once more stood up.

"Well, okay, I would say that the motion is almost unanimously carried." Laughter erupted. "Now, all we have to do is figure out our next move. Stroma, you are used to dealing with all kinds of community fundraising. What should we do?"

"Well, first off we need to have some kind of working committee to coordinate and at least start the whole process." I knew deep-down, never mind his pleas for more community help, that the weight of the work would fall on Ellen, Maureen, Auntie Lottie and me anyway. At least twice before, I had been unofficially nominated to take control of fundraising for projects. At least this time, I had been asked for my contributions.

It happens in any small place. I know this from all the committees I have set up through my work. Even though I'm a realist, I still waited and willed some fresh faces to offer to take on some of the responsibilities. I knew in my heart that wasn't about to happen though, and I was right.

So once again, the main instigators would be Ellen, as nothing in the area happened without her, Auntie Lottie, as she had become one of the hardest workers in the community since her return, and Maureen would be communications officer, as she had her ear closest to everyone in the area. Paul would also be heavily involved but wouldn't take on a formal role, as although nothing was done without him, he didn't like to wear an official cap.

I cringed inwardly when I heard a chair scrape along our nice wooden hall floor. I looked over to see Rap was standing and offering to help in any way he could. The atmosphere suddenly changed. People shifted in their seats and either looked at their feet or fixedly at Rap. *Who did this newcomer think he was? We played in these woods as children. Who was he to think he could help? If anyone was going to help it should be us.* Anyway, everybody knew that Ellen and her inner circle would get things done, like always. Only, hadn't Paul said they all needed help now, at the start, not later when the funding had already started to come in?

There was another scraping sound, and Jill got to her feet, also pledging to help. Other villagers started to stand up and volunteer. It seemed that the woods had the power to draw in more of the community than we had dared hope. Many locals felt, in their own different ways, that they had a special bond with our woodland. As I mused this over, another thought entered my head.

I stood up, "You know, Paul, I think we need to get in touch with the selling solicitors immediately and see if anyone has put in a bid for the woods. The Development Trust can take the lead on that. We will also need to be seen to be working along with other local organisations."

There was a general groan before Old Tam responded. "Weel thon widnae be difficult seein as whee'll be talkin tae wirsels, ye ken."

Laughter followed his observation before Maureen quipped. "Well, anybody else feel free to join us. I'll get in touch with their solicitor. His dad was related to my dad, just through marriage like. His secretary, or PA as he likes her to be known, lives next door to my cousin."

That gave her at least two ways to fathom out what might be going on. In the meantime, I would be spending even more time on my computer looking into community-owned woods, development trusts and, of course, funding for the purchase of said woods. Before people headed home, a meeting was arranged for the following week.

&a.

The Smith's children were ecstatic when they found out there was the possibility of buying the woods. They threw themselves wholeheartedly into the cause, beginning with persuading Karen, at the end of her babysitting stint on the night of the meeting, to hold a school fundraising event.

"Thank goodness the community decided to take this forward," she said the next time we met. "I had them and then my own children harassing me to do something to help. I've raised it with the head, and we are going to nominate a couple of the older pupils to come and sit on your committee if that's okay. They can feed back into the school, and we can build a whole environmental project involving all the pupils. It will be a great learning experience for them."

So that was it – even the primary school was behind the project. Now, all we had to do was find out if the woods were still available for us to purchase.

Maureen, unsurprisingly, came up with the information we needed. Two days later, after an excited phone call from her, the new committee was ensconced in Ellen's kitchen.

"These scones are just out of the oven and that jam was made from the wild raspberries from the woods, so I'm hoping you have some good news for us, Maureen."

"Well, you never would believe it if it wasn't me who was telling you but..." This couldn't have been further from the truth. True, Maureen was the best person to get news quickly, but as often as not, you had to decipher what had actually been said and what was conjecture on her part. "It turns out that Campbell Fraser has indeed left the woods to that cousin of his, but there was a clause in it that said if the woods were to be sold, the community should have first refusal."

"What, what? Why weren't we told about that? Surely the solicitor should have informed us before they were put the land up for sale?"

"Well, as you know, he's a bit of a rogue himself, old William the Wig. The closing date is tomorrow at noon." The jovial atmosphere changed into one of concern. Ellen, as usual, brushed our worries away and came up with a workable plan.

"Okay, Lottie move over a bit closer to Stroma so I can get alongside. Right, let's get this wording right for our bid. That way Stroma can get our e-mail off tonight. Maureen did you not say you were off to Inbhirasgaidh tomorrow?"

Maureen was quick to understand. "Aye, I am that." Before she could say any more, Paul stood up.

"Right, ladies, Rap, you seem to have all this under control. I'll be off then if that's all for now. I've things to do." Paul winked across at me before leaving the kitchen.

I opened my laptop and began typing. It had become obvious that the meeting was breaking up. *Here we go again*, I thought, just when I was beginning to enjoy not having to deal with so much Development Trust work, I was being dragged back into another cause. A worthwhile one, but when would all this community stuff stop? Maybe I should have taken a leaf out of my younger sister's book. Iona had moved away and just graced Blàs with her presence on holidays. Then, like her, I'd be greeted with love and few expectations of doing anything for the community. I could just enjoy all its benefits, at least for a short while. And there was the rub. I didn't want to enjoy Blàs for a short while; I wanted to enjoy it for the long-term. Being involved in all these community developments and continual fundraising was just the price I had to pay for living here. And even Iona had eventually succumbed to the community funding bug. Hadn't she raised £10,000 with her sponsored walk across Scotland from west to east in memory of our bard, Angus? Even leaving the area was no defence against becoming involved, it would seem.

6

"I need a dog." Auntie Lottie sighed.

She had been looking a bit sad lately. Despite keeping busy, she just wasn't looking her normal happy-go-lucky self. Both Mary and Ellen had taken me aside and asked if I knew what was wrong. Since Mary's party, Auntie Lottie had been sailing through life cheerfully. If anything, she had appeared almost too happy. Then suddenly, the smiling and laughter stopped. Even her banter had disappeared to a large extent. Now there was this declaration about wanting a dog. As far as I could remember, she had never owned one. In fact, I remembered her saying her lifestyle wouldn't allow her to have one. Then again, she wasn't going off abroad anymore. Perhaps she was right. It could get lonely, even in a community where everyone knew all about you and your next move.

GLADS, the acronym for Gaelic and Language Development Schemes, the organisation I worked for, had embraced our initiative to develop and deliver courses on culture and history for tourists as well as locals. Even given the travelling to each area to deliver these courses, it wasn't a full-time concern for Auntie Lottie. I could barely keep up with the admin and interest the courses had generated myself, especially the one that combined Gaelic language and whisky.

On top of that, I still had the responsibility for Gaelic pre-school groups and anything else involving Gaelic that might arise. My schedule was full to brimming. I had to acknowledge though, that due to the time of year, we hadn't been on many sessions lately and none were due for weeks. I had been neglecting Auntie Lottie and taking our relationship a little for granted lately.

"You okay, Auntie Lottie, you seem a bit down?"

Maybe she was suffering from SAD – Seasonal Affective Disorder. Our long, dark winters didn't allow the sun to shine on our skin for long enough to produce enough vitamin D. The lack of this can affect moods and rob us of the feel-good factor in winter. Maybe that is why we all start smiling the moment the sun comes out. Our moods are restored and off we go on our merry ways. I hoped Auntie Lottie was not about to succumb to this form of depression.

"Ach, I'm fine, just fine. Don't you go worrying about me. Just thought I could do with something in my life that was loyal, showed me unreserved love and wasn't afraid to let anyone see how happy he was to see me," she answered.

"Ah. I see. Well, wouldn't a cat do just as well? You wouldn't need to walk it, and we could go off on courses without worrying about leaving it behind. Less responsibility really."

"For goodness sake, Stroma, what is wrong with the people here! There is nothing, absolutely nothing wrong with taking on responsibility on a personnel level. A cat! A cat? Do you really think I need a cat? Those selfish, I'm- alright-Jack animals who only choose to love you when they see fit. I don't need any more of that sort of affection in my life. I've had enough of that kind of selfish, that 'I'll see you when I see you' kind of attitude. And furthermore, I'm a single, unmarried woman of a certain age, and the last thing I want to be known as is 'that poor spinster with the cats'. No. A dog it has to be, and not a great, smelly sheepdog. I want a dog with character who loves me, not one who is friendly with everyone and can't say no when shown any sort of attention by just… well, just anyone."

Auntie Lottie was flying through pages on her phone in high dudgeon. I was getting the distinct impression we were not having a conversation about owning a dog here, but I wasn't too sure what or who we were talking about. Although, I was beginning to have my suspicions.

"There, there is the dog I would like. Small, affectionate to me and… well, look, how can you not smile when you see it?" Auntie Lottie was holding up a picture of a strange-looking dog. Long-bodied with big eyes comparable to those of a baby seal, it had an enormous tuft sprouting from the top of its head.

"Ha ha! You are joking. I can't quite see that thing fitting in here. Looks more like it belongs in a show ring."

"Don't be so quick to dismiss it. It made you laugh and what more can you ask? Of course, that one is brushed up for a show, but mine wouldn't be so spruced up." I was remembering her obsession for hairdressing so wasn't so sure about that. Any dog that Auntie Lottie owned would be groomed to within an inch of its life.

"It sounds like you have already made up your mind. What is it anyway, a something-doodle?"

"No, they are way too small to be a doodle of any description. I'll have you know, it is Scotland's oldest terrier breed. It's a Dandie Dinmont terrier, better known as a Dandie nowadays."

"Okay, I know I am not the best-read person, but even I know that is taken straight from Sir Walter Scott's *Waverley*. So come on, what is it really?" Thank goodness for my English teacher, or I wouldn't even have known that, truth be told. I did know nobody would name a dog breed after a character in a book though, I mean, really.

"Here, see for yourself. The Dandie Dinmont terrier, the only dog named after a character …" Auntie Lottie handed over her phone, and there it was in black and white, or as in the Dandie

Dinmont terrier case, mustard and pepper, a dog called after a character in a book.

"Wow, well you learn something new every day. It says here that there is a whisky named after it too, and it has its own tartan. Please tell me that it wasn't the whisky that swung you in its favour?"

"Don't be daft. Although that is a distinct advantage in its favour. I just love how it looks so strange. It would love me, warts and all. I just know it would. It would love going out with me, would welcome my cuddles... *wherever* we were, wouldn't be afraid to show how much it loved me or wanted to be with me... *all* the time. I can't wait to belong to it."

"It says here there are hardly any breeders, and you could end up having to wait a while for one. If you went for something more rugged, you could probably get a puppy quite soon. There are always litters around the district. Any dog could give you all that."

"Not any dog, Stroma. Some love everyone they meet. Look at Shep – he's loyal to Old Tam I'll give him that, but he couldn't care less who takes him out as long as he gets out. And I've already registered an interest with the Dandie puppy coordinator. I'm just waiting to see if there are any litters coming up that will have some puppies available, or I could offer a home to any who needed rehomed. I don't want a show dog. I don't care if it's mustard or pepper. I just want something of my own to love."

I put my arms around Auntie Lottie. "You are loved, Auntie Lottie, and not just by me. The whole community loves you. How many people do you know who are called Auntie by near the whole population?" I handed her a hankie.

"I know, I know you are right. I'm just feeling a bit emotional, that's all. But I'm still not taking my name off that list for a Dandie. It could take ages anyway."

After she left, I put in a few phone calls to find out if any puppies of any sort were due soon in the area. Even if she didn't get a puppy in the end, it was time we both went on a road trip together. The weather and dark nights were drawing in. She had barely left the village, that I could remember, since summer, and if previous years were anything to go by, she needed to get out before winter blew in. So puppy-hunting it was. It would be a break from looking into buying the woods and researching grant funding.

The letter and e-mail we had agreed on had been sent to the solicitor. It had worked better than we had hoped, and a hold had been put on the sale of the woods until the community could get itself organised to put in its bid. Maureen, the fount of all knowledge, had reliably informed us that Campbell Fraser's cousin was hopping mad at the delay in the sale.

"But he deserves nothing more. Sitting over there, pulling our strings and affecting our lives while he counts his money. Not done a thing for the community either. Shouldn't have tried to pull the wool over our eyes. Campbell Fraser wouldn't have been happy if his wishes hadn't been carried out. He was a rogue of the first order, but he loved living in this community. With the money he left, he could have gone from here for an easier life anytime."

Things were moving at their own pace. Every time I got the answers to one question, it just added more to my workload. Then again, that was nothing new, and it wasn't as if I hadn't been down this road before.

7

We passed a very mature rowan tree as we entered through Ellen's back door into her kitchen. Initially, the meeting had been called to discuss our latest fundraising event. However, Maureen's last delivery as the bard had brought things to a head. She wasn't happy 'spouting a story like a damned actor'.

"You know me. I don't mind giving out information, letting everyone know what is happening, but I'm not an artist or storyteller in the way Angus was. Well, nobody is really. I feel right sick before I have to step up, and I don't enjoy it one little bit, but I don't want to let the community down. Someone else has to take it on."

We all knew Maureen was right. She was the fount of local knowledge that was true, but she was painful to watch in front of a large audience. It was Mary who came up with what we hoped was a workable solution.

"I'm that happy you took on this role, Maureen, but my Angus wouldn't have wanted you to suffer in his wake, so to speak. You know all the stories, and I've seen your appetite for more. He would have been proud how you have searched around, taking note of all the old ones and some forgotten ones even my Angus hadn't heard of I'm sure. You are the best one for that job, there is no doubt, no one would argue your expertise." Mary smiled across at Maureen who preened under her friend's praise. "But we don't want to make you ill. I think, for all that's best and good, we should look for someone you would be able to work along with. You could still be our story-gatherer and keeper of our folklore. What we need is your twin in a story-telling sort of way. Someone who's not afraid to give a performance, someone who is used to talking in front of people, someone who has a larger-than-life personality, someone who never mind how many people are in a room gets noticed by sheer strength of personality, someone, in fact, who even when I am trying to be the main focus of everyone's attention is, this very second, drawing eyes by her continual movement and, shall we say, impressive sense of… dress."

We all turned as one to look at Auntie Lottie who smiled benevolently at her captive audience. Maureen drew her eyebrows together in a slight frown. They were the best of friends, but their rivalry when it came to routing out the latest news and dispensing it around the village was becoming legendary. We all knew that Maureen was the fount of local knowledge, true or untrue, but it was Auntie Lottie who had the best delivery when it came to actual storytelling. All we needed was for them to agree and work together as the local bards.

Mary had decided her proposition was going to stand, so she filled the brief lull before anyone tried to contradict her. "Ah, I see you both agree by your uncharacteristic silences. My Angus would be right happy with that."

I wasn't so sure that is what their silence meant, but neither one would upset Mary by refusing her suggestion.

"Right." Ellen interrupted the pause. "I'll leave you two to sort out how you will work together. Now that is settled, perhaps we could move on to discussing the event itself." No one disagreed. "We could offer hot chocolate and baking. Maybe even buy some artificial lights to hang from the trees and have some extra that folk could buy at a slight price increase." Ellen was right into her subject. "Could you get hold of some costumes to dress up in, Lottie? I may have something if you can't. We could light up the pathways down to Ban na Luis. Charge an entrance fee to raise money for the purchase of the woods – that seems sort of poetic, don't you think?"

I hated to put a dampener on Ellen's idea, but as we did not own the woods yet, we could not really ask for an entrance fee or technically use the woods in this way. Maureen, however, came up trumps as usual.

"Well, after that little incident with the solicitor where he didn't tell us about our right to put in first bid on the woods, I did some digging of my own. It would appear that he has another little... or should I say, not so little thing, if her big blonde hairstyle is anything to go by, on the side. Apparently, his missus doesn't know, but she could... if he was to make things awkward for us."

I was so glad that Maureen was a friend and on our side. Blackmail was not above most in the room depending on the circumstance. I mean, if I needed Iona home for a certain reason, I was not immune from using emotional blackmail on her, but still, this was something a bit more sinister.

"I think we should save that for another more pressing time," Ellen said. "Maybe we could ask for a donation and have collection boxes, then everyone can pay what they can afford or want. We could advertise by word of mouth. Make it feel sort of like a secret and suggest an appropriate amount to donate."

"That's a better idea. It would make it all seem a bit more magical and special. Okay, what's next to organise?"

The meeting continued well into that night, until everything that could be arranged had been.

"Damn, I've dropped my torch. Remind me why we are here again in the pitch dark?" Ellen's voice broke our silence.

I smelt the earthy ground beneath us and heard the twigs break under our feet. Moonlight shone through the branches and illuminated the area far better than my torch had. I decided to keep it off and followed Ellen and Mary along the path in the woods to the clearing. We took our time as Mary, although spritely for her age, was not as sure on her feet as she once was.

We were in a place that held no concerns for us. On this clear, bright and cloudless night, thousands of tiny lights twinkling overhead, we felt part of our environment. It didn't matter if anyone saw us entering the woods. The community knew what was happening. Unlike that stormy evening when Mary, Angus and I had become the opposite of grave-robbers. Angus was no longer with us, but it hadn't stopped Mary from participating in outdoor activities after dark it would seem. Our former bard remained with us in spirit though as his legacy lived on through all the stories that were constantly told about him.

Old Tam, Mary and Maureen were often seen chatting and comparing the numerous versions of Angus' tales that laced around the community. I wondered as we tramped along if there was a way we could maybe start an official archive and perhaps offer a storytelling workshop. Funding could be found some-where, I felt sure, that would allow us to run courses or even just display our folklore.

Maureen could be found recording conversations all over the area anyway and would love to be included in something like that. Being officially recognised through her recordings as a woman who was clued-up on all the old stories and the new ones too would definitely appeal to her, even though she wouldn't be happy having to deliver them more creatively. Hopefully, if tonight went well, that would no longer be an issue.

I turned around and saw shadowy figures flitting through the trees on either side of us. Everyone seemed to have their own special path that led into the woods, but all eventually wound up at Ban na Luis. It was a special place. A clearing in the woods surrounded by rowan trees.

On a night when the moon was full, it was believed that fairies could be seen dancing around these rowans. It was also said, if you were in great need, a door could be opened to the fairy world from the rowan grove. Although many shrugged at these tales of superstition and myths, it was surprising how many rowan trees were planted near doors or garden gates into properties around the area. They had, for generations, been regarded as a form of protection against evil and bad luck.

We found ourselves somewhere to sit within Ban na Luis, not as in olden days awaiting to see the Queen of Fairies but awaiting the more generous proportions of Auntie Lottie. Both she and Maureen had been locked away for the past two weeks at every chance they got. Maureen passing on her wealth of stories, and Auntie Lottie rehearsing her delivery of them.

A tangerine spark from the crackling fire brought me back to focus on the clearing. Shadows danced in time with the rhythm of the fire over the small patchwork tent that stood silent in the one darkened corner. The buzz of conversation all around replaced the hum of the insects that would have been heard earlier in the year. Now it was the hum from the community as people busied themselves finding a warm, dry place to sit while they communicated with their nearest neighbours.

Small colourful lights started to go out around the clearing stilling the nervous laughter of the children. Voices hushed as the remaining lights dimmed. The moon, like a natural spotlight, illuminated the area in her soft, brilliant glow. A log fell from the fire, throwing sparks that twirled and flew away into the night sky. As our eyes were drawn again toward the fire, we could make out a dark, hooded shadow standing beside the tent. Her ragged cloak was draped over her arms covering the bottom of her face.

Auntie Lottie stood, commanding the attention of even the

youngest of our audience. She swayed and moved around in a spell-binding performance, weaving and swirling her story into the night air. No one uttered a word, but gasps and laughter erupted as she led us all on a journey back through time to an era where magic, folklore and humans all combined to live spiritually side by side. Barefooted, she stamped her way across the clearing, pointing out the rowan trees and warning of dire consequences if any were felled. Her hair flew about her face as she turned and peered viciously straight at Paul of the Sheds, warning of loyalty and love, and the need to honour those whose spirits could be found in all living things. She was earth mother, she was magnificent, and she was a woman to behold, fear, respect and love, a reincarnated fairy queen of old. And then suddenly, it was all over.

She was gone, the clearing stilled, the remaining lights disappeared. One small voice could be heard in the clearing, whimpering, "Mum?" And then the lights came on, the applause began, and Auntie Lottie, returned to her original form, stepped out of the tent.

She drank in all the rapture thrown at her. It was a magical night. We had, for a brief moment in time, been transported to a place hidden well within us during our everyday lives. It was certainly worth the money that was raised. More important was the message that Maureen and Auntie Lottie had weaved so successfully into the tale, and the delivery. We were so much more with nature in our lives. Spiritually and morally, we had to save these woods, not just for the children, but for our community, our way of life and for our own mortal souls.

If Maureen and Auntie Lottie had taken up politics together just think what they could have achieved, I found myself thinking, as we all wound our way back to the artificial lights of our homes. Many in the community who hadn't considered the purchase of the woods before tonight would be joining our cause one way or another by the morning, I felt sure.

8

I thought I had managed to put Auntie Lottie off a trip to the Borders. Over the intervening weeks, since she has voiced her longing for a puppy, I had made the effort to take her with me on my visits around the Highlands. I had made a particular effort to get her to accompany me to places where I knew litters of puppies could be visited.

Not one of the adorable dogs that we had seen would do. If it had been up to me, I would have bought at least one from every litter. Somewhat hypocritically, Auntie Lottie wouldn't allow me to purchase any of the pups.

"You don't really want a dog, Stroma. You are just being taking in by these lovely wee bundles. I would never forgive myself if you got a puppy because of me and then lived to regret it."

She was right of course. I had had no real desire to get a dog, but it was so difficult to walk away from all those lovable puppies. It didn't seem Auntie Lottie had nearly so much trouble turning them all down. For her, it was a case of a Dandie or nothing.

I had just arranged a visit to Inverness to see a project officer about our intention to buy Coilltean Sìthiche. The next thing I knew, Auntie Lottie was bursting through my door.

"I met Maureen." *Here we go*, I thought. "She said you were going to Inverness. How about adding in a trip to the Borders since we're going that way anyway?" I opened my mouth to comment, but before I could, she raced on. "Oh, come on now, Stroma we've got to go to Inverness anyway. What's a little trip to the Borders from there?"

"Try about a four-hour drive depending on traffic, in the wrong direction. And that's just one way. We would have to overnight it," I replied, but Auntie Lottie was not going to be put off. Before I knew it, I found myself putting our overnight bags into the boot of my car as part of the preparations for what had started out as a quick trip to the Highland capital. Somehow, she had worn me down and convinced me to take a 'little' detour home via the Borders.

Our meeting with the project officer was about our feasibility study. I hated feasibility studies, but every organisation seemed to ask for them. For communities, it meant we had to find extra funding. Normally, at least another £10,000 on top of what we had originally budgeted for. For the organisation that may agree to fund us, it meant us paying one of their ex-staff members, who now worked as a freelancer, for the work. All very convenient for them, but for us, it felt like we were just moving money around from one part of their organisation to another, with us doing all the work in between.

Although, if we were clever with the questions we asked and spoke to enough people in the community before completing the study, we could more or less get it to say what we wanted it to say. This was just one of the many hoops we would have to jump through in order to get the money, or in this case the woods, safely in our hands.

As we were heading south, the woods were being surveyed for valuation. It wouldn't be long after that before we'd know exactly how much we were going to need to raise. Everything was beginning to line up, ready for our enormous fundraising campaign to begin.

૪ৡ

"Well, that was a turn up for the books." We were on the A9 heading south. "I think all the available women in the area will be happy to have him as our project officer, wouldn't you say?"

"I think that is a bit sexist, Auntie Lottie, don't you." She was right though, I had to admit. Jim Main was under forty years old which was a bonus in itself. He was full of good ideas and enthusiasm toward our project. His blue eyes had stared intently as he informed us of his timescale and how exactly he envisaged going about his research. He oozed charm and was obviously just as at home in an office environment as he was outdoors. As he followed us out of the offices, I had noticed that he was well over six foot tall and kept himself in good shape. Not a paunch in sight.

"He liked you, I could tell. Maybe we won't just have our business plan at the end of all this. Play your cards right, and maybe you could have a bit of fun when he comes to do our research."

"At the end of this, all I'm looking for is a workable plan that will help us buy the woods, run it without getting us into debt, and then pass it on to the next committee."

"Oh, Stroma, don't set your expectations so low. Right, how long before we get to a Dandie?"

૪ৡ

Once we had left Inverness, I had to admit the scenic drive alone made the journey worthwhile. I hadn't been down south in a long time and had forgotten just how beautiful it was. Each little town had made an effort to enhance what they had to offer. In many ways, their community spirit was not so unlike ours. I was pretty sure we could adopt some of their improvements and tweak them to suit our area.

Our little trip to the Borders took us exactly four and a half hours, due to roadworks. Only slightly more than I had originally expected. We'd booked into a nice little hotel near where the breeder stayed, at least that's what the satnav told us.

Given the time of year, we were taken aback to see so many colourful flowers displayed all around the centre of the town. We didn't have nearly so many still growing up north by then. The frosts had already picked them all off.

"That's unusual." Auntie Lottie was pointing at a sign on the pub door.

Dogs: homemade dog treats available for your four-legged friend to munch as you eat your meal.

It turned out that was not an unusual sign in the Borders. Lots of shops, restaurants and pubs had similar signs on their windows and doors. I had never seen anything like it before. This was definitely dog-friendly country.

"Maybe we could learn something from this doggie-friendly atmosphere and have something similar up the road," suggested Auntie Lottie.

"Auntie Lottie, we only have one pub in the village, and it doesn't need a sign to say it's dog-friendly. Old Tam and Shep are the best advertisement they have. They are in there most evenings. Shep has even got his own bowl behind the bar. The shop could be a bit friendlier I suppose, and the cafe."

I was mulling it over in bed that night, trying to come up with a way of raising more cash. Could we somehow latch on to the dog culture in the country to increase the viability of the woods? We definitely needed to have some sort of income to maintain paths and manage the woods into the future. Was there some sort of fundraising opportunity we were missing out on because we didn't advertise that we were already a dog-friendly area? We had lots of walks around the district. In general, the beaches were pretty safe, and Auntie Lottie was right if we could persuade the cafe to allow dogs inside that may well encourage more tourists.

I awoke the next morning, no clearer in the head, to Auntie Lottie knocking at my door.

"Good morning, good morning, time to get up. Come on, we need to get breakfast, then we can get off to see if I can rescue a Dandie."

"Okay, okay, just let me grab a quick shower. I'll see you in the dining room in fifteen minutes..." She left happier than I had seen her in months. It was only as I was locking the door that I realised she had said 'rescue a Dandie'. As far as she had led me to believe, we were here to check out Dandie puppies. There was a long waiting list of potential owners keen to get their hands on a Dandie Dinmont terrier puppy. She was still on that list as far as I knew. Perhaps it had just been a slip of the tongue.

We paid our bill and put our bags in the car before we double-checked the directions to the breeder's house. It had to be around the back of the main street, as we had walked all around the middle of the town, keeping an eye out for the right house the night before, but we hadn't been able to locate it.

The previous night after we had settled into the hotel, eaten a delicious dinner and had a few relaxing drinks, we realised we were not quite ready for sleep. Although the drive had been tiring, we both felt the need to stretch our legs.

"We might as well take a walk around and see if we can find where we need to go in the morning." Auntie Lottie followed this up by saying, "You never know, if we find the breeder, she may let us in for a wee sneak preview tonight."

It was a lovely night for walking. Finding the breeder, however, was not as easy as we had thought it would be. Auntie Lottie had us up closes and down cul-de-sacs. We sneaked off the main throughway, along dark lanes and narrow, cobbled avenues to no avail. We whispered into the deepening dark. It had got late, and most of the town's folk were in bed.

"Can you read the number on that door?" Auntie Lottie had asked.

"Are you daft? I can't see my own hand, never mind read a number on a door a metre away."

"Come on, we can try down here." Down here consisted of walking through a dark stone corridor where we could just about make out a row of cottages huddled together. No lights were on inside, and there were no street lamps to guide us. Creeping forward, Auntie Lottie grabbed my arm, asking in a stage whisper, "Do you think we are trespassing? Could this be someone's garden, do you think?"

"How would I know? Shhh! I think I hear someone." A blinding blaze hit us right between the eyes as a security light flooded the area.

"Quick, quick, come on." Auntie Lottie grasped my arm and pulled. To the sound of our running feet, I heard Auntie Lottie gasp. "Do you think anyone saw us?"

"I don't know."

"I got such a fright at those lights coming on," she said, "that I just wanted to get out of there. I don't suppose you noticed the name or number of any of the houses there."

"No, I didn't, and I've had enough of creeping around this town in the dark. We'll end up getting lifted by the police if we're not careful."

"I just wanted to see where we were going to tomorrow and to see if we could maybe meet the puppies tonight. I'm just excited, that's all." Auntie Lottie didn't look as contrite as she tried to sound.

"I know, but we really should be getting back if we want an early start. You'll see them in the morning. Come on, let's go and get a nightcap at the hotel before we go up. Maybe they will have your Dandie whisky there."

"Stroma, are you listening to me?" Auntie Lottie broke into my daydreaming. I locked the car and took a deep breath, enjoying another bright and fair morning.

"Sorry! I was just thinking about last night. Hopefully, we can find the breeder this morning. It feels like we've already looked everywhere in the town."

"Well, yes, we certainly gave the area a good checking over. How on earth are we going to find that puppy house? I thought that satnav of yours said we were near. Maybe we should just ask someone."

"Hold on a moment, let me get back inside the car and see if I can work out where it is trying to send us." I opened the car door again and switched on the electrics. "Okay, I think maybe it could be right behind the hotel, so we will need to go back out this way and then take a left then left again. As I am driving, you need to keep looking at the satnav and read out the names of the streets"

We headed out of the town, doubled back on our original position and ended up directly at the back of the hotel.

"It's no good, Stroma, we should be there by now. I can't see any street names, and I can't even hear any dogs barking."

She was right. Oh, to be back up north where landmarks never moved, and there was always someone around to ask. Even with the windows wide open, we couldn't hear even a whimper coming from any house nearby. Surely, if we were in the right place, we would at least have heard one bark.

I looked up the phone number and dialled. At least mobile signals were almost guaranteed here, which was an improvement on back home. The call came through the loudspeaker. Now we could hear barking dogs. In fact, that's all we could hear down the phone. Eventually, there was a loud bang then some muffed barking as someone shouted down the phone.

"Hello, yes, hello, sorry, my husband has just shut the doors on the dogs." Even with the doors shut, we could hear loud, muffled barking. How many dogs did they have? They couldn't all be Dandies surely? There had to be some big dogs among all that commotion to cause so much noise.

"We need directions to your house. We can't find it. Can you help?"

Once the breeder realised where we were, she told us how to find her.

"Okay, go to the end of that street, take a right then a right again, and you will be in the main street. You can park near the hotel. We are four doors up from there, through the large, green, wooden gate. It looks like a front door. Just open it and follow the path. We are the third cottage on the left. Sorry, but you can't bring a car in here."

Four doors from our accommodation! Of course there was no sign to say that a street or any homes existed through the green door. Only the locals and the postie knew they were there and what the street name and numbers were. A 'hidden street' – these houses should be used for witness protection.

"Are you sure you want to see these dogs? They seem to make an awful lot of noise for something so little. I could barely hear what that woman was saying."

"We have not come all this way for nothing. Now, come on. I've a Dandie waiting to see me."

Knocking on the door, the noise level increased again. Dogs were coming from around the back to the garden at the side. Luckily, they were stuck there. Only three, and they made enough noise to awaken the dead. The puppies inside didn't. Tiny, fat bundles, sniffed and snorted their way around.

"Aah, would you like a hold of a puppy before I introduce you to the others?" The breeder smiled and plopped a small mustard female into my arms. It snuffled down and immediately fell asleep. *My willpower would have needed to be extra strong to walk away without one of these cuties*, I thought. *Just as well they are all reserved already.*

"No, no, I'm fine. I'm anxious to see the three-year-old female." Auntie Lottie looked around.

"Of course. Why don't you sit down there?" The breeder absently scratched the belly of a Dandie who was lying tummy up on a soft chair, before she removed the little dog. "That is their default position, you know. Any excuse, avoidance, saying hello, anytime and anywhere, roll on their backs, they will, and present their tummy for a rub. Never known a breed like it." She laughed and lifted a wee mustard adult into Auntie Lottie's waiting arms.

It looked up into her eyes, took a big breath, sighed and cuddled into her chest. That was it, the moment I knew I had lost the battle. There was no way me or anyone else would be able to separate those two. It had been love at first sight for them both. I was now panicking a little, as that little lady obviously belonged to the breeder. It would be going nowhere with us, and none of those puppies would be either. We were here so Auntie Lottie could see and feel them first-hand before she purchased one. This was just a checking-out the breed mission, nothing else.

"Okay, I have all the information here. Some food, a little custard for the journey in case you need it. A few little treats for her, and some of her toys to take home. I've also bought her a new one." Auntie Lottie shifted the Dandie slightly, so she could take hold of the pack without dropping her precious bundle.

"Thank you, that all looks grand. Did you get the remaining amount yesterday? I got the bank to send it a day early. I wanted you to know I was a serious buyer."

"Yes, yes, everything went through. It was fine. No more watching her online for you. Thank you so much for offering her a home. We don't often have Dandies needing to be rehomed, and most new owners would like a puppy rather than an adult. On saying that, it is never difficult to find new owners willing to take one on. It was such a shame she lost her owner, but these things do happen from time to time. Now you have her in your arms, it must feel nice."

"Yes, yes, it does." Auntie Lottie's gaze had returned to the Dandie.

After a session of questions and answers, a cuddle with the rest of the puppies and dogs, we finally said our goodbyes and walked slowly back to the car. Auntie Lottie with the new love of her life trotting happily beside her. Our arms were laden down with water, food, toys and packs of forms and paperwork. I negotiated opening the boot and put the whole lot inside.

"Here, hold her a minute, will you?" Auntie Lottie carefully placed the lead in my hands. I bent down to pat her new companion. She was a lot more solid than I expected. Dandies may be small, but they're sturdy and solidly built. She was also cuddly and warm and totally melted away any resistance I had left. It did not really surprise me when Auntie Lottie opened her case, took out a small bowl, a bottle of water, a few treats and a nice warm fleece blanket.

"You know my motto: 'be prepared'." She smiled at me and gently removed the lead from my grip. "Come here, little one. We'll soon be home."

9

"Well, there's a sight for sore eyes on such a dull morning."

It was winter, it had to be as Jill was out and about collecting anything that the frequent storms would have thrown up on the beach. Her remark wasn't aimed at just any old little treasure she had found. No, this was a hunk of six-foot manhood tightly wrapped up in high-tech outdoor gear.

"Who is he?"

"Our project officer. He's been having a look at the woods and talking to people about their expectations. Did you not fill in the survey?"

"Oh that. Yes, weeks ago. How long will he be here?"

"Well, I'm surprised he still is. He showed us his findings last night at the meeting. We're hoping to hear about the next phase of funding in the new year. If all goes well, we expect to have everything in place for the buyout soon. Having the Development Trust already up and running has shortened the whole process, otherwise we could have been waiting months."

"So, we may be seeing more of him then. That would be nice." Jill nudged my elbow as Jim made his way toward us.

"Good morning. I was just speaking to Thomas MacDonald.

He has a wealth of knowledge. We could use his insight when putting together the information boards for when the community owns the woods."

Two blank pairs of eyes stared back at him. Who on earth was this bearer of local knowledge who we had never heard of?

"I was out walking with him this morning with his old sheepdog. Shep, is it? He's full of stories about this place. Shame no one ever found that pot of stolen gold though. Now that would have gone a long way toward purchasing the woods. Stroma, if you have any more questions regarding the study or the application, let me know – you've got my e-mail, though I aim to be here in person more often. It's great to get away from the city."

We watched him striding away.

"Bet he says that to all the communities he works with." Jill nudged my arm again. "Aww, come on, Stroma, why don't you ask him out for a drink sometime when he's over. What harm would it do?"

"Not my type."

"Who's not?" Auntie Lottie had crept up behind us. I should have noticed Whisky softly patting against my shin. Her dog had settled down well and had grown in confidence, although not in height. Her short legs barely held her off the ground. She wiggled backward and forward in time with her wagging tail. The use of her tail had increased greatly since living with Auntie Lottie.

Once Whisky finally got control of her body, she jumped up and placed her two front legs just below my knee.

"Aww look, Stroma, she's smiling at you." Whisky's teeth could be seen as her lips pulled back in her attempt at a doggie smile. It was not a pretty sight; she just looked odd. If that was her smile, how terrifying must she look when she snarled?

"Stroma was just saying that Jim, our project officer, was not her type. Well, you can throw him over here if you don't want him. Although he may be a bit young for me really."

"I don't blame you, Stroma. You are way better off with a dog. No more waiting around for when they can fit you in. You know you are loved every time you look into their eyes, and best of all, they are totally loyal and unselfish."

Jill and I looked at Auntie Lottie in awe. Was this really the woman who had always wanted to set me up with any, and I mean any, male who was not attached within a fifty-mile radius? I had never heard her so despairing of males. Lately, I often wondered, halfway through a conversation with her, what we were actually talking about. Jill looked at me and shrugged. Auntie Lottie turned to leave.

"I'm off then. Can't be seen wasting time chatting. I'm way too busy. I'm off to meet a friend in Inbhirasgaidh if anyone asks. A really good friend who I have been seeing a lot of recently." Off she trudged with Whisky bouncing along at her side.

"Have I missed something? What were we just talking about, do you think?" Jill was looking almost as perplexed as I felt. We'd just had another one of those conversations with Auntie Lottie that seemed to be about something completely different from what she was actually saying.

"Call that thing a dog? What is she playing at? She'll be lucky if it lasts out the winter." Paul of the Sheds had walked up beside us.

"Hi Paul, what did you make of the meeting last night? Thanks for your input, by the way. It really helped." I said.

"So where is she off to in such a hurry? She's never about these days, always here there and everywhere with that daft wee dog of hers. Don't know where she goes." Paul shook his head, a bemused expression on his face.

"I think she is kind of cute," I volunteered.

"Well, I don't think cute is a word I would use to describe her, but she is a fine figure of a woman. Frustrating, totally illogical and downright annoying, but did you see her in full flow at the storytelling in the woods a few weeks back? What a woman."

"Emm, I was talking about the dog, Paul."

Colour oozed into his face as he blustered. "Aye you're right, I suppose, if you're liking wee dogs. And you're welcome, Stroma. Hopefully, we'll have the woods in our hands soon. I've got another donation from the fisherman to give you yet." Off he wandered, his eyes flicking toward the retreating figure of Auntie Lottie. Was her normal walk just a little bit more exaggerated as she sashayed her way home, I wondered? Could she feel Paul of the Sheds eyes burning into her back?

Jill smiled "You don't think... Could they possibly...? Oh, I am surprised Maureen hasn't cottoned on to this one."

Oh, I *did* think, and it certainly made sense now that I thought about it. My face flushed as I remembered one very early morning, or in my case, a very late summer's night, sneaking home myself. I had watched Paul of the Sheds furtively creeping around the back of the cottages near Auntie Lottie's house. I had just assumed he had been visiting one of the holidaymakers that he dallied with throughout the summer. Being preoccupied with my own little secret that summer, I had dismissed it from my mind. But if my intuition had finally kicked in, then these two had been together for some time before whatever it was broke them apart. No wonder Auntie Lottie had been sad. She had obviously been hiding a broken heart.

The darker days of winter had led to a sadness creeping throughout the village. Crystal-blue sky had been replaced with dark brooding grey upon grey. To make matters worse, despite the arrival of four new pupils for the local school, rumour was rife that we still needed one more student or else we'd lose a teacher. Disappointment and dissatisfaction were skulking around looking for new members.

"Have you heard, have you? There is talk about closing the bank in Inbhirasgaidh. The bank, of all places. Job losses not to mention how we get our money in and out," Maureen had told me earlier.

It was a worry – not only did the bank employ local people from here in Blàs, but the nearest branch to us after Inbhirasgaidh was over an hour away. Many in the community were too old to travel that far and didn't want or couldn't go online.

"It will be a mobile one for them next, take my word for it. It will pop in just like the mobile library we get, but I don't think the locals will be as glad to see that service. I'm off to write a letter of complaint. It is bad enough we have to travel to Inbhirasgaidh for a proper branch. It's time that we looked at a cooperate bank, or whatever it is you call them." Off Maureen had gone. Driving her wheelchair as if she was in a rally car.

I hoped she was wrong. The last thing we needed when we were busy fundraising was the closure of another bank. A mobile one was all well and good, but it wasn't as flexible or accessible as having a physical branch close at hand. People had been putting small amounts of money into our fundraising account when they popped into the Inbhirasgaidh branch to do their banking. I hoped this was one of Maureen's half-listened-to stories.

Our next fundraiser was due to take place soon. Hopefully, it would cheer up the community after such a dark and dreary winter. Snow – heavy, cold and white – at least brightened up the look of the place. Normally, that would then be followed by blue skies, which always brought a holiday atmosphere. We'd had none of that throughout this winter, and we missed those clear, cold days. The community had become dour in the constant heavy downpours and blustery winds. Heads had been forced down by the weather, and once it had passed, the effort to lift them again became almost too much for the majority of the population.

Checking my computer when I got back, I was relieved to find that, thankfully, our town crier had got it wrong. Inbhirasgaidh was not on the hitlist of bank closures. Blàs had already gone through the closure of our little branch years ago with the promise that the cash machine would still be available. That promise had been broken only a few years later. The inconvenience to holidaymakers was undeniable. Crafting had taken the biggest hit as most people wanted their sales to be in cash. The village shop had stepped in and persuaded a different bank to install a cash machine on the side of its building, but we lived in fear that, someday, that too would be taken away.

Early spring had not dispelled the general melancholy that often hung about as winter ebbed away. Even the news that the bank was under no threat didn't appear to lift the spirits much. Yet, as hats and scarves were disregarded, so hearts and minds would lighten and look ahead. At least villagers could look each other in the eye now that the cold wind no longer forced their heads down.

The wind finally dropped, but not before it had cleared the dreary clouds away. Everything felt a bit brighter – the sun might still be low in the sky, but it was shining. As I made my way to the hall to check on the refreshments for our latest event, I couldn't help but notice the village was finally coming out of hibernation. It was as if everyone had waited until the wind had moved off before they came out of their confinement. The pupils had been industrious outside the school, I saw as I walked past. I was so busy admiring their work that I walked straight into someone.

"Ach thars nae need tae apologise, lass. Eh dinnae think ee wid mind." It was Old Tam and his dog. Or rather, it was a scarecrow made to look like Old Tam and Shep. Only it was Old Tam who was speaking.

"Meh, thay hiv done meh likhness affy weel. Auld Shep here waz that excited tae see eezsel. Fair prud o th honour, wer ye no?" Shep was leaning heavily against Old Tam's leg, looking like he always did – old, shaggy and odorous. Thankfully, the children hadn't gone in for smelly-vision on their exhibit. "Teacher telt meh tae come awa in so the bairns cood hiv a guid look ower us. This is whut thay came up wi'. Eh lent em some o meh auld clathes that meh Morag wanted tae thraw oot, glad eh didnae. Hiv ye seen th ane next tae the shoppie yet?" I hadn't but decided to take a walk around to see how many more extra straw residents the community had placed around the district.

We had planned for, optimistically, about forty scarecrows and had drawn a map that people could follow to see them. In the end, I counted an extra ten to our original number, which I dutifully added onto the sheet for copying. There was a straw man reading a newspaper outside the shop. Two were having a chinwag at one of the tables outside the pub. A trio of children, frozen in time, played on the beach. I'm pretty sure that was Jill's work as each was beautifully decorated with seaweed, shells and flotsam from the sea. Even the distillery had taken the time out to produce a scarecrow in white overalls with a notebook and pen. The health centre had a dentist, nurse and doctor all suitably decked out in overcoats, swabs and face masks.

Scarecrows of all shapes and sizes were dotted around, some in boiler suits and wellies. Others had used that only as the base and had gone on to further decorate them in various ways, including using homemade flowers and colourful clothes. Politics and satire had not been missed out either, some of them making me laugh out loud. The one that made us stop, stare and wonder though was the scarecrow at Rose Cottage. The Smith family had gone their own way, as usual. Each child had made an animal to represent their name. Their scarecrows were surrounded and enclosed by a woman scarecrow with long, flowing hair made out of moss, seaweed and straw. Her body contained a bird's nest complete with tiny birds, and her clothes were made of fishing nets which helped to house a whole variety of little creatures from mice to butterflies. In her hand had been placed a fairy. It looked like an illustration from an old-fashioned children's book. They had managed to make a hay-filled scarecrow look so gentle and appealing... It was amazing. It would take some beating. Thankfully, I was not one of the judges.

By the time I was finished checking everything at the hall and was heading home, the sun had been replaced by a golden moon. Stars studded the night sky and heralded the arrival of the first competitors for the event. Some hardy souls were camping that night in the field. Now, a campervan would not have been too much of a hardship, but a tent, that early in the year, would be cold and too uncomfortable for my liking.

As such, many did not bother with bedding down. Instead, they stayed up and enjoyed the campfires, stories and the odd dram. The campers had reasoned that the cold would have kept them awake anyway so why not indulge and have a good time. Tractors could be heard arriving all through the night. Their noisy engines growled into the wee hours until the sun blasted across the sky to herald the new dawn.

The stalls were all located inside the hall. This early in the year, we were lucky to have such good weather. We could have had snow. I'd had nightmares about that for weeks. Next year, I vowed, we would have this event later in the year. Early spring was far too risky a time to hold outdoor events.

Ellen and Mary were safely ensconced in the warmth, looking after our forest stall. Jams, jellies, cordials and chutneys made from the various berries and plants foraged during the year could be sampled and bought. Mary had also baked loaves of bread from corn flour. Wild-grown mushrooms she had picked and dried from the woods earlier enhanced their flavour. Rowanberry jelly and silver-birch syrup, both old favourites of mine, took pride of place. Also on sale were wild garlic pesto and Mary's special rosehip syrup that she swore kept her in good health. For the children, there was toffee acorn brittle and tasty small tarts made from acorn flour and crab-apple puree which Mary had kept frozen since harvest.

The school, when it heard that the community was hoping to buy the woods, had elected to run a project about them. Once the children had become involved, you could spot them heading down there to take surveys of the various plants and animals they saw. Their favourite project had been making toffee apples from the apples that Mary, specially drafted in for the occasion, had helped them to forage. The children had used their data and pictures to provide an exhibition that was being displayed near the forest stall.

Helen, Ellen's partner, was home from her rotation on an oil rig. A gifted photographer, she was busy cataloguing the day's events. Some of the photos were to be added to the forest exhibition, while others would be used as publicity and evidence for future grant applications.

No one could fail to miss why we were fundraising. Any grant-funding body could easily see that the community was heavily engaged in the project to take over the woods. Our event had been advertised as far-and-wide as possible, and we hoped for the arrival of some early tourists with money to spend.

Tractors of all ages, shapes and sizes were ready. Many had arrived late, having spent the previous day working on farms and crofts. Each one had been spruced up, cleaned, and shone in the morning sun. Drivers were dressed in different themes to match their machines. We hoped to pull in the crowds that would normally attend vintage car rallies, as well as those who would go along to see floats. We had combined this with the first of our local markets.

Everything was there, ranging from homebaking to illicit gin. Auntie Lottie and Maureen had placed their stall next to the foraging one. They had used the berries from the juniper bushes that grew all around the area to make their gin. Sloe gin was also there for those that preferred. Bramble and crab-apple liquors were presented in beautiful, small, recycled-glass bottles. Slightly larger bottles of bramble whisky rose above them all. Many different wines, contained in dark green bottles, were labelled as rhubarb, elderberry or nettle.

Strangers to the area could be forgiven for thinking that both Auntie Lottie and Maureen were quite the drinkers, but I knew who had orchestrated the theme of their stall and who had been behind most of the recipes. It was evident to the locals who knew her best, thanks to the birch-tree wine which stood in pride of place in beautifully hand-decorated bottles. Jill had done Mary proud with the design. The wine shone out as a luxury item, a special gift on that boozy stall. Mary, together with her Angus, had collected the sap and fermented their special wine for years. Here she was paying homage in her unique way to her late lamented husband.

It wasn't just their scarecrows that made Rap and his children's contributions to the day stand out, but also their stall. They had made homemade lemonade and some unusual, strange-looking biscuits. The Smiths had set up their table selling homemade colourful lemonade. Ranging from a light pink elderberry to a brilliantly orange carrot, the sizzling red watermelon and raspberry lemonade was particularly eye-catching. The only flavour that seemed to be missing was plain lemon lemonade.

Paul of the Sheds and Jim, who had come across for the occasion, were to judge the tractors and their trailers. Auntie Lottie was busy sipping hot tea – it was black, so I'm pretty sure some of the gin or even a dash of whisky had made its way in there.

Vintage and new tractors grumbled past, some massive, some smaller than the average 4x4 car. All were decked out in colourful flags, balloons and streamers as they roared past, making their way through the village, paying homage to the motley range of scarecrows as they passed. The noise was reminiscent of the bikers' 'thunder in the glen' held each year in Aviemore, only this was more like 'growl in the gorse'.

"Damn."

"What's wrong?"

"Fly just committed suicide in my tea." Auntie Lottie threw away the last of her laced drink. "Well, Stroma, it looks like another successful fundraiser. Do you think people will liven up a bit now? It's been such a dreary place lately. Oh, look, there's Paul and Jim. Should we join them?" Off she strode without a backward glance, Whisky, her ever-present companion, bouncing along at her side.

"So, the big romance is back on then." Ellen stood beside me watching the body language between Paul and Auntie Lottie.

"You knew? I only worked it out after they had split up. How did you find out? They kept it so quiet. I didn't think anybody knew, apart from me and Jill, that is."

"Poor Maureen – it has been killing her not to gossip about them. I threatened her with death if she so much as breathed a word to anybody. They got together very quickly when Lottie first arrived. They only split up because Paul thought they were getting too comfortable. Mentioned it once to her in passing, stupid man, and off she went, left him stranded without a paddle. Lost without her he was. It has taken him months, and a new dog on her part, to mend their relationship."

"What? Paul bought her that dog?"

Whisky was greeting Paul like a long-lost lover.

"Well, not actually bought it for her, but let's just say he had contacts and managed to pull a few strings, so one became available for her. So yes, between Lottie finding that out, and a lot of grovelling on his part, she has finally forgiven him. Maureen best be brushing up on her wedding routines before the year's out, mark my words. That man has finally found his match, much to the relief of us all."

I watched the pair flirt outrageously together, right there in the open, in front of everybody in the community. There would be no need for Maureen to spread the word now, as Paul bent down and placed a light kiss right on Auntie Lottie's lips.

"Yuck, look at them, they're way too old for that," Lark remarked as he sauntered by.

"God, I'm just relieved. That could have been our dad," Swallow replied.

I raised my eyebrows at Ellen.

"Not in a million years. They were made for each other those two. No one else was ever going to get a look in once they both finally gave in and admitted that to themselves."

That day may not have been the best fundraiser the community had ever seen, but in other ways, it would be remembered by some for a lifetime.

As early spring flowed into lambing season, the weather broke again. Moods in the village had lifted by then though, ensuring fundraising would continue with sufficient enthusiasm. We were well on target, and it seemed nothing could possibly knock us off. We had been so efficient that we were doing better than even our most optimistic predictions. Due, no doubt, to the fact that we were already well-organised with the running of the Development Trust. It hadn't been that long since we had finished the housing project, so it been a simple case of getting everybody back into established rhythms again.

That was when Maureen was called upon to perform a service, and unfortunately, it was not a wedding as Ellen had hoped. Instead, disaster struck right in the heart of the community. Helen was killed on her way home. Just one of the many motorbike accidents that cover half a spread in the local newspaper before being replaced by some other equally horrible event in someone else's life.

To our little community, it was devastating – not only because we had lost a dear friend but also because we had to watch Ellen work her way through each day that followed, merely functioning. All events and functions stopped. It was weeks before Ellen was able hold any sort of funeral, as much to allow for relatives and friends to arrive as anything else.

Maureen could be seen driving past at all times of the day and night, gathering as much information on Helen as possible. Mary decamped to Ellen's and barely returned home. Relatives arrived like moths to a light, desperate to have some contact with someone who could keep Helen's spirit alive for them. Ellen slogged and slumped her way through each second and minute of the day. Drenched in sorrow, grief emitting from her every pore. An uncomfortable perfume that we will all emit at some point and, therefore, instinctively recognise.

Newcomers like the Smiths were shielded from all this community outpouring of grief. They knew of Helen, but her job had meant she was away so much that they hadn't had time to get to know her well. Rap understood Ellen's grief only too well, but his children didn't seem to notice. The youngest children, as they so often do, played, argued and went on with their lives, treating everybody, including Ellen, in the same way as normal.

"Dad said there is going to be a walk. Will it be a big walk, and will you bake those special cakes of yours for us?"

"Sorry! It's a wake you idiot, not a walk. Ellen isn't going to bake for anyone, especially not you. We have to bake for her." Only one of her siblings could get away with insulting Fawn so openly.

"We do? So, what would you like us to bake for you? Swallow can bake gingerbread men, and me and Stag can put fhings on them to make them look pretty. Would that do?"

Ellen looked down at Fawn's earnest little face and dredged up an attempt at a smile.

"That will be fine." It was the most animated she had looked since she'd been bereaved. If only we could have taken a leaf out of the children's book and acted normally around her, it might have helped. We couldn't of course. Every time we looked into her eyes we saw the pain, hurt and anger that swirled around in a tornado of grief-stricken confusion.

This was to be Maureen's first go-it-alone funeral. She had been involved in a few before, but this was her first solo performance. Maureen wanted to make sure it would be a funeral to remember, not only as a commemoration of Helen as we all remembered her, but Maureen also longed to capture the very essence of who Helen had been. She desperately needed to help Ellen find her path to recovery, a path that would allow her to emerge as one complete person, instead of a grief-stricken half of a partnership. Being Maureen's first funeral, it would always have special significance for her, but with the deceased and their partner being her friends, it would carry even more meaning. She had been quite willing though for someone else to take over at the start.

"It's a bit too near to my heart. Perhaps, we should ask one of the other humanists to do it," Maureen had said at one point.

In a flash of anguish, Ellen spat back, "Maureen, I'm the one who has lost everything, *everything*, do you hear?" Tears streamed down her face. "I'm sorry, so sorry. Please, please, I want you there at the front; I want you to hold the service. You of all people, you know everything about everybody. You are our friend; we need you to do this for us, for her and for me."

That was all it had taken to shake Maureen free from the initial shock of Helen's death. Now she had a focus, she threw herself into the task.

Every bed available had been taken in the area. Friends and colleagues from work had arrived, mostly the night before. As the last of the relatives arrived so the last of the beds disappeared. It was not just the bed and breakfasts that were full. Mattresses had been pulled out from under beds, sofas had been made up, and even the few rooms at the pub had been taken. Visitors not involved in the next day's event could have been forgiven for thinking that some sort of celebration was taking place. Relatives who had not seen each other for ages linked arms and downed a few pints together, and friends who had lost touch years before became reacquainted.

The village took on a strange atmosphere. Ellen was cocooned from it all as much as possible.

The over-optimistic, hoped-for sunshine the next morning did not materialise. Small, bitter snowflakes hurled themselves from the sky. There were not enough to cover the ground and make it brilliant or picturesque, just enough to make it freezing and damp. Plans had to be changed, and the outdoor celebration of life was abandoned.

Luckily, Maureen had a contingency plan in hand. I had been woken by the familiar knocking of her walking stick on my door at six that morning. The sun hadn't even got out of bed yet, but there was I opening the door to a bright and breezy Maureen. She was clad head-to-toe in warm, fleecy clothes, all of which were coated in a thin covering of snow.

"Morning, Stroma, I need your help. Everything has to be moved to the hall. This horrible snow is going to turn into cold, horrible rain soon. It's going to be too wet to have the service outside. It's okay, I had already spoken to Ellen about what we'd do if this happened. She doesn't want anyone else dying so won't risk anyone catching pneumonia at this do today."

"What exactly are you needing me for?" A horrible thought had entered my head. Surely, she wouldn't expect me to lift the coffin? Well, I certainly wouldn't be able to do that on my own. She gave me a knowing look.

"Nothing heavy, you understand, just the frills and things. Helen is at home with Ellen. That's all arranged – she was always going to be leaving their house this morning wherever we held the service."

All this information was flung at me before I had even put the kettle on. "Tea?"

"Aye, that would be grand. I wouldn't mind a bit of toast if you have any. I haven't had time to get mine yet. Too busy watching the sky and listening to the early weather forecast.

Can't have my tummy rumbling halfway through the service,
now"—her voice broke a little, then with great effort, she pulled
in her emotions—"now can we?"

We'd finished sorting the hall in time for the first people to
arrive. After the initial shock, the mourners naturally migrated
toward the many photographs that surrounded them on the
walls. Pictures of the colourful characters who brighten our
community, ruins and new-builds, washing lines and fishing
boats, all with the people who lived and breathed in the community where Helen had lived. Among them were photographs that
had been taken offshore. Men and women in boilers and
uniforms, dramatic skies and industrial rigs. Helen had taken
hundreds of photographs over the years. She had documented
her life here and at work. I saw myself through her lens – at
stalls and standing up at meetings. I never had a clue she was
even there, let alone had taken my picture. The best pictures
were without question those she had taken of Ellen, Mary and
Maureen. Love and friendship shone out of their eyes. They had
got so used to her with a camera over the years that they had
barely noticed she had one. Although we had seen the occasional
photograph, no one had seen this collection. It was a beautiful
gift she had left for the community – I wondered if she had
known that.

As everyone settled back into their seats, we heard a roar
outside. Ellen arrived accompanied by the ever-present Mary.
Two lines of bikers walked in behind her and sat in the back two
rows. Maureen turned her wheelchair around and looked
straight at Ellen who nodded slightly.

"Ellen and the family would like me to thank you all for
coming and welcome you to Helen's portrait of her life here in
Blàs. You can see from the photographs just how much she loved
living here. Ellen can also see how much you all loved and

adored Helen in return. Helen was from a local family…" And from there, Maureen went on securing and tying Helen's place and life into the community. It was a history lesson on her family tree that only Maureen could have known well enough to pull off. Funny anecdotes and music lifted the atmosphere, celebrating her life. By the time her straw coffin topped with cream and pink roses left the hall, there was still a sense of sadness, but there was no longer the utter despair there had been at the beginning.

Two lines of bikers followed her to her resting place. Ellen sat behind one of the bikers, and Mary was lifted by two burly men onto the back of another bike. Then it dawned on me it was Scott, Ellen's nephew, on the bike. I hadn't seen him since our fling last summer. Maureen pulled in at my side.

"Well?"

"Well what?"

"Well, how was it for you?"

"I beg your pardon."

She followed my gaze and let out a big sigh.

"Not him. Not everything is about your love life, you know… well, maybe it would be, if I were Lottie… How was the *service*?"

"Sorry, yes it was fine… actually, more than fine, Maureen. You did a really good job."

"Thank you, but I'm not finished yet. Got to go and zoom after that lot. I'll see you in the pub afterward? We're setting off some rockets later tonight, just as a final farewell."

Later that night, I found myself standing next to Scott watching the rockets head high into the sky before bursting with colour. Never one for more words than were needed, he turned to me and said, "Stroma."

"Aye, Scott."

And that was it once more until morning.

Helen's death seemed to ignite the flames of romance and commitment in the community. The need to carry on living and make the most of what life could offer was running like a river in spate. A blossoming romance between Rap and Jill had developed which quickly grew in intensity. Much to the joy of the children, or at least the younger Smiths, Rap had proposed. Or more correctly, Fawn and Stag had done it for him, if Maureen was to be believed.

"He was taking a bottle of wine up to where Jill was painting out on the point. You could see the twins trailing behind him with a basket of picnic food. I saw him trip and fall before he even got to her. The twins thought he was proposing before they caught up, so Stag was shouting at Jill to say yes. I could hear him shout right enough from where I was on the sea wall, but I couldn't hear what he said, unfortunately. Anyway, Fawn got in on the act too – they are like a tag team those two. She even said 'please' if Stag is to be believed. 'Please will you be our new mummy?' I mean, how could she say no?" Maureen was loving this. She had been close enough to witness it herself. Still, if you heard Rap's version, it was more of an accident than a foregone proposal.

"I was going to ask her eventually; the twins just beat me to it," he supplied. "I had just been hoping to enjoy a quiet picnic, the two of us together. I told the twins it was a special picnic with Jill and myself. They had already eaten and almost cleaned me out of food. I persuaded them to leave us in peace to eat, by saying it was a special day, and they got the total wrong end of the stick, but I couldn't be happier."

You could feel spirits in the village lifting again, any excuse to celebrate life was grabbed. Jill and Rap wanted a quick ceremony with not too much fuss. It was hard to believe that Jill had lived in Blàs as long as she had and yet still believed she could get away with that. People were desperate to confirm they were still alive, and a good party was just what was needed.

Luckily for the village, the children were determined to be involved, and that meant there would indeed be an excuse or two to make merry. Fawn expressed her personality as strongly as ever, wishing to be dressed like a fairy with wings. Stag wanted a kilt and a sword. Rap had compromised by allowing him a *sgian-dubh* (a ceremonial Scottish dirk) in his sock, as was the tradition. However, it would be a fake. Lark and Swallow were more laid-back about the whole affair as befitted children of their age. Unfortunately, for both Jill and Rap, Mary had taken a surprisingly strong interest and was meddling happily.

She was sat with us, retelling tales of her youth when weddings were the culmination of a drawn-out process following a long list of traditions. Maureen helped herself to another piece of cake as Karen and Grace arrived. They had managed to grab an evening without their children and merrily joined us in Mary's garden. The twins' presence, however, ensured our gathering was not without the odd child or two. *Poor Karen*, I thought; *you may have escaped from your own children tonight, but you can't get away from your pupils so easily.*

"Now the blackening," Mary said, her eyes sparkling as she enthralled the twins with stories of her youth, "was originally held by the women of the villages. My blackening as a young woman was a much different thing from what happens nowadays. It started, I'm sure, because we didn't like to wear those horrible uncomfortable shoes. We preferred to walk around in bare feet when we could." She pulled Fawn up onto her knee. Both Stag and Fawn's eyes lit up. Not having to wear shoes sounded like a good idea to them.

The twins' habits echoed the wildcats found hereabouts, stalking the village, never going where invited, opting instead to give the pleasure of their company wherever it was ignored. We were all good at pretending not to notice as they crept in and about. When they couldn't be found at Jill's, they were normally either in the woods or at Mary's. Her calm disposition attracted them like midgies to warm blood.

"What's a blackening now fhen?" asked Stag as he stuffed the last bite of a cake into his mouth.

"Well, it's a tradition that has sort of turned totally upside down on what it used to be."

"What's that mean then?" Stag pressed.

"Here, let me explain a bit more. It used to be done, as I said, the night before the wedding. In my day, all the women of the village would gather in the bride's house and wash the bride's feet. That's what happened to me and my two unmarried bridesmaids. Bridesmaids had to be unmarried of course. Then the young married women of the village would come in later on, and we would have a wee drink and a laugh and joke, and tell stories. It was lovely. A right women's night of sharing and joy."

"Wash your feet – yuck! That is horrible. I don't want to wash Jill's feet."

"Well, for one thing, Stag, you are not a girl, so you wouldn't, and another, they don't bother with washing feet anymore. It's a shame really; it was a lovely bonding moment for me with the other women of the village."

"Were your feet very dirty, Mary?" Fawn whispered.

"Well, yes and no, my lamb. It's not that I didn't have shoes, only it was that nice walking through soft grass in the spring in bare feet. Mind you, in late summer, the longer grass could cut your feet sore, so it could."

Fawn looked around at Mary and touched her face gently "The blackening sounds really nice to me, Mary," she said.

Mary smiled as she continued. "Nowadays, if you have a blackening at all, it is the direct opposite of what it once was. Is that not right, Karen?"

"Yes, it is. When I got married, they grabbed me and put me in a cart. Then they got hold of Jack, and we were pulled throughout the village. People clapped and wished us luck, and some threw all sorts of smelly stuff on us. If you look at some of the photos up in the hall that Helen took, you can see us all covered in horrible, smelly gunge."

"That was you fith all that muck on you?" Stag asked, looking at his teacher in awe.

"Yes, it was. Helen liked to take black-and-white photographs. That's probably why you didn't recognise me."

"How did you get all that muck off?" he asked.

"Well, once we got as far as the harbour, they just tipped up the cart, and we fell into the water. The cart followed us, as it was even smellier."

"Wasn't the water cold then?" asked Stag. His mind was trying to fit all the pieces together in the hope he could do the same to his dad.

"Oh yes," continued Mary, "but it was a great blackening, even though it was back to front. Now, it is about getting the couple as dirty as they can be, but there is still the cleaning element, right at the end and then a wee party. After your teacher and Jack were dumped into the water, we all headed back to the pub and had a drink to warm us up. Karen and Jack joined us later, after… well, after they had heated up."

Karen flushed a bright shade of red and coughed.

"Was it hot chocolate?" Fawn asked eagerly.

"Sorry, wee lass, was that hot chocolate, you said?" Mary asked.

"Yes, of course, it was," said Karen. "With lots of fresh cream and marshmallows."

"I didn't know the pub did..." Maureen began then stopped. "Oh, I see, yes. We all had hot chocolate; it was grand – just the job when you are cold."

"I'd like that," said Stag. "I'd like to drop dad into the harbour. It would be great fun." The twins looked at each other and smiled.

"But would Jill still want to be our mummy if we threw her into the harbour?" Fawn was taking no chances that Jill would change her mind.

"Oh, I think Jill would want to be your mummy whatever you did," Mary said, a grin spreading over her wrinkled face. She had decided at some point that she wanted there to be a blackening for this wedding. The first part of her strategy was to inform the twins, and then I suspected she would leave it to the rest of us take it forward. She was off to a good start. Fawn slipped down from Mary's knees and ran off with her brother to find their older siblings.

"Actually, I'm with Fawn here," I said. "That whole washing of the feet and having a women's night in sounds quite nice."

"Is there something you would like to share with us, Stroma?" Mary twinkled.

I felt my face burn up red and cursed my stupidity "No, nothing, nothing at all. I just thought it sounded a lot nicer than getting bombarded with smelly fish."

"Are you trying to keep our traditions alive through them then, Mary?" Maureen asked.

"Well, someone has got to do it. My Angus would have been the first to encourage them. I'm just helping them along."

Poor Rap and Jill had no option after that.

Right on schedule, a week before the wedding, Paul of the Sheds turned up at the Smith's household with a car and trailer. The inside of the trailer was covered in plastic as were the two throne-like chairs that were secured to the floor. Scott, Ellen's nephew, had stayed on after the funeral. He produced two disposable coveralls that would allow the couple some relief from the onslaught to come. There had been many discussions about this. The children, apart from Fawn, felt quite strongly that their dad and Jill shouldn't be allowed to wear anything but their own clothes. Fawn didn't want Jill upset and would have rather, on the whole, gone for the feet-washing ceremony. She was still nervous that Jill would somehow change her mind and opt out of the wedding altogether. The males of the village didn't think that coveralls should be allowed, but most of the women felt the opposite. Jill was thankful that the women won in the end. She entered into the spirit of things by adding handmade crowns for herself and Ralph. Their headgear consisted of workmen's helmets ringed with a wreath of leaves and flowers. Their welly boots had been sprayed bright silver and sparkled in the sun.

Their children were excited and had the honour of throwing the first buckets of smelly gunge that had been fermenting outside for days. After much laughter, the car was driven off around the village stopping at various spots so the inhabitants could cheer, throw more buckets and follow the cart as it made its way to the harbour.

Cars joined in behind the trailer, at a safe distance so as not to get covered in the invasive, smelly gunge. By the time they made it to the harbour, the sun and smell were high as the mixture of fish, seaweed, flour, eggs and various other ingredients started to bake in the heat. Lark and Swallow, and their brother and sister waited excitedly at the harbour. There was much laughter and joking among the crowd when they parted to let the cart through. Amid the shrieking and crude comments, the smelly but happy couple were dumped unceremoniously into the harbour. Within seconds, Lark, Swallow, Stag and Fawn had leapt into the water to be beside them.

As the couple and children dried off, the pub served hot chocolate as requested. The merriment and singing went on through the afternoon and into the evening. Everyone agreed that the marriage would be a huge success, given that the blackening had gone so well. Now they only had to survive the wedding the following week.

Apple blossom draped the trees in whites and soft pinks. A small fairy-like figure danced with a slightly taller wingless spirit. They fluttered like giant May butterflies around a tall slender woman in a mid-length, pale green dress. Her hair shone in multi-coloured, short layers held down by a bridal crown covered in leaves and meadowsweet blossom. My breath caught in my throat as they walked toward me. A fairy queen and her followers.

"Do you like my wand, Stroma? Look, Swallow has one too, but I'm the only one with wings," Fawn chatted excitedly.

"Yes, I do. I see you and Swallow are real flower fairies for the day," I replied. "And just look at you, Jill – you look amazing."

"Ach, it was just something I threw together the other night." She laughed. We strolled together toward the hall where Maureen would perform the service. Latecomers running in ahead of us made their way in. Others came out their doors, handing flowers to Jill and wishing her good luck as we passed. Joy and sunshine shone out as Auntie Lottie hastened toward us.

"Can you walk around the block again, please?" she gasped as she reached us.

Jill frowned through what was now an arm full of flowers. "Why what's wrong?"

"We're not in a car, you know, Auntie Lottie. We can't just drive around the corner."

"Sorry, but it's Rap and the boys; there has been a bit of a holdup. According to Paul, something about smelly feet and the blackening."

"I told daddy last night," Swallow stated, "before we went over to Jill's. The boy's shoes were stinking still. They chucked them out in the garden after the blackening and only went looking for them last night. Dad said he was going to have to put them through the wash."

Jill started to laugh, probably with some relief. "Ach well, I'm sure they will find something else to wear."

"I hope so," Swallow said, scrunching her nose. "I'm not standing next to them with their feet smelling like they did last night."

"Look, look, here they come." A large 4x4 drove past with the boys pressed hard against the window pulling faces at their sisters. The girls giggled and pulled some in return.

"Ah well,' Jill said, "I will just have to get used to this, I suppose," laughing along with them.

We watched as two kilted figures got out of the car, and Rap and Paul rushed into the hall. Trees showered cherry and apple blossom on the well-wishers and the bridal party as we made our way toward the boys who were to accompany Jill down the aisle.

"What on earth have they got on their feet?" Auntie Lottie asked, staring at Lark and Stag.

"It looks like their slippers," Swallow said in awe. "Yes." She giggled. "That's Lark's bigfoot slippers and Stag has his batman ones on." We all started to laugh as we drew nearer to the boys.

"Like your snazzy footwear," Jill said, "goes really nicely with your kilts."

"We didn't have a choice," said Lark; "our trainers are still stinking. Dad said you wouldn't mind. Do you?"

"Not at all."

"We wanted to slide down the hall in our stocking feet, but Dad said we could leave that till the ceilidh dance tonight," added Lark.

"And we couldn't put on our wellies as then we couldn't have worn our *sgian-dubhs* down our socks. We have to wear them. Mary said it's trade distional, and anyway, how do we protect Jill if we don't have our *sgian-dubh*?"

"It's traditional, you idiot. How come you can say the Gaelic words, okay, and you can't use English right." His brother nudged him.

The pipes started, and Jill quickly got her Celtic escort organised. They set off down the hall. Jill followed in the wake of her baffie-wearing, kilted little warriors. A soft chuckle echoed across the room, which immediately changed to sighs of "ah, will you look at her" to "they are so bonnie, just look at the bairns."

What followed was a magical day of joy, fun and laughter, and of course, lots of dancing. The youngest bairns were eventually carried home to bed by Paul and Scott. Auntie Lottie and I settled into the Smiths' home for the night to allow Jill and Rap one night without interruption at Jill's cottage. It was to be remembered by everyone as an enchanting wedding.

13

Nobody had taken much notice of the strangers who had been wandering around the area, taking photographs and measurements, asking locals who owned what, and where the best sunrises and sunsets could be had. Even enquiring about decent hotels and bed and breakfasts didn't raise much interest. We were all used to visitors asking such questions and looking around our village.

Working and living in the amazing countryside didn't make us immune to its beauty and unique appeal. Rather, as locals, we were well-aware of what we had and wanted to preserve it, even if it meant being frozen to death and drowned like a rabbit during the somewhat pernicious weather. The pink and violet days in winter and the long, lazy, blue evenings of summer more than made up for it. We were, however, astounded to discover that these strangers were from a television company. Maureen, of course, was the first with the gossip.

"Six foot and long, lazy hair. Got that Celtic look, you know – dark hair, pale blue eyes and bleached white face. Would have been able to rock red hair too with that combination. And he's not even an actor, such a waste! Anyway, he's here for filming a new series about a small community. One-off, he says, but who knows. Oh, Stroma, but he is a fine figure of a man. Do you want me to introduce you?"

"No, and no again, Maureen. I have too much to do without hanging around a film crew like some groupie."

"Well, you won't need to 'hang around'. He is staying at the old estate house."

Now *that* I hadn't heard.

"The owners have rented it to the film company for the next two weeks while they get it in the bag, or should that be 'the can'? It's a shame Ellen isn't back; she could have done with the distraction. Could have started her new B & B she was talking about."

Soon after the funeral, Ellen had upped stakes and disappeared. Mary wouldn't say where she had gone and wasn't sure when she would be back

"It's what she is needing, too many people here about rely on that poor woman. She needs to get away before she makes any major decisions. Do us all good to sort things out for ourselves."

She was right of course. Mary had gone through much the same herself. Married for years to the local storyteller, historian and all-round character of the area, she knew how difficult it was to adjust to being one person, on your own, an individual answerable to no one for anything, not even whether you stayed or went. Mary, however, had not run away or even mentioned the possibility of going away for a holiday. She needed to stay where she was firmly rooted in the earth and soul of the area. This was where she could connect with Angus. Blàs was where their spirits entwined, and where she could seek him out in her heart and mind.

Helen, on the other hand, had spent her working life away. Although she played a big part in the community, she had led a life outside it too. Ellen needed to connect to that part of her life, away from here and its people.

There were times when there was nothing better than being somewhere everyone knew you, and people would hail you and catch you up on news about family, friends, themselves… However, there were other times when all you wanted was to be the stranger in the woods, the foreigner without a friend, the daytripper with no knowledge or understanding of the language and lives of the individuals who lived here. You didn't want to know that the person you had just spoken to had been to the dentist the week before and had a tooth pulled, or that the woman who had just asked after your family was having a torrid affair with one of the fishermen or one of the local ghillie's, or that one of DJ's clients had just shot the biggest stag seen in these parts for years. All of which could have been found out about before breakfast depending on whether you had run into Maureen or Auntie Lottie, first-thing.

"I don't think Ellen would have been up to looking after anyone right now."

"Aye, well, perhaps you are right at that. You know they will be looking for film extras, don't you? Walk-on parts and the likes. You could get a nice wee bit of pocket money. Put it toward your Christmas presents, or a nice wee holiday," Maureen suggested.

It wasn't the thought of me affording a holiday that was putting a glint in her eye. I knew she hadn't given up on finding me a suitable male friend. She had been spending way too much time in Auntie Lottie's company. I was their joint project now.

I decided to try and get her to see my point of view. "When would I have the time?"

"Ach, I'm sure you could fit it in. You work from home."

"Yes, and the key word there is *work*, which I should be getting on with right now, so I'd better go."

Maureen had got me thinking though. I knew of many people throughout the Highlands who had taken part as extras in films that had been shot near or here about. From what I could remember, the money they got paid for appearing in a crowd scene or, more precisely, battle scenes and walking around a hill-top, was not too bad. Auntie Lottie would have already looked into this, I felt sure. After prodding the thought around for a while, I arranged a wee get-together with her to find out what she knew.

Auntie Lottie arrived early, a couple of nights later, cake in one hand and bottle of wine in the other.

"Find the glasses. I've a wee proposition for you." This was from Auntie Lottie before I even got a chance to question her about the whole 'extras' thing. She never did get around to asking me why I had asked her over and what I wanted from her. But then again, Auntie Lottie and Maureen had become their own tag team since Ellen had left. There was always one of them nosing around or giving advice to the inhabitants of the village. Most people seemed to accept this new role they had taken on. Their past rivalry over who could find out the best news in the area had been forgotten. Instead, they had become a formidable team – our very own community agony aunts. Even if you didn't really want their advice, they freely gave it and expected you to make use of it as payment for their interest.

Many households, I suspect, were visited by them across the area from Blàs to Inbhirasgaidh. They persuaded individuals and, in some cases, whole families to apply for positions as extras in the filming that was taking place. I often wondered if the two of them were on some sort of commission, or had set up their own agency for the sole purpose of providing extras.

The programme was a pilot for a proposed new drama series. It meant, for the next few weeks, we locals would have a life of early starts, late nights, heavy make-up and pampered hair. On saying that, Auntie Lottie's hair did not end up looking that much different from how it always did. I met many people from quite a few of the communities around and about who I would only normally have seen at meetings. It sometimes took a while to recognise them as they strode around the hills and, some-times, Inbhirasgaidh in strange and wonderful forms of dress. Even our relative newcomers, the Smiths, had got in on the act. The twins enjoyed the attention and having their faces smeared in what looked like dirt all day. Fawn and Swallow were prone to getting fed up with all the hanging around, but soon got over that when they realised what they could buy with the money they were earning.

The actors, technicians and the rest of the staff got on with their work with the minimum of fuss and very little wild partying. It was us locals who partied into the night, changed our conversations from discussing the weather and the crofts to talking about the light, the make-up, and the lines some had acquired. The only exception to what appeared to be total engagement in the whole process was Paul of the Sheds, who already had numerous jobs of his own to get on with. Even Old Tam and Shep had a walk-on part and would be seen in the background. Luckily, they were keen to have old Shep in much the shape he came in, so no bathing was required.

One day we were all busy developing our method acting and totally immersed in the project, the next, everything had disappeared. Vans, sports cars, extra big lorries, expensive trailers and the hundreds of people, all just disappeared into the mountain mist

14

Sun shone late into the evening and birds filled the air with their songs. There was a lazy feel sprinkled around the village. People sat in gardens or on the numerous benches scattered around the area. Light clothing and hair lifted in the gentle breeze that meandered its way through the community. The hustle and bustle atmosphere had left with the TV company, and what passed for normality had quickly reasserted itself.

Of course, the peace and tranquillity didn't last long. Just as I was bathing in that lackadaisical feeling, up popped Auntie Lottie with news of her own. Not even Maureen had dropped a hint about what had been going on. It must have been killing her not to tell, but it did explain why I hadn't seen her for a while. She hadn't trusted herself not to say anything.

Auntie Lottie came marching up my garden, homemade cake in hand, with instructions to put the kettle on before I even had a chance to greet her. She delivered her news before my first bite of cake.

"So, you see, everyone will hear about it soon enough. Only I thought I'd better let you know first, and besides, Maureen is giving herself an ulcer having to keep it all a secret."

Once Auntie Lottie and Paul of the Sheds had so openly let

the community know that they were an item, things had moved on at pace. The initial surprise had been followed up by lots of head nodding and knowing comments:

"Ach you could see how they flirted at Old Mary's party, 'twas obvious to me."

"She had looked that heartbroken these last few months. Even got herself that silly-looking dog to try and mend her broken heart."

"Man, explains why Paul of the Sheds has been that touchy. Haven't been able to pass the time of day with him without him asking if I've seen Lottie here there or anywhere, and if I said, 'Aye, saw her in Inbhirasgaidh,' he would near take my head off then stamp away muttering to himself so he would."

"Thank goodness" Maybe things around here can get back to normal. I was in danger of losing my crown for being the bearer of all news here..."

The latter was, of course, Maureen's contribution as she filled the community in about their meetings, stolen moments, and how she had known all along about the couple but had been sworn to secrecy by Ellen. "I was just being a good friend to them you see, didn't want to scare them by letting on." I knew the truth of that statement, of course, and her silence had had nothing to do with protecting their relationship. Rather, it was fear of Ellen wrath, if Maureen had so much as breathed a word to anyone.

Paul, the foresworn bachelor, the envy of quite a few married men in the area who thought of his existence as carefree and independent, had finally succumbed to matters of the heart. The disappointment in him for giving up his freedom could be seen in the shake of their heads when Auntie Lottie and Paul of the Sheds walked past, hand in hand. The men weren't alone in their negative response – many single women over the age of forty stared daggers at their retreating backs. They were well in the minority though. The community in general was delighted that these two singletons had both found their match. Now that the pair's relationship was out in the open, they saw no need to wait to move on to the next logical step. Paul of the Sheds, within days of their reunion, had gone down on one knee, in the old-fashioned way, and asked Auntie Lottie to marry him.

"I have to admit. I was a little taken aback, but how could I refuse when he asked so nicely?"

"Auntie Lottie, are you sure? Only, you don't sound so convinced?" Along with the sparkle in her eye, there was a hesitancy in her voice.

"Well, I am sure that I want to spend the rest of my life with him, but do we really need to get married to do that? I mean, I have had many, and I mean many, wonderful lovers, but never contemplated spending my life stuck with them, so I know Paul is different…"

"Have you spoken to him about this? He may be happy to wait a little or even just for you both to live together." There were times, still, in in my relationship with Auntie Lottie, even given her twenty years seniority, that I somehow felt like the only adult in the room.

"Well, of course, I sort of have."

"And what do you mean by 'sort of have'? Did you actually use words like, oh I don't know… for example, 'Wouldn't you rather move in together? Since we are both so committed anyway, we don't need a ring on our fingers.' You know, stuff like that," I offered.

"Ooh, that's very good, Stroma. And no, no, not really. More like, 'Well, we could always wait a wee while.' And of course, 'I love you,' and, 'Yes, I believe in marriage and sharing things is so important in any relationship,' but he just didn't seem to want to understand what I was hinting at."

I wasn't surprised – even I wasn't sure what she had been trying to say, and I *knew* what she wanted to say.

"Look, Auntie Lottie, if you have any doubts about marriage, you have to tell him, but be careful or it could all blow up in your face. You don't want to hurt his feelings or lose him now, do you?"

"Oh, no, of course not. Maybe I should just keep quiet and not say a word. It is just… well, you know, marriage, changing my name and moving out, or him moving in permanently, not just shifting around together. And you know, in some ways, he is quite old-fashioned. I am the only one he has ever asked to marry. He wants everyone to know we are committed."

"I think people can tell you only have eyes for each other. As long as you haven't set a day yet, you can just make it a long engagement. Do you think you can handle that?"

"I never thought… Of course! That could be the answer. Why didn't I think of that before?"

"Before what, Auntie Lottie?"

"Well, before I spoke to Maureen, of course, and booked her for our wedding."

"Oh, for goodness sake! You have booked Maureen already? When you weren't even sure you wanted to get married? Well then, when is the date? Maybe you could postpone it for a few years?"

"I don't think so. You see, she is so busy, and well, after Paul asked me, Maureen happened to be wheeling past, and we were a bit caught up in the moment, and well, we just sort of jumped the gun and—"

"Auntie Lottie, when are you getting married?"

"Four weeks. We are getting married in four weeks, and I don't want to. I want to stay as we are for a while. What am I going to do? You have to help me, Stroma, please."

I agreed to help Auntie Lottie then sent her home with instructions to come back to me in the morning. Of course, she opted to go and see Paul instead. Why two supposed grown-ups couldn't sort this out for themselves was beyond me. But then again, neither of them had managed any sort of long-term relationship or had even wanted to have any sort of committed relationship before, so I suppose it was all new to them. I found myself wishing for the return of Ellen, and not for the first time either. I missed her presence in the village, in my life, her interference, her ear always open to me, her unquestionable love and her incredibly good baking. This was just the sort of situation where she would have calmly sorted out the whole scenario, without too much heartbreak.

I walked into the evening, still almost daylight at this time of year, and found myself in the only other place I could have gone. I opened the back door and was surprised to hear voices so late on in Mary's kitchen.

"Aah, there you are," Mary said as if expecting me. "I've just put the kettle on for some nice hot chocolate, what with the hour being so late."

"Sorry, Mary, I can always come back in the morning. Hello, Maureen, you will be filling in Mary with your news then."

"I was that. What a right pair, would you believe they have booked me for four weeks' time? Well, I can tell you if you could have seen both their faces when I said I have a slot in four weeks – which I do, but I was only joking with them. What a picture! I thought Paul was going to pass out and Lottie have a heart attack. Her eyes were out on stalks. Made we want to say, I'd made a mistake and that they would have to wait, but they both turned away so quickly, laughed, kissed, then went off together. What are they playing at? You'd think, by the time they got to their ages, they would have more sense and wait a wee while to get used to the idea of marriage. Love makes a fool of us all, I suppose." Maureen took a slurp of her hot chocolate.

Well, that answered a few questions right away. It wasn't just Auntie Lottie who was a bit concerned about them tying the knot so soon.

"There you go, Stroma," Mary said as she placed a steaming mug in front of me. "I was saying to Maureen here before you came in that it was about time I had Paul and Lottie over for supper. It is a while since I've had the chance to catch up with Lottie, and I've got a few things I need mending that I'm sure

Paul would do for me. Maureen here is going to give them my invite on her way home. Isn't that right, Maureen?"

"It is too, and you and I, Stroma, are going to be back in, the night after tomorrow for a little after-supper drinks with our friends. Once, of course, Mary has sorted them both out."

&

Two nights later, when Maureen and I presented ourselves at Mary's kitchen table once more, we were relieved to see a happy couple with contented smiles on their faces.

"You have to congratulate us, girls," Paul said, holding up a small dram. "You two are the first to know – Lottie and I are moving in together—"

"One week at my house the next at Paul's," Auntie Lottie interrupted. "Then, when we have worked out which house suits us best, we may set a date for our wedding. So sorry Maureen, we won't be wanting that date you originally gave us."

"Not a problem." Maureen winked over at me. "I have another couple waiting, hoping for a child's naming date event that day anyway, so I can confirm their booking instead."

"Right, well, sorry to have to break up this little party, but I'm off to let Grace and my grandson know the good news. You coming, Lottie?"

"Well, you give that little grandson of yours a cuddle from me, and tell Grace I'll catch up with her on Friday as agreed."

"My," said Maureen after they had left. "Ellen would have been proud of you, Mary. You seem to have sorted them out right enough."

"Ellen? Tell me, Maureen," Mary said, laughing. "Who do you think taught our Ellen in the first place."

We smiled together, raised our glasses and toasted, "To absent friends and loved ones."

15

"Oh my God, I thought she was too old to get pregnant"

"Who would have thought it at her age? Must be some kind of miracle."

The male population, of course, was giving all the kudos to Paul.

"Aye, life in the old dog yet."

Rumours were running rife after Maureen had burst into the village shop one morning to impart her news.

"I see our latest couple to set up home together are to become parents then. Due in the not-too-distant future, so they tell me. They are fair excited about it. Well, Lottie most of all, needless to say. I wonder if it means they will finally start sharing the one house."

By the time Maureen had made it back to her own doorstep, Old Tam and Shep were awaiting her.

"Ye widnae hiv a cup o tea gaein, wid ye, Maureen? Eh heird some affy surprisin news."

"Well, if it is about Lottie and Paul, you are too late. But you are welcome to come in for a cuppa. I'm sure Shep won't say no to a biscuit."

The pair were locked inside for the rest of the morning,

putting the world to right, no doubt. I saw them saying their goodbyes as I returned to the village after a visit to a group. I had barely got out of my car before I was stopped and told the good news by a less-than-happy ex-partner of Paul's.

"You'd think at his age he would have more sense."

"I'm sorry, but I'm not following you. Who are we talking about exactly?"

She had been moaning about the pair living together to anyone who would listen. As Auntie Lottie's almost relative, I was, of course, the one to take responsibility for listening to all the reasons as to why they were so unsuited.

"Paul and that… you know, your so-called auntie, his so-called common-law wife."

"That would be Auntie Lottie, Paul MacQuin's love of his life and partner?

"Yes, yes who else could it be? Comes flouncing back here and steals the man from right under my nose. He loved me once, you know, and still would if it hadn't been for that… that woman." The truth, of course, was nothing of the kind. She and Paul had a minor flirtation that lasted perhaps four weeks, and it was long enough ago to be historic. I don't ever remember them being a couple as I was so young at the time.

"Just ignore her," Maureen had advised when she'd accosted me previously. "She never got over him, silly woman. Chased him for years, so she did. Him running away like his life depended on it. Told me once he only went with her in the end in a weak moment. Nothing weak about it. She handed herself to him on a plate, and he wasn't one to turn down an offer. Mark you, that was about twenty years ago, before we had all the tourists flocking here."

Maureen had never succumbed to Paul's charms. When she was in her teens, her family had moved abroad, along with her future husband's. They had married young, and a few scant years later, widowed and broken-hearted, Maureen had arrived back in Blàs. Like Lottie, she had been in school with Paul, but unlike her friend and countless others, she had never fallen under his spell. "Ach, he was a right spotty teenager before I left. Always smiling and trying to charm his way with the opposite sex. Apart from the spots, he hasn't changed overly much in my mind." Maybe that was how she had stayed so immune to his obvious charms.

"Are you even listening to me?" barked Paul's wanna-be girlfriend.

"I'm sorry. I'm just back from work and really tired. Was it something important?"

"Important! Well, not if you think a woman of that age becoming pregnant is normal. I bet the conniving wee besom got IVF without telling him so he would feel obliged to move her in. Poor Paul, stuck with her and that child."

"I'm sorry, what are you saying? You think Auntie Lottie is pregnant. Well, first off, if she is, it is no business of yours, and secondly, I would be the first to know about something like that... after Maureen that is, and thirdly, even if it was IVF, that would be their choice. And lastly... well, I have never, never, you hear, not in my entire life, including my parents I may add, never, have I seen a couple so much in love. Have you got that? Never in my entire life." I sent a small apology to my parents, but I was *seachd searbh sgìth* of listening to this woman moan and malign Auntie Lottie. Someone needed to tell her she should get on with her life and leave them to get on with theirs.

I stomped up the path and slammed the door. I could barely believe what I had just heard. Surely not. It's not that I could never envisage them as parents. Paul was already a great dad to Grace. Any child born to them would be very fortunate, but neither of them was young. Paul was already a grandparent, and they weren't exactly within the age bracket that you would expect a couple to be starting a family. Then again, lots of couples had late children. They had taken a long time to admit to each other how they felt. This could be the first and last chance for Auntie Lottie to have a child. I wondered what Iona and

Grace would say, if it was true. Grace already had a child who would be older than… their aunt or uncle. And Grace herself would then be a whole generation older than her sibling. I longed to speak to her but thought I had better wait to hear it first from the happy couple. After all, it wouldn't be the first time the village had become all fired up about something that was not even nearly true. The last time it had been about Mary.

Half the village had been convinced she was moving away with a younger man. When it turned out, all she had done was offer a distant relative bed and board in return for him helping her do a major clean out of stuff from the house.

I was just settling in for the night when Auntie Lottie knocked on the back door and came in with Whisky wiggling along beside her.

"Put the kettle on, or would you rather a different sort of brew? I've something exciting to tell you."

Could it be true then? Was she pregnant?

"Okay, I'm ready."

"We are going to be parents. Me and Paul. We are expecting some babies in about two months." Auntie Lottie's eyes were shining; she looked so happy. They say that sometimes, don't they? That your hair and skin can shine with health. Karen always looked great once she stopped being sick when she was pregnant, so I guessed it must be true. *Wait a minute… babies? More than one*, I thought as her words fully processed.

"Wow, congratulations! That must have been a shock though. Babies, you said?"

"Thank you, yes, but not that much really. He's quite a stud you know. Known for it, you could say."

"Auntie Lottie, that is way too much information. I mean, I know you are thrilled, but I wouldn't go around describing your partner like that."

"Like what? I've not said anything about Paul." She looked at me with a puzzled look on her face just as Maureen thumped her way into the room.

"Well, just look at you, pet. What a clever girl. I was just telling everyone about your lovely news." She bent down and ruffled Whisky's hair in greeting.

"We can't wait. We didn't think we would be so lucky the first time," trilled Auntie Lottie.

Yuck, I knew there were besotted with each other, but that was way too much information. Maureen, needless to say, didn't look even remotely put out, but then again, it was just more fuel for her as town crier.

"How many are you expecting? Paul hinted at three," Maureen added.

"Glass of wine, Maureen?" I tried to change the focus.

"What? No thank you, Stroma, it's just a quick visit. I just wanted to congratulate this lovely mummy-to-be. Clever Whisky, who's having babies then, clever girl?"

"Oh! Oh, right! Good girl, Whisky. So Whisky is the mummy then?"

"Of course, she is. Who did you think we've been talking about? Oh no… Ha, ha. Really? I'm flattered, Stroma, but… Ha, ha. No!"

"You can blame Maureen – she told everyone you were going to be new parents. The whole village thinks it is you and Paul."

"Wait a minute. I never at any point said that Lottie was pregnant. I just said they were to become parents because Whisky is expecting. Who in their right mind could think that Lottie would conceive at her age? Oh, this is priceless. Lottie with child."

"Okay, Maureen, I think you have made your point." Auntie Lottie huffed, the suggestion that she was too old for anything destroying her mood.

Perhaps Maureen had got it right. After all, exactly how many of us can be regarded as in our right minds… for long.

16

Funding had finally come through, and the woods were ours. There was still more money to raise though as the running costs would need covered. As with most ventures, the initial purchase was easy compared to finding the cash to pay the ever-increasing day-to-day costs. Even woods required money spent on them. One of the best outcomes of the whole process was the full integration of the Smith family. Jill had established herself in the community years ago. Now, Rap, Swallow, Lark, Fawn and Stag were also firmly bonded into the community. The burns and rivers that flowed through the woods were as much a part of them as the blood that ran through their veins. If more ideas were needed to raise the money, they were the first to come up with them (not necessarily all usable, of course).

After much consideration, we had foregone the mud match suggested between Blàs and Inbhirasgaidh – much to the twin's disappointment and, it must be said, some of the adults as well. The race with a sheep on your back was similarly disregarded. Although it had been rumoured that some of our teenage boys had attempted their own version under cover of darkness one night. Whisky had become a minor celebrity now that her confinement was getting nearer. People were betting on how many puppies there would be, how many would be boys or girls. Not to be outdone, the Smith children had set up 'guess the puppy names'.

One puppy would be staying with Lottie and Paul of the Sheds, so not too many other homes were needed. Dandies were renowned for their small litters. The twins had refused to take any guesses on where the other puppies would go, as they were of the strong belief that one would be coming their way… when they could get their dad to agree, that was. In among all this activity, something quite unexpected came about. Not a death, birth or marriage then? Nope. Something was found that nobody knew had been lost. A most unusual find as it turned out, and it was all down to the children and their love of the woods.

The Smith children had continued to play, explore and generally claim a large part of the woods as their own. Rap had long-since stopped trying to keep them out. However, he had insisted they carry a mobile phone and come home when he called them. It hadn't seemed to curtail their freedom overly much. If anything, they appeared to spend even more time there than before. Jill, on the other hand, could be found back in her cottage, getting her stock ready for her summer markets.

Heading back from the shop, I was congratulating myself on missing Maureen and her update on who was doing what to whom and why, when I heard a voice yelling. It was Lark, running, swerving and sweeping along like his namesake… only, there was nothing musical about what was coming out of his mouth. Even from a distance, I could clearly hear the panic and fear. Old Tam was first to stop him. Dirt and dust mingled in his hair carried on going when the rest of him came to such an abrupt halt, flying from his head in a cloudy mess.

"Jisit tak yer time, boy. That's it, breathe deep like, and agin. Aye, that's it. Noo, whut's aw th commotion aboot?"

"It's the twins. It collapsed, all of it, it collapsed. We told them not to go on it when it started to wobble, but they wouldn't listen. It collapsed."

"What collapsed and where?" I asked.

Maureen had appeared and was already phoning Paul. Even though we didn't know exactly what had happened yet, Paul and his many hats would be needed in one capacity or another.

"The big hill. You know the big hill? It fell down, and the twins are inside it."

"Where the hell is the big hill?" DJ, down from the glen, had joined the growing circle of worried faces.

"Please, please you have got to help them. It's the big hill, the big hill."

I bent down to Lark whose face was streaked with big muddy rivulets running down from his gritty red eyes.

"What do you call the big hill, Lark? It's your special name, isn't it? What would me or Auntie Lottie call it?"

He looked blank for a moment. "Dun, the old dun. Swallow is waiting there. We tried to find them, but we couldn't."

Paul's 4x4 screeched into the road. Within five minutes, all who could were in his and DJ's cars heading into the woods. The others left behind were collecting shovels, blankets and anything else that could prove useful. Lark had refused to wait. He had jumped in beside Paul.

"I got a phone call first from Rap. He will be up there by now. Swallow had the good sense to phone him as soon as Lark ran off to get help. I've got loads of equipment in my car that should help. Under the circumstances, I thought it better we check it out first to see the lay of the land."

Once inside the woods, we marched as quickly as the paths would allow to the old hillfort or dun. It had been a favourite for all the local bairns for generations. If you didn't know what you were looking for, you may well have marched past it. Over the centuries, the undergrowth had grown more into overgrowth. It was just off a path, a rounded hump. Looking closely, some big stones could be seen, and if you walked around the top, it was obvious that some sort of structure had been built there years before. What remained now was a grassy round with a few loose rocks on the top.

That was before this cave-in. Swallow was kneeling, shouting down into a large hole that had not been there a few days ago. The ground was brittle. It had been an exceptionally dry summer, and the rain had been an infrequent visitor.

"It looks like the soil has shifted with all this strange weather we've been having lately." Translated, this meant our weather had been boring compared to normal patterns. Not many storms or gales, blistering sun, even fog. Each day was the same, eerie in its sameness, not something we were used to at all. The earth was bone-dry and cracking.

"Swallow, Swallow, come away now, there's a good girl, it might give way again."

"I can't, dad has gone down. He's got the wee ones. I've got the rope, but I can't pull them up. I've tried, but I can't get them up." Poor Swallow was crying in fear and frustration. Her grip on the rope never loosened. Paul and DJ sprinted up the mound and took stock.

"Aye, she's right there. She would never have been able to pull them up. But you have done well, lass, very well – you've got them stabilised. Well done. Here now, I've got the strain." DJ gently took hold of the rope. Swallow collapsed on the ground the stress of keeping that tie to her family taking its toll.

Paul took charge and quickly assessed the situation. The ground felt pretty stable, but Paul warned us that if we felt any movement we were to fall back immediately. The damage had already been done. We could hear Paul talking to Rap who had his twins firmly placed beside his feet. They appeared relatively unscathed, considering the cave-in. Once the earth had started to move, they had managed to squeeze themselves under a flat low-lying rock that sheltered them from most of the debris. Stag sounded amazingly chirpy given their ordeal. Their older siblings had taken it much worse, being the ones who could do nothing but watch helplessly, not knowing what had happened to their brother and sister.

"I think I can get a grip on these rocks and pull myself and Fawn up no problem. The rocks are almost like a staircase."

"It may look like that but use the rope. We don't know how stable all that is under the first layer. When you get close enough, pass Fawn up here. Then, depending on how the fall-in has behaved, you can go back and get Stag."

"I don't need help. I can do it myself, wait and see," came Stag's confident voice of youth.

"You just wait there, young man. We don't want any more accidents. Hold fire till your dad gets to you."

Fawn emerged, looking like some mystical, dirt-covered fairy rising from the earth. Unfortunately, most of that earth chose to stay attached to her, but Auntie Lottie gave her a quick once over.

"I think this knee could do with a little attention. Maybe even need a wee trip to have it X-rayed, just to be sure." She wiped as much of the loose soil from Fawn's face as she could. Bits of stick, grass and leaves were intertwined in her hair. "We will have you right in no time, little one." The lack of conversation or any other sort of vocal input from Fawn was giving the rescuers some concern. Silence was not a normal state for this outspoken young girl. Her eyes were huge, staring straight into Auntie Lottie's. She spluttered and coughed then gripped Auntie Lottie tightly, burrowing herself as close as she could get into the caring woman's neck. Rap finally emerged from the pit, hauling Stag behind him. Stag didn't look any different from his twin with his matching forest creature's hairstyle. His clothes were the same dirt-covered mess. One of his legs was bleeding in a few places, but it all appeared superficial.

"You should have seen it. Like a waterfall it was, grass falling and stones, and look, look what we found." Out of his shirt, he produced a skull.

"Oh my God. Yuck! Put that back. Please tell me that isn't human." Auntie Lottie took an involuntary step back.

"And fhis. Fawn found fhis. We was digging it up when everyfhing fell in beside us." Stag produced what looked like just a lump of dirty stone. On closer inspection, we could see the edges of a circle, part of a design running around it.

"Now, that could be interesting. Did you really find that here, Fawn?" Rap asked gently, taking his daughter into his arms. She managed a small nod of the head then buried herself into his neck. "I think this can all wait until later. We need to get my lot seen by a doctor. Stag, you leave that thing with Paul. He will look after it for now."

Paul carefully removed the skull from a very reluctant Stag.

"You will look after it, won't you? Do you fhink he was murdered and dumped here? Do we need to tell the police? I bet I could find the murderer all on my own? Are you—"

"Stag, that's enough. Now come on, my lot, we have to get these scratches checked out."

Rap and his rather grubby family headed off with most of the helpers. It appeared that the children were relatively unhurt. Paul took out his phone.

"Well, here we go. We will see what Constable Jim makes of this. I'm thinking the next call will be to the archaeology department."

Constable Jim arrived in no great hurry. After all, it was obvious to all that the remains were not fresh. Anyway, he had been busy in Inbhirasgaidh where a couple of fishermen had decided that fishing was less lucrative than drug smuggling. He was not at all happy to leave all that excitement behind to the experts, while he had to look at yet another ancient skull that would, in the long-term, result in him losing another case – this time to the aforementioned archaeologists.

17

It was beginning to look like the old skull had less value than the 'stone' brooch which Fawn had found – at least to everyone except Stag who was determined to get his find back. Stag bounced back pretty quickly from the cave-in, but Fawn had lost much of her sparkle, turning into a very quiet and subdued little girl. She still followed her brother around but was very reluctant to go into the woods, even with her older siblings. Rap was becoming more and more concerned about this change in his once precocious child.

"I don't know what to do. She has latched on to Lottie and follows her and that little dog around all the time. The doctor doesn't seem to be worried, but it's not her normal way of things."

"Ach, she will be fine." Maureen was giving out her tea wisdom. It was cafe day in the hall. Consequently, most of the village elders were present. Those who worked from home or were able to build some flexibility into their day were often to be found there as well. It started mid-morning with coffee, cake and the craic – this being a good catch-up on what was going on in the area. For those who could hang around, this simmered along into soup and sandwiches served at lunchtime. Only a short sip, toilet or nappy change later, and it would be time for tea and cake in the afternoon. The older residents walked, wobbled, rode and shuffled along mostly for the lunch and stayed for a blether and catch-up with their hot drink and chosen afternoon treat. The homeworkers, mothers and babies tended to arrive for morning coffee and headed away after lunch.

Maureen's news round-up from around the area and its content often dictated whether it was worth staying around for another cup of something. Fortunately, the cafe was held on the same day the local paper came out which allowed for debates and updates on the stories. Maureen, of course, was the lynchpin in all this. She knew a little fabrication and speculation could go a long way.

Time was always put aside for the older generation's main topics of conversation, those being their own updates on their health, their medication or who had died. Sometimes, it felt like there was some sort of hidden competition, the winner was the one left standing or, more accurately, still breathing. Unfortunately for the winner, being the only one of their known acquaintances left still alive meant there would be no one around to witnesses their victory.

A bare month after the cave-in, there was still lots to examine and debate over. One of the favourite topics was who the skull belonged to. Could it be someone's ancient relative? There were many helpful suggestions.

"Why could they not get that wifey from Dundee to take a look? You know the one that sounds like the Terminator – we can rebuild it."

"The Terminator doesn't say that, you daft eejit."

"Aye, aye, he does. It's his catchphrase. 'We can rebuild it.'"

"No, it's no. It's, 'I'll be back.' Everybody knows that. What films have you been watching? We can rebuild it – what sort of hero says that? Away and don't be so daft."

More helpful advice and thoughts went along the lines of, "Why are they bothering with all them archaeologists when

Maureen could probably take one look at the skull and tell them exactly who they were related to in the district. And if she can't identify it, then common sense tells us, it must have been a stranger to these parts." Their faith in Maureen's ability to know everything about everybody knew no bounds. Other more pressing questions also needed to be answered – like, was it some sort of burial site or, worse, some sort of ancient ceremonial site that dealt with fairies and the like? Would removing the skull, therefore, bring about bad luck?

"Oh, Eh'm tellin ye, it wull be bad luck that befas us, noo thay hiv takin awa thon skull. It broucht us luck, you ken."

"And what luck would that be then, Tam? Can you name me any?"

"Noo, Mary love, ye ken fine weel, if that husband of yers hadnae gone an deid, ee'd hiv telt aubody stories aboot thon place!"

"Stories is it? Well, you'd be right there, Tam, but as to whether they would be true or not ... well, he wasn't called a storyteller for nothing. He's told me many a tall tale before now." Laughter erupted around the tables, many remembering the wild tales that Angus came out with. One thing Old Tam was right about though was that Angus had been the keeper of the district's history in a manner of speaking. Much of it had been embellished with heroism, acts of complete stupidity and downright impossibility, but wound up in among it all was a modicum of truth. The fairy tales and folklore liberally passed on through his storytelling possessed enough of an essence to know what names were around from ancient times and whose families were interlinked generations ago. They were reminders of who used to own what land, and perhaps how they had improved on their fortunes or lost it all. The facts may have been debatable, but the era, names and who possessed what were, on most occasions, correct.

"I'm tellin ye, tis only a matter o time afore someane wull dei or rot awa," Old Tam insisted, once the merriment had abated.

"Well, Tam, given our ages here today, excluding Stroma and the young mothers, I think that is a fair bet." Again, the 'lunchers' cheered and laughed together as only the elderly are allowed to about their nearness to death.

"Oh, come on, Tam, you didn't even know that skull existed before, so how would you know if it brought good luck? You are worse than my Angus was. It's as well he isn't here. The pair of you would be off snooping around that dun right now."

"That's maybe noo a bad thing, ye ken. Wha's comin wi' me?" There were no takers this time. Mary was right – Angus would have been knee-deep in soil and rumours. Most, of course, would have been started by him. I found myself contemplating that it wasn't just Mary's life had been left with a great gap in it, but the community's too. Maureen had seemed the next best fit, with all her local knowledge, to take up the gauntlet of the local storyteller and keeper of knowledge. Her love of gossiping, however, added a different element to the telling.

Angus had been a lover of doing things, feeling, tasting and generally getting himself into bother, but all without any sort of malice. Laughter had followed him around as he bathed in the light of his listeners.

Maureen's recollections often came out of the shadows, somebody's brother died who was related to someone else who had probably committed a murder. Nodding heads followed her around, and not much laughter. Until, that was, Auntie Lottie had joined her in the shared role of the local bard. Even Maureen seemed happier in her delivery of news now.

The clumping of heavy feet preceded the entrance of four people leaving a trail of dust in their wake. They ordered four teas and some cakes into the silence that had formed around them.

"Hello, I'm Maureen, and you are?" Before they could answer, she had gone on to explain she was the local humanist and knew most people around these parts if they needed help with anything.

"It's okay, we are fine. We're from the Archaeology Institute at the University of the Highlands and Islands. We've come to take a look at your dun."

Maureen manoeuvred her wheelchair closer, finding a small space at their table. The general hubbub around the room picked up again. I watched Maureen expertly cross-examine the students and their lecturer.

"You'd better keep your kettle hot tonight. She'll be over to tell us everything that's going on later." Auntie Lottie whispered in my ear. She had enthusiastically embraced her return to the village by taking part in most things. Including, it must be said, some hare-brained schemes of her own. Paul, in his many ways, was the best partner she could have, as he could be relied upon to provide any machinery, contacts and, if necessary, rescues that may be required.

She had only recently told me how she had embraced technology wholeheartedly and was busy taking down all the stories and tales that Mary could provide. She had every intention of chasing after Angus' friends and accomplices to verify and add any missing details. Between her and Maureen, hopefully, they would be able to collect most of the stories that Angus had had in his repertoire.

"Well, I don't know about you, Stroma, but I have work to do. Little Fawn has asked Swallow to show me how to e-mail. Have you got any message for me to pass on to Rap or Jill?"

"Not right now thanks, but no doubt, once we've had that visit from Maureen later, I probably will. See you tonight then."

Auntie Lottie made a slight detour to where Maureen sat talking with the students. Maureen looked up after Auntie Lottie had said her goodbyes, raised her thumbs, nodded, smiled and held up eight fingers to indicate when she would be around at mine that night.

1 8

"Would you believe it, that's the farmhouse booked out again? It's getting difficult to find anywhere to stay around here for a short while. It's the university of course. Coming for the dig. I suppose the students would be a bit young for you Stroma, but there could be some lecturers free."

Why I continued to meet up and have tea with Auntie Lottie, Mary and Maureen I could never quite understand. Each time it was the same topic of conversation: what man may be available to lay down at my feet. They just didn't get the concept that really when all was said and done, my generation was quite happy to be on our own. Well, a lot of us were. I was particularly disappointed in Auntie Lottie given she had backed out from the last male who had asked her to get married. I felt she was displaying rather double standards towards me. Although she was blissfully happy living together with Paul, as far as I could see, she had no intention of giving up her independence anytime soon. So why was she so determined to marry me off, I never understood. I had lost my greatest ally as soon as she had moved in with Paul, or rather they have moved in together, while flitting between their different houses.

115

"Ellen's coming home." Mary's voice dropped as she disclosed her news.

"Are you sure, I've never heard anything? Have you Auntie Lottie?" she shook her head.

"It's Scott, he is taking her back here next week. He always keeps in touch. Nice boy." Mary looked across at me and smiled one of her 'I know what you've been up to' smiles." She couldn't, I was pretty sure, but it was enough to have me dropping my eyes and shifting in my seat. Great, I had probably sealed my guilt. Thankfully, the others were too busy pondering Ellen's return to take much notice of my discomfort.

"I've asked someone to air the house and just give it a freshening up for her." Mary continued.

"I'll pop in some flowers and stuff for the fridge so they can at least have a cup of tea when they get in. Any idea what day they will be back?" Auntie Lottie added.

"Tuesday, Scott is looking at staying with her for a few months at least. Or so he says in his e-mails." I was still trying to get my head around the fact that at eighty-one Mary had succumbed to technology and had a phone that not only sent e-mails but that she had a Facebook page as well. It wasn't that long ago that she had bought an automatic washing machine for goodness sake, and now she was more up to date than either Maureen or Auntie Lottie. "Well, it doesn't matter where he works, does it? Not now we have high-speed broadband here." This woman was truly amazing, before we knew it, she would be telling us all that her posts had gone viral!

"You know, if she's coming back, we should get her to start her B and B. With the interest in the dig, it would be a good time. We don't want her to get lonely." Maureen suggested.

"That's if she's planning tae stay. She might be right fed up weeh ous. Hud a taste o life wi' oot ous. Another ane lost te ous, ye ken."

"Afternoon Tam or should I say Harbinger of doom. Of course, she is staying this is her home."

"Eh, ach wi oot her bidie-in, she wull be off eh'm telling ye, an thain whar wull weeh be, nae decent baking left aroond here."

"Well, you can just hand back that piece of cake right now, being as it's not up to her standard, the cheek of you, come on give it back." Maureen was advancing towards Old Tam in her wheelchair, one hand held out for the plate.

"Leave him be Maureen. We all know Ellen's cakes are the best. You have said it yourself, away Tam and have your tea and by the way, Ellen is as part of this community as you are. They couldn't keep you away, and nothing will keep her away now that she has had some time on her own."

Old Tam shuffled off with old Shep trailing behind him. He poured some tea into a saucer added milk then placed a small piece of cake on the side.

"That man treats that dog better than he treats himself. Look he has obviously brushed the poor thing which is more than can be said of his hair."

"Ach don't worry about him. His granddaughter makes sure he is fed and watered. Being a midwife, I bet she can force him to have a shower on occasion too."

We talked some more about the interest the find had been creating before we went our separate ways. It still amazed me just how much attention the dig was generating. I had been up north for a quarterly visit the week before and even they were talking about it.

"Do you think they had like wild dances and sacrifices there then what with all the bones they have found?"

"Ach, that doesn't sound any worse than a normal Friday night here."

"Right getting back to the 4th item on the agenda, fundraising." I interrupted the flow, as it turned out to no avail, as they started mixing together possible fundraising into what was happening back in Blàs

"We could always have a sponsored walk from here to there and say it was an old traditional path or something like that."

"We could even dress up." *Oh God, not again.* I could just see them turning up at my house again in some crazy costumes, with a bucket full of money at some unearthly time during the night.

"How long do you think it would take to walk?"

"Probably about a week."

"Oomph, not a chance. A day or even a night I can do. A week, jeez, we will think about it."

So I wasn't totally off the hook then. I was hoping the time it would take to complete a walk from the top north-east coast of Scotland to Blàs would be enough to stop any planning, but who knew. When my north committee and friends came up with an idea for funding anything could happen. The trouble was they were quite capable of organising anything. If questioned, on the sense or validity of an idea once they had muted it, they never came up with a good enough reason not to do it. Once completed it generally led to great celebrations which in turn, habitually resulted in yet more fundraising. Often this would include a bucket to fill with coins during a pub crawl to celebrate the success and completion of the last event. They were a force to behold. I both loved and feared working with them.

That was the trouble with working with the committee and its members. One was as endearing as the other and seemed to get away with things nobody else could. Forward planning was needed, I thought, I'd better make sure that my spare bedroom was kept ready just in case. Auntie Lottie had been with me the last time they had turned up out of the blue late at night. They ended up sleeping on my couch.

And just like that without any warning, my mind slipped back to the last time my couch was used for any sort of sleep-over. It had been quite some time. It was the mention of Scott that had done it I knew. He had intimated that he was thinking of coming here to stay when he had come back for the funeral. Not just for a holiday either, but for good. However, people say lots of things during the high emotions of funerals. Time often filtered passion, and distance can cool both the head and the heart. Scott hadn't been in touch since he left after his prolonged visit following Helen's internment, and now it looked like he may have decided to come back and stay. Had I figured into his decision-making? Perhaps he wanted to keep his aunt company now she was on her own in that big house. I could be just a fringe benefit on the side. Play it cool my mind said but I knew hidden, cosseted within my soul, I was already in way too deep. I could keep things at bay knowing he was here for short periods, but knowing that he may well stay could put a completely different perspective on the whole thing.

19

"I cannae gae hame." Old Tam and Shep were sitting on the bench hiding behind the local newspaper. That was the only paper he was prepared to spend his money on. "Them folks keep stoppin meh and askin if eh was thon auld mun wi thon shaggy dug in thon TV show. Wha dae they think they are cawin Shep shaggy? It taks meh ages t comb eez coat, so it does. It's thon craitirs' fault. Eh telt ye all, ye ken eh did. Bad luck it is, bad luck, eh cannae even git hame fae th croods." Old Tam lifted the paper again and sighed like the world's problems were on his shoulders. There was no denying that Blàs was busier than usual, but nothing should have stopped him from going home.

"I'm afraid you've lost me there, Tam. Why can't you go home? I know there are a few more cars, but you can still cross the road." It was noisy though. You could taste the fumes from the minibuses full of sightseers.

"It's no th traffic, tho it is affy noisy and peur auld Shep is findin it difficult to cross th road fast enough. They dinnae stop for ye, ye ken. No, no, lass, it isnae that at ah."

I waited patiently, but Old Tam wanted me to ask the question, so I did.

"Why can't you go home then, Tam?"

"Thon daft bairns that done it. Not only did they find an loose thon cursed skull to thon research folkies, but they went and telt them other craitirs, them people that watch thon TV show, jist whair eh lived." Old Tam dropped his normal speaking voice, gifted to him by his mother who was born and bred in Dundee, and attempted a slightly higher pitched one that grated on the ears and sounded strange uttered from his mouth. "'Where does that smelly old man and dog live?' they asked Stag. Eh heird them, eh did, wen eh was peroosin th newspapers, ye understand, in the shop and afore Swallow cood stop eer brither ee wuz pointin oot whair they cood find meh. So eh hightailed it here. Eh didnae want them turnin up at meh croft, eh can tell ye. Peur auld Shep wid tak ther leg af, if thay came near."

Poor old Shep sighed and lay down beside the bench. I rubbed the dog's ears.

"So, you haven't gone home to see if anyone is there?' I asked.

"Course nae, ye ken Shep here wid savage them, then the polis wid be involved, an it is aw thon dam skull's felt."

"I'm really trying here, Tam, to see how having telly fans walking around the place is that bad or indeed the skull's fault."

"If it wer nae fur th skull thay widnae be here, ye ken that."

"But they're not here for the skull, Tam; they are here because of the TV show."

"Aye, weel, that is whut thay wid likh ye to think, is it no. They foond th skull, then thon TV folk came. It was a warnin findin thon skull, and naebody paid ony attention wen eh telt them. Eh shouldnae hiv taken pairt in thon show. Noo, how am eh goin tae live wi all thon cratirs chapping on meh an Morag's door, eh?"

"Come on, Tam, I'll walk you home and make you a cuppa. If anyone asks, I'll tell them it's not you." I don't know what had been going through Old Tam's head, nor how he thought he had somehow generated a fan base so dedicated that they would come to his door. He'd only played a little cameo part, but he was genuinely shaken.

Unsurprisingly, no one stopped us as we made our way back to his house. He was right though, there were a lot more people walking around. I could pick out guides pointing out landmarks that were in the show and talking to their followers. It seemed a little surreal. Guides in kilts with the Saltire flying at the top of a crock that would have been better placed at the sheep pen. It reminded me a little of my last holiday in Italy, where we were herded around by our guide as lots of other flocks of tourists followed their own leader. Of course, the scale in Italy had been much larger, to say nothing of the many sights and historical buildings available in their cities. Here, the visitor milled around the village, taking in sights that were really just the ordinary houses, pub and beach, no different than they had been the week before the show went out. It surprised me how quickly the small tour operators had picked up on this new opportunity. *In the Darkest Depths* had only been aired a few weeks ago but had caught the viewing public's imagination. Within a week of its airing, we had seen our first 'Screen' tourists.

As it turned out, Old Tam did not have a fan base that was into 'old smelly men' and their dogs. Old Tam had, in fact, dropped his keys. By the time the finder had managed to cross the road to give them back, Old Tam had disappeared into the shop and hidden. The kindly people had then dropped the keys off with Morag, his granddaughter, who had arrived home after delivering yet another baby. She greeted us and listened with a smile on her face as I told her about Old Tam's reluctance to come home.

"Oh, Grandad, what are you like? Come away in. I'm in need of a cuppa myself after that all-nighter. You will have all heard by now, I reckon—" Morag stopped, just in case the grapevine had somehow not grown at its usual pace.

"Ach, aye, not to worry, Morag. Neil told Maureen earlier, so we are all aware of the twin's early arrival and how they are doing," I said.

"See, see, eh telt ye. Thon peur bairns born early. It's thon skull."

"Oh, for goodness sake, Grandad, they are doing fine, and twins often come early. Anyway, I would say, given that some kind stranger handed in your keys, perhaps finding the skull has given us good luck." Morag winked at me, used to dealing with her rather dour grandad.

"Ach, awa wi ye, lass. It was ye doing yer job so weel that saved thon bairns, despite thon skull. As fer as meh keys… weel, eh've nivir dropped them afore, so why noo? Twas thon skull that forced them oot meh pocket, eh ken that fine weel."

Morag planted a kiss on her grandfather's head, ruffled Shep's fur, smiled and handed me a cup of tea.

"Well, Stroma, a piece of nice news, I hear. Maureen was telling me Ellen and Scott are arriving back tonight. Now, that's what I call good news, don't you agree?" Morag's eyes twinkled across at me as she smiled. A depth of understanding and a spark of wildness dwelt there. There was a flash of Mary about her. A hidden liveliness flamed within her soul. She could lead the unsuspecting astray as sure as Mary could. Not surprising really as they were related in some roundabout long-distance way. Morag, in another fifty odd years would, I'm sure, look and act very much like her distant cousin. Travelling with her along that path would be lots of fun.

20

Ellen returned like a whirlwind. The morning after she arrived with Scott, we all received our summons to the house. The freshly baked scones came hot out of the oven just as we were trooping in the door. Before we had finished our tea, she had managed to outmanoeuvre us at every turn, steering the discussion firmly in the direction of subjects of her choice and nothing else. Her bereavement and grief were clearly off the menu. Thankfully, her hot, buttered scones were not.

"Right, I've been keeping tabs on what's being going on since I left. Mary has kept Scott and me informed about the TV programme and the landslip. I was thinking the Development Trust could benefit from all this drama, get a little nest-egg going which we can hopefully use to leverage matching funding from somewhere. I'm open to ideas, but I thought having a wider range of stalls at the market would help bring in more buyers."

The old Ellen appeared to be back, although it was obvious she was fighting hard to stay organised and professional. After a short pause, we gave Ellen a more in-depth report on how the market was performing, our good sellers and where we felt the gaps were.

"As I thought – we have a space for luxury chocolates. I've

someone in mind I could contact. Leave that with me, and I will get back to you. Okay, if that is us finished then—" But before Ellen had the chance to end the meeting, Scott strolled in.

"Oh, there you are, Scott," Maureen interrupted. "I was wondering when you would put in an appearance. Not so young as you once were, but still free and single, I hope?" Maureen winked across at me. Did she have no shame?

"I forgot you were quite the matchmaker, Maureen. Let me make this absolutely clear to you now: I am not looking for any romantic connection while I am here. I am already more or less committed to someone, so leave me well and truly out of your plans, and that goes for you too, Lottie. Okay, ladies, have you got that?" Scott planted a brief kiss on Ellen's head before helping himself to coffee.

"You are such a spoilsport, Scott. I've never seen what your aunt sees in you personally."

Scott walked over, took Maureen's face in his hands and looked directly into her eyes.

"What can I say, Maureen? If only you were about forty years younger."

"Forty years! You cheeky beggar." Maureen laughed, shoved his hands away and blushed deeply "Away with you. He's worse than that bidie-in of yours used to be, Lottie."

Auntie Lottie smiled, acknowledging the fact that Paul had changed his ways. They were still flitting between Auntie Lottie's cottage and his house. He just couldn't leave his beloved shed. Well, where would Paul of the Sheds be without his most favourite building? There was no way he was going to leave that behind for some other male to enjoy. Auntie Lottie was used to holidaying away and shifting between Blàs and the city. Moving between homes was not such a difficult thing for her. Paul was finding it more difficult. Rumour had it, he was considering moving the shed brick-by-brick and rebuilding it in Auntie Lottie's back garden. This, as it turned out, was pure speculation.

If they do move into one house, I thought, *maybe they will consider renting the other one out.* Despite our housing development stock, we were still short on affordable homes for rent for local people. If the increase in tourists continued, that could mean even more of our housing stock going for holiday homes, leaving the locals fighting for what was left, yet again, or worse – being forced to move away altogether.

Each week, more tourist buses than could fit comfortably into our wee burgh squeezed along the streets. Apart from the bed and breakfasts and the holiday rentals, nobody was happy. Holiday accommodation had always done well, attracting families looking for somewhere close to nature, a decent place to sleep and a clean toilet. Unfortunately, our quiet holiday destination was fast becoming an overcrowded tourist spot.

Cars crawled through the village bumper to bumper. Fumes tainted the air. A quiet walk was no longer possible with the noise of horns and smell of engines polluting the atmosphere. Seabirds still swooped and spun, but nothing could be heard of their call. People ducked as the feathered divebombers hunted for the food in their hands. Residents didn't bother stopping for a chat as nobody could hear anything over the traffic and thumping music. Walking along the streets and lanes was hazardous thanks to cyclists speeding past the cars with no consideration for the lack of pavements. Blàs now felt like a city in rush hour, but without the bonus of theatres, restaurants and shops. It wasn't even benefitting the market because potential buyers couldn't find anywhere to park. No one could stop and shop, let alone gaze and buy. Something would have to give.

"Can weeh no jist ban th buses. Ye ken, stick up a sign: Nae suitable fae cars or th lot of yees either." Old Tam was not a happy man. Nothing unusual in that really. "Peur auld Shep cannae git walkin, whut wi all these vehicles aboot. Eh jist wish thay wi gae awa. Eh telt ye awh an ye jist ignored meh. Thon bloody skull. Naethin wull be th same until we git it back."

It was as if the village was under siege. Locals stopped going out during the day. Even our yearly returning tourists were heard complaining of the loss of their 'quiet hidden part of Scotland'.

Once the last bus of day trippers left each day, villagers would start creeping out of their doors like nocturnal creatures seeking safety and solace in the growing dark. Groups huddled on street corners and outside the local shop. The pub became the unofficial meeting place to voice concern over what was happening. Not that the landlords were bothered by the crowds – their takings were well up. But they knew that these new visitors could disappear just as quickly as they had materialised, then it would be the locals who would return to providing their stable income, so they weren't going to voice too much complaint about the community debating their fears for the future over their pints.

"I cannae go fishing anymore, all the boats are constantly booked out. How am I supposed to spend my weekends with no boats to fish from?"

"Ach, Archie, I'm sure that wife of yours will find you something to do," his companion said.

"That's the whole point of me going fishing, you idiot!" Archie returned.

"Never mind that. You can't find a spot to sit on the beach either. Dogs, litter and music screaming at you. The sun's blaring down and I'm stuck inside."

"Eh cannae wuak aboot wi' auld Shep here. Peur wee dug, wi' cars comin up ahind us, wi' thar horns gaein, it's affy. It's jist... weel, it's affy nae guid. Right thain, eh'm off tae Mary's. Thar's a meetin oan."

"Well, you tell them, Tam, we are not happy, not happy at all that we can't get on and do what we want because of all these people. I want my old life back. I want to go fishing."

"And I want to go to the shop and find there is still milk and bread and things for my tea, instead of everything fresh being bought by all those visitors."

"And I want to go into my back garden and not find someone has done the toilet in it."

"Aye, and left their tents and litter all over the place."

"And partied outside my house till three in the morning."

"And…"

"Stop." Old Tam held up his hand. "Thar is nae point in moanin at meh. Eh telt ye all, eh did, way back wen thon wee laddie foond thon skull. Eh telt ye thar wid be trouble. Ach, naebody waz listenin tae meh. Weel, eh'll tel aubody at the meetin whut ye hiv aw seid. Ach, mark meh words, until weeh git thon skull back, this trouble wull stay."

Old Tam arrived full of news and comments from the pub. He had wanted to hear the opinions of the locals there before he came along to the meeting. Or rather, that is what he *said*. I think a quick pint would have had as much of a draw as the chatter about how this invasion of mob tourism was affecting the villagers.

"Karen and Grace send their apologies but have offered up their thoughts," I informed the meeting as Old Tam and Shep settled down. "Karen is concerned about the safety of the pupils walking to and from school with all this extra traffic about. It's not so bad first-thing, but by the time the bairns are leaving, it is horrendous. She also said we have to remember that our children aren't used to all this traffic. Grace added that pre-school children are just at car-exhaust level, whether they are walking or in a buggy. Many of the mums no longer allow their children to walk or run as they could end up under a car."

"Eh telt ye, eh telt ye, and ye widnae believe meh. Thon skull, eh—"

"Okay, Tam," Auntie Lottie interrupted. "We know how you feel about that. But maybe you can fill us in on what the craic was down the pub."

In between Old Tam voicing his opinion on the skull's influence, we managed to glean what others from the community were thinking.

"Okay, Maureen, maybe you could repeat all the concerns that have been raised tonight," Ellen suggested.

"Well, danger to children from excess fumes and too much traffic, anti-social behaviour from campers, including litter of which some is broken glass, all-night parties, excrement in people's gardens and wherever the tourists camp, villagers not being able to leave or get home due to campervans and parked cars."

"Worryingly, this has impacted on emergency vehicles being able to get through as well," Paul of the Sheds added.

Maureen scribbled some more. "The shop running out of fresh supplies, destruction of habitat, negative impact on our wildlife, also the students say people have been lifting away stones and other things from their site. Lastly, I would add general noise levels and total disregard for and destruction of our quality of life." Maureen finished, laid down her pen and looked at us expectantly.

There was a stunned silence while this list of offences settled into our thoughts. We had lost our gentle way of life. It was as if a volcano has erupted within our midst. We were buried under other people's muck and fumes. The silence grew as we considered what we had lost.

"I'd offer you all a hot chocolate, but there was no fresh milk left at the shop," Mary said, bringing out a bottle of homemade spirit. "Here, I am sure my Angus would want you all to have a wee nip. It's good for shock." Even after the list's devastating impact, we had enough self-preservation between us to know not to gulp down one of Angus' brews. As we each took small sips of the sweet, strong liquid, we contemplated our sorrow at the loss of our way of life. Our village was like Pandora's box. The lid was off, people now knew about Blàs. How could we return to what we once had?

"Ach, if only thon people wid gae awa things whut be an affy lot better." Old Tam said as we all nodded in dejected agreement.

As if his wish had been granted, it wasn't long before everything had quietened down to a more respectable level again. What was the cause of this little miracle? If Old Tam was to be believed, there was no doubt it was due to moves being made to return the skull to the site by setting up a museum or at least an exhibition. For the less superstitious among us, it was the end of the English school holidays that heralded the change. Most within the community were thankful that, although still a shade busier than before, the village had more or less returned to its normal seasonal rhythm.

It was time to call a new meeting about the market.

"Well, at least we can now get down our street." Maureen helped herself to another slice of Ellen's drizzle cake.

"Maybe we should decamp to Inbhirasgaidh." There was a sharp intake of breath. Rivalry between Blàs and Inbhirasgaidh was almost a religion for some. Moving the market over there could well look like we were giving away one of our assets to the opposition.

"Look, it's not as bad as it sounds." Ellen handed out more cake in an attempt to sweeten the less happy among us. "They are struggling to offer tourists the things we have right here on our doorstep. Laura Mackay, from their council offices, phoned me. They love the idea of the market and wondered if we would be willing to take it there, if not every week, then at least twice a month in an attempt to pull in some trade. We are already up and running for this season, so it makes sense. I haven't told her how difficult it had become for people to stop, look around and buy here. This could be the answer to the problem. At least there, they have wider roads and parking, not to mention a larger population to sell to."

"An pavements, dinnae forget th pavements. Weeh cood dae wi' a few here th noo." Old Tam bent down and scratched Shep's ears. "Weehr missin wir wee wuaks are weeh nae, boy."

Myself, I had no problem relocating the market to our neighbours. I worked within both communities and could see the benefit for each. The Development Trust would still get the rent from the stalls, so we wouldn't be any worse off. The stallholders would probably sell more in Inbhirasgaidh, so they would be happier too. We debated the idea before deciding it was worth at least a trial run.

"Wait a moment, Ellen." Mary had sat forward and was watching Ellen intently. "I think I speak for a lot of the ladies here tonight. What we really want to say is, as long as Elaborate Chocolate is still going to be represented, then we are quite happy. I don't think we could live without our little taste of luxury now, could we, girls?"

"It's nae jist ye wifies," Old Tam added. "Hiv ye tastet eer rum an raisin liquor chocolates? Aye, but they are guid."

"Okay." Ellen smiled. "As long as we can get our chocolate maker to agree, we can go ahead and add Inbhirasgaidh to our market, which brings me nicely to this." Ellen pulled out a small tray of chocolates. "I thought we could finish tonight's meeting with these. It seems appropriate after our wee discussion. A nice wee taster for you all. It's a new recipe Giulietta is trying out. She calls it Highland Heather Delight. It's a heather and honey chocolate, so comments please for improvements if needed."

Mary helped herself to one. "I'm sure, like Giulietta herself, these will be loved by everyone here." Her eyes sparkled at Ellen as she popped one into her mouth.

Wow was the mutually agreed comment from everyone. The chocolates were indeed a delight.

2 1

At a time when we would normally expect the village to begin its lazy autumnal decline into shorter days and longer nights, the community was once again crackling with excitement. The pilot show of, *In the Darkest Depths*, was such a success a series had been commissioned.

Bed and breakfasts and the old estate house were all full again. Villagers were once more decked out in full make-up and strange clothes (at least for that time of year in Blàs), although there wasn't the same take-up of extras needed or, truth be told, locals who were willing or able to take part. It hadn't taken long for the same rhyme and pattern to occur, though on a smaller scale than before. After all of Old Tam's worries about being recognised and harassed by his fan base, I was surprised to learn that he had taken up with the TV company again.

"Aye, lass, weel ye ken, it helps taeward meh wee dram an th likh. Noo Shep here, weel ee waz missin awh thon company an asides, Morag telt meh it does meh guid to be doing someit productive, likh, instead o hangin aroond waitin on th lambin."

I was tempted to ask him what the skull would think of that.

Old Tam continued. "Eh've a feu apples left ower, wid ye be

wantin some? Dinnae want tae waste ony an eh've made enough cider fae mehsel, ye ken."

"Ach, that's right kind of you, Tam, but I've got some already from Ellen. Thanks for the offer though." I had been caught out before with Old Tam's kind offers, however we, including Jill, had forgotten to warn the rest of the Smiths about this yearly event. Now that Old Tam didn't run his croft or sheep, he had no outlet for any excess produce from the crops that he still grew. It didn't take long for the consequences of our mistake to materialise. I bumped into Jill later the next day.

"That old man is incorrigible. He finally got rid of his extra stock. Poor Rap doesn't know what to do with it all." Jill went on to tell me what had happened.

Old Tam had been talking to the twins. "He asked if they liked apples, and when they said they did, he promised to take a few along to the house later that day." Jill explained that the children were ecstatic when Old Tam turned up in an old, grey Ferguson tractor, or 'Little Grey Fergie' as they are affectionately known. These machines had become much sought after again and were entering the realms of vintage collectibles. They were worth far more than when they were first built in the forties and fifties. Old Tam, though, had had his from the beginning. It was well used and had been repaired countless times. It didn't quite come under the banner of 'great condition, as new, only one owner'. It was more 'great workhorse, owner used it continually, washed when neighbours complained about the smell'. Behind it, he pulled a trailer containing his 'few apples'. Old Tam didn't like to see anything going to waste. He needed to know that every apple would be used and not just as feed fodder for some animals.

Rap's gratitude for this free gift had rapidly vanished when he realised that *all* these apples would now be his. Every one of them would need to be peeled and cored, or squashed for juice.

"What he is going to do with them all before they go off is

beyond me. Why can't Old Tam just stop growing things and stop making everybody's life so difficult?"

I could understand Jill's frustration. Old Tam had given up the sheep, but he still owned a large amount of land where he grew apples. He also produced enough tatties and turnips for himself and most of the village. Many of us had woken up on a morning to find a large pile of turnips or tatties barricading us into our homes. He just couldn't quite stop himself from growing something, and he couldn't scale down his operation to garden-size. Morag believed it kept him fit, occupied and out of too much trouble, so she couldn't be relied upon to stop him. Most of us over the years had learnt not to accept his offers of gifts for fear of finding ourselves knee-deep in produce.

Maureen appeared at my house later that day. She thumped on my back door as I was tidying up from tea. I was looking forward to a nice quiet read beside my fire.

"You are needed at Mary's. Ellen has called a meeting. Oh, and bring a wooden spoon."

"What?" But Maureen was off, making her way along the road. After grabbing a wooden spoon, I shivered into my jacket and headed out.

Autumn was blowing her worst. Leaves swam and dived under my feet and pasted my face. I thought lovingly of my warm seat beside the fire. But I knew better than to ignore a summons from Ellen. The wooden spoon had thrown me a bit though.

Ellen, Mary, Maureen, Lottie, Jill and, much to my surprise, Giulietta from Elaborate Chocolates were sitting around Ellen's table.

"Ha ha, you actually brought a wooden spoon. I can't believe it. Must ask you to bring something even dafter next time." Maureen chuckled.

"Don't you listen to her, Stroma. It's just the thing as it turns out," Mary riposted with a sparkle. "You won't be needing it tonight though, but maybe tomorrow. Isn't that right, Ellen?"

"We need to help the Smiths out of their predicament. It is all our fault, really, for not warning them about accepting Old Tam's offer of a few of anything that he grows."

"I second that," intercepted Jill. "We are totally snowed under with apples. Once they start going off, we are going to have all sorts of trouble with rats, smell, mush, slushy apples – yuck."

"Yes dear, we know – that is why we are here, after all. Now if you would let Ellen continue," Mary said.

"Ach, Jill, you are just scared you will be the one left to cook them all or clear them up. Oh, don't look so affronted, of course, we will help. I was only jesting," Maureen stated.

"Anyway, back to apples please, everyone. I have put out a request in the neighbourhood for extra demijohns and empty bottles and tops. Maureen has also put the word around, and Lottie has asked Paul for a shot of his apple press and capper."

"Okay…" I had no idea what they were all talking about. Well, apart from knowing that the Smiths were drowning in apples. "Emm… you are wanting to make some apple juice to help use up the Smith's gift?"

"No dear, not apple juice. Now, how long would that last? We would be drinking continually, till we were all sick." Mary shuddered.

"Cider, Stroma. Wake up! We are going into cider making, on a large scale." Auntie Lottie smiled across at me.

"We'll have to be going into it on a *really* large scale to use up all their apples," I replied, while wondering whose idea this had been anyway. Then I noticed the small smile and amused expression on Mary's face. Of course, she and Angus had often made cider, but nothing like on the scale of this. There would be a mountain of apples waiting at the Smiths' for us.

"Well, I calculated we could get approximately 100 demijohns, given that there are 4.5 litres roughly in each, we are looking at 4,500 small bottles of cider, less if we use bigger bottles. Of course, we could leave some of the bottling and do more as needed, or until we get enough bottles or containers. Mary has a nice pottery cider jug that holds at least 3 litres of cider all on its own. Don't you, Mary?" Ellen glanced over toward Mary.

"That I do, Ellen. Me and Angus used it every year. It would be nice to get regular top-ups when I needed it though."

I looked around the room. I was beginning to feel like I was on another planet. I mean, really – 4,500 bottles of cider. Just how long would it take to get through all of that, never mind the time it would take to actually do the whole bottling and capping process? I didn't doubt Ellen's calculations for a minute. She was an accountant, for goodness sake.

Ellen's voice brought me back. "Obviously, the amount will also depend on how many of the apples we turn into chutney, sauce or sweets of one kind or another. Some of these we can try to sell at the markets. We could always sell some to the local pub maybe next summer, can't see Ben the Froth complaining if we give him a good price. A little 'donation' for the Trust. The cider should be at its best by then too."

"I am developing a chocolate using apples. In the meantime, I can help the children make toffee and chocolate apples we could sell at the next market," offered Giulietta.

"Thank you, Giulietta. I'll also bake some apple and caramel tarts. I'll put some in the freezer, but I will also need to put some in other people's freezers that have room."

"So that will be yours then, Stroma. You never have much in that freezer of yours. Just don't invite Iona home too much, or she will be handing it all out to her friends or anyone else she thinks would like it. We can also sell lots of apple baking over the next few months to the students at the dig when they come to the hall for their breaks," Auntie Lottie said.

"Right, we have a plan. Most of any money raised will go to the Trust once expenses are taken off. Jill, can you go and put this all to Rap? We could be up and running for the weekend. We should have loads of volunteers if we offer them some bottles when it is ready or cakes for the non-alcohol drinkers among us."

෯

Rose Cottage's outbuildings were teeming with activity by the weekend. Volunteers had been arriving since first light. Most had come armed with demijohns and buckets. One demijohn to take home once it was full, and the rest to add to the mountain that was steadily growing behind Rap.

A line of trestle tables heaped with mounds of apples, knives and boards awaited the helpers. Buckets stood to attention beside fence posts along with other long, wooden objects to crush the fruit. Three presses had been located in the end. Two from Paul of the Sheds. One he used each year, and an older machine he had completely forgotten about until he found it in the back of his most ancient and least used shed. Maureen surprisingly had managed to locate the third, through one of her complicated friend-of-a-friend-of-a-distant-relative connections. This allowed the whole operation to be completed in one weekend.

Village children were engaged to run between the tables and the apple mound, replenishing stocks for adults to cut. Older children bashed the fruit in buckets with the post, just as it had been done for years. Children were kept occupied and engaged in the whole process while their parents and others fed apples into the presses then draped muslins over buckets to strain the juice before pouring the cloudy liquid into demijohns.

The atmosphere was full of joy and the sweet smell of apples. Then there was a lull while we waited for the first lot of muslins to strain the juice. I couldn't quite believe we had managed to get enough material to strain all the liquid, but once more, Maureen had been amazing. Together with Ellen, they had approached all those they could think of who, over the years, had at one time made their own crowdie, chutney, jelly, beers or wine. Muslins and strainers had been pulled out from the back of cupboards, boxes and top shelves, long forgotten about but still usable.

The water urn, cups, tea, coffee and other paraphernalia needed for refreshments had been removed from the hall kitchen and were ready to offer hot drinks to anyone who needed or wanted.

Ellen had gone back to Old Tam and suggested he gift them a few tatties and turnips that could be used to make some industrial-sized pots of soup. They were careful to check how much he was giving *before* it left his croft. Rap, Jill, Mary and Ellen then made enough soup for everyone to enjoy during the day. Giulietta had also appeared, looking both elegant and ready for work, with trays of treats to enjoy. Laughter, fun and stickiness surrounded everyone.

Mary started to sing some of the old Gaelic working songs that matched the rhyme of the work. Others joined in, either singing a traditional verse or making up a new appropriate one to add to the history of the event. Everyone, as was the tradition, joined in for the chorus. The song mingled with the air swirling around and up into the rafters, linking centuries-old traditions with the new happenings in the byre. Most of the women had tied their hair up in cloths. It rendered the whole scene old-worldly. As the day rolled on, new people stepped into spaces behind cutting boards, buckets and presses made available by others taking a break. Old Tam and Shep joined everyone for lunch.

"Wull if eh'd kent this waz whut ye were gaein tae dae, eh cood hiv given a wee bit extra tae the Trust years ago."

"Thank you for the thought, Tam, but I don't know if the Trust could have managed to pull pulled this off before now. But if this goes well, maybe we could consider it as an annual event. What do you say, Rap, would you be happy to lend out your byre every year?"

"I would find it impossible not to after you have saved my

family from drowning in a sea of apples—"

Rap was interrupted by three of his children's eager shouts of, "Yes, Dad, please, come on, Dad."

"What do you say, Fawn?" Rap asked his smallest child. Fawn's face was covered in a glue-like film of apple juice. Her flyaway hair was no more. Instead, it stuck out in all directions bound together with gooey juice. She stared earnestly at her dad and solemnly nodded her head. Rap smiled sadly at his daughter and ruffled her hair. He quickly realised his mistake and rubbed his hand on his shirt, grimacing. "Well, it seems we have our answer. If my children are happy to do this again, then so am I." The Smith children hugged their dad and ran off to play among the apples and their friends, eager to tell them we would be doing this again next autumn.

As the light started to seep away from the sky, yeast was added to half of the filled demijohns. Camden tables would be dropped in the next evening. Rows of containers filled with sandy-coloured liquid lined one wall of the byre. Many villagers had already gone home for a shower, food and a good night's sleep before returning to finish up the job the next day. Mary sat and drank sweet tea as she watched the rest of us clean and wash down the equipment ready to start again.

The next day followed much the same pattern. The villagers who couldn't commit to two days had been replaced by a second shift. It was not so noisy, but the same friendly atmosphere, created from everyone working toward the one goal, cemented the bond that already existed in Blàs.

I watched as my friends, Karen and Grace, along with their families, joked and laughed together while they crushed the apples. Their children tasting the delicious apple juice that gave them sustenance, much like the renewed community spirit that grew and deepened within them, flowing seamlessly into their psyche. The last apples were squashed, the last demijohn was filtered and filled, and the lasting collective spirit of Blàs was well and truly preserved within the next growing generation.

2 2

"Did you see me? I was the man sitting in the pub nursing a pint."

"Not much acting called for that then," laughed his companion.

"Well, you would think with us all playing our parts, more people would be interested in us, instead of that hell hole of a town Inbhirasgaidh."

This mumbling had been going on for weeks now. Although many of the shots for the pilot programme had been filmed around Blàs, the filming for the actual series had taken place in and around Inbhirasgaidh. To add insult to injury, Inbhirasgaidh had then been thanked in the credits with a simple 'and surrounding area' meant to cover our own little village. Given the constant rivalry between our two communities, some likened it to Blàs having lost a battle. However, many more of Blàs' inhabitants quietly saw it more like we had won the war.

"Maureen says." *Well, this should be good.* "Maureen says that her cousin-once-removed's nephew's wife's sister... that's right, isn't it, Maureen?"

"Yes, yes, Julie, that's her."

"Well, she works at the Inbhirasgaidh hotel, so she should know."

"For goodness sake, woman, she should know what?"

"Well, that the hotel is already full for the holiday season, and people are already booking up for next year. All on the back of that TV programme." Of course, the title of the show was now never uttered, if at all possible, so giving it less status in the eyes of the Blàs populace.

"You don't say."

"Aye, and where are our bookings then?" Of course, these were the same individuals who had been complaining about how busy and noisy Blàs had become. After all the upset caused by the hype and the screen tourists after the initial episode of *In the Darkest Depths* had been screened.

What these few locals didn't know was the television company's move to Inbhirasgaidh had had a wee drop of help.

It was Mary who had come up with the initial idea.

"You know," she said, one afternoon during the regular tea party at the hall, "I have been thinking. I reckon Inbhirasgaidh has many more suitable locations close by for all that filming than we have here in Blàs."

"Ach, awa with ye, lass. Aubody kens that Blàs is bonnier an better than Inbhirasgaidh ony day o th week." Old Tam regarded Mary in disbelief.

"Even with all these sightseers and screen tourists, or whatever you call them, cluttering up our roads, so it's not safe for a man and his dog to cross. To say nothing of them selling out of newspapers at the shop." Mary's eyes twinkled. She knew as well as anyone that Old Tam always had a read of the daily papers before he replaced them on the shelf. The only paper he actually paid for was the once-weekly local one.

Maureen stared at her elderly friend before adding "Can you

imagine what it would be like at the pub, not having to queue for a pint?"

"Oh," added Auntie Lottie, cottoning on, "what I would give to enjoy a nice stroll along the beach without sharing it with all these extra people and their dogs. No more big dogs chasing after Whisky… or any other local dog for that matter." If there was one way to persuade Old Tam of anything, it was through hinting at an improved life for Shep. He had had some run-ins with bigger, faster dogs, and Old Tam was not happy about it.

"An jist hoo wid weeh gae aboot changin them TV folk's mind." He stared at us.

"Ach, Tam, we know you are friendly with Willie Murray. I've heard the two of you can't stop gassing when you meet up. I hear he has the ear of one of them on the crew. Finds his old tales amusing, so I heard anyway. I'm sure you could mention a few more suitable areas nearer to Inbhirasgaidh for filming to him."

"And jist why wid eh do that? Ee'd ken somit waz up."

"Well, I dare say," Mary said, "you could say something like, 'I only hope the film crew never find out about wherever,' or 'Could you imagine how angry Blàs would be if the film crew ever found about…' Oh, I don't know, the corrie, for example. Way more suitable and dramatic than what Blàs can offer."

"You know," added Auntie Lottie, "I bet I could get Paul to suggest a few places himself to the fishermen. They all tend to meet up in Inbhirasgaidh for a few pints after they tie up."

"Well, I know that Rumba Tracy has a list of where they are thinking of shooting the next series. She has to sort out the traffic and things. So she must know the crew quite well. It is probably time we had a little catch-up." Maureen smiled.

There followed a clandestine campaign with a few chosen locals leading the charge. Carefully chosen words in the right ears were designed to hasten the desired effect.

"Can you imagine how great it would be to have all the filming done in one area? I hear they are talking about just using Blàs from now on. Saves on too much moving around, you know, to say nothing of how bonnie it is. So, if I were you, I would just tear up that list you have there, Tracy. Can't tell you where I got the information from, of course, but I *can* tell you, the community of Blàs will be right happy about it. Just think – all that money going into the locals' pockets. It will be great for us. Loads of people coming along afterward and spending their money in the village – can't wait. It's a shame Inbhirasgaidh will lose out, but then again, we can't all be winners, can we?"

Rumour had it that, before Maureen had even exited the building, Rumba Tracy had danced her way quickly upstairs to her boss, Peter the Peacock (named so due to his puffed-up manner), the Lord Provost. It was a ceremonial title, but he was also the senior official in Inbhirasgaidh. It was only after the filming had started that it became clear that no scene whatsoever was being shot in Blàs this time, and not that many close by either.

Our campaign to surreptitiously push the filming away from Blàs had been even more successful than we could have wished. Now we only had the tourists who were interested in the discovery of the dun, brooch and skull to consider, and their threat to our way of life had decreased naturally. The initial flock of holidaymakers and daytrippers interested in the site had dropped to a level we felt we could deal with. Well, one soil-covered object looked much the same as the other. The skull, on the other hand, was being kept in the papers mostly, it had to be said, because of Stag's fight for its return. It had fuelled debates in the pub, in the hall and around the area about what should become of it.

The Development Trust eventually contacted Stag, officially, after an impassioned plea from Rap who was, as he stated, "losing his own head" due to the constant complaining from his youngest son. It was Fawn, though, who was still causing him the most stress, having still not returned to her previous self.

"Aye thon peur wee mite. She winnae git weel thou. I telt eem, no until thon skull is returned." Old Tam was back to his favourite subject of the past few months.

"Oh, for goodness sake, Tam, give it a rest. It's the fright the poor bairn got, not any power that skull has over anyone." Even Maureen, never known to refuse an excuse to develop any stories she could, was losing patience with it all.

"Dinnae mock meh. Ye wull see. Ye wull awh see. Eh, been talkin tae th wee laddie, eer brither, eh telt eem awh aboot it." Well, that would explain a lot. If Old Tam had been filling Stag's head with all his ludicrous beliefs from the beginning, it was no wonder the boy was in such a state about the skull. Maybe someone should have told Rap right then, but it could only have made matters worse. Once Old Tam had made his mind up about something, not even indisputable proof would change it. We would have to find another way of stopping his stories from affecting Stag.

The Development Trust sent a letter to Stag, stating they were looking into setting up a museum or exhibition, either within the hall or somewhere nearer the original site. It had already been discussed anyway, but we hoped this personal communication to Stag, would help. Of course, we told him, all this would take some time, but funding was being looked into right at that moment.

Rap was ecstatic when his son read the letter out to him. He looked forward to no more mentions of the skull. Unfortunately, all it seemed to do was shift Stag's emphasis slightly. The Trust then received a request from the twins to rent a stall at the next indoor market. They intended to sell fresh lemonade, like before, but without the help of their dad this time. All proceeds were going toward the funding of the 'return of wat is mines and Fawns'. I delivered the letter myself to the chairwoman of the

Trust, who handed it right back to me and told me I had to deal with it.

"And just how am I going to do that, Ellen? They are just bairns. What do I say that's not going to break their hearts?"

"Sit them down with their dad and explain that there are all sorts of health and safety issues that they would need to adhere to. A responsible person over the age of sixteen would have to be present at the making and distribution of the lemonade. If I remember rightly, their lemonade stall did very well last time. It complimented the individual snacking cakes we were selling."

"Ellen, focus. So, are we letting them make it or not?"

"I would like to see them there, but not unless the health and safety conditions I mentioned are agreed to, and they have to have an appropriate supervisor. Otherwise, we could find ourselves in all sorts of trouble."

I had one foot out of the hall when I spied the twins lurking in the bushes outside. Making my way to what was once Jill's cottage but was now her studio seemed the best possible action to take. If they followed me, perhaps we could both talk some sense into them. You never knew, perhaps it would force some sort of reaction from Fawn. It would be good to hear her babbling around the place again. The twins had always been inseparable, linked together since they had arrived when both had appeared as lively as each other. Stag now took the lead in everything. Fawn was like a shadow at his side, ever-present but sadly quiet.

I rapped on Jill's door. She could still be found at her cottage most days as all her work materials were there. However, plans were afoot to convert one of the outbuildings at Rose Cottage into a new studio. Until that was complete, she retained her cottage as her workspace. While I waited, I noticed that her window frames had been painted. That had never happened before. All the colourful arts and crafts had been removed to allow for the revamp. It did look a lot more weatherproof, but the cottage had lost something with the removal of all that colour, reflection and shapes.

Jill opened the door, and before I could stop myself, I burst out with, "Where is all your stuff from the windows? Are you putting them back up?"

"I thought I would take some of the older ones off and add them to my stock. I've got some nice, shiny new ones to put up in their place. Well, not here, of course; I'm hoping my new studio at Rose Cottage will be ready soon enough. Do you like the colours?"

I had to admit they were lovely – all the different tones of the sea with flashes of red that accentuated the different hues.

"Right, come away in and tell me what I can do for you? I hope you are not after more stalls or stock. I am flat-out, trying to keep up with my market commitments."

Explaining about the skull didn't take long. She didn't seem surprised or even worried about the possibility of the twins taking on a stall.

"I knew about it. The whole thing is really worrying Rap. He is getting desperate about poor Fawn. He thought she would gradually come around by herself and start talking. He has had to finally admit that Fawn needs more help. He has spoken to the GP, but there is a waiting list for this sort of thing, even if you are a child. Only now that he has accepted there is a problem, he is impatient for Fawn to get that help. Anyway, I've spoken with Fawn. I wasn't sure if she was maybe scared of the skull, and that's why she wasn't speaking so much. As it turns out, she wants it back too. Seems like Old Tam has had an effect on them both, and they think bad things will happen if it is not returned. Well, I suppose it was bad luck for the person that lost their head in the first place. Not that I said that to them. Look, the stall was sort of my idea. I thought if they felt they could raise some money to help get the skull back, it would empower them. And you never know, perhaps it would help Fawn to feel more in control of things. I am their step-mum, after all, so I can keep an eye on them from my stall." She grinned happily and continued, "You can put them next to me, and I will look after them. Make sure nobody gives them any trouble. The older two will be with them as well. Put that to your committee and see what they have to say, then let me know."

I heard a door close. The twins had followed me inside. Two little heads peeked around the side of the door.

"Did you tell her about us? Will they let us do it?" asked Stag.

"I've got to put it to the market committee first. But your mum thinks it's okay, so that should swing it in your favour."

Suddenly, there it was – the return of that wide, cheeky smile from Fawn. No words yet, but just to see her smile again made all the hassle of having them at the market worthwhile.

All our markets were to be held indoors until at least spring. Inbhirasgaidh had the perfect place to hold them – an old Victorian-style building that had originally been used as a sort of covered bazaar. Stained-glass windows and wrought iron twists could be found throughout the space. It sported a large, vaulted ceiling that supported a circular domed roof at its centre that allowed light to flood in. It wasn't the warmest place for the stallholders, but it was certainly warmer than outdoors.

True to their word, Stag and Fawn had made their lemonade again. There was the addition of apple lemonade this time made from juice they had frozen. Looking around, there were a fair few apple products featured on the stalls from Blàs. They ranged from apple muffins to apple crisps. Giulietta had been true to her word and had developed a new apple, cinnamon and salted caramel chocolate and called it 'Mela Blàs'. She was doing a fine trade, especially from the locals in the village, together with some students from the dig. The natives of Inbhirasgaidh itself weren't so keen to give it a try. Why promote their nearest rivals and why, if it came to that, wasn't there a chocolate from their town? Giulietta was doing enough trade not to feel their slight regarding her new delicacy. Those who couldn't bring themselves to try it could, however, buy her wonderful hot chocolate which she served with the help of Ellen. They were doing a roaring trade, helped no doubt by the cold weather outside. As Ellen had offered to help on the chocolate stall, I was left to deal with any issues that occurred on the day.

"Oh look, it's that nice-looking man again, Stroma." Mary had come through with Maureen to see how we were all getting on.

"Jim, it is good to see you again. We were just saying that, Stroma, weren't we?" I narrowed my eyes at Maureen and attempted a smile in Jim's direction. Our initial flurry of meetings at the beginning of the process of buying the woods had come to a sudden stop after we acquired them. All contact since had been through phone calls and e-mails. We had gone from an intense working relationship to almost nothing. This was probably how the members of my committees felt after we had worked toward and completed projects. It was a strange feeling for me to be on the other side.

Now we both smiled shyly at each other, and truth be told, I felt a bit awkward which is probably why I said, "Hi, stranger, we've just about forgotten what you looked like in Blàs. What's Inbhirasgaidh done to grab your attention then? Bet you are surprised to see us here." I meant it as a joke, but it came out sounding needy and not very friendly. My face flared, my insides squirmed, and that hole I prayed for in the ground didn't open up and swallow me. I remembered, belatedly, why I always prepared speeches and practised my first lines before I entered rooms or meetings.

Mary was first to rescue me. "I expect you heard about our markets from Ellen and have come to take a peek. Have you tried our new chocolate named after our village? And you really should taste some of the apple juice on sale. I'm sure Stroma can take you around and tell you all about our cider weekend." She twinkled her eyes at me. Mary was prepared to throw out a life jacket, but it was up to me to grab hold of it and rescue myself. There was no way she was going to let me run away from this. "Off you go, Stroma. If anyone needs you, Maureen here will come and find you."

I spent an excruciating ten minutes introducing Jim around the hall before I felt someone at my back.

"I'm Scott. I expect Stroma has told you about me." Scott leant over me and held out his hand for Jim to shake.

"Actually, no she hasn't. Are you on the committee that acquired Coilltean Sìthiche?" he replied as he shook the proffered hand.

"Well, yes and no. I was late arriving for all that. But I have involved myself now. Just moved permanently to the village. I'm looking forward to working more closely with Stroma and the others."

He took a step closer to me. I was beginning to feel a little hemmed in with the two of them towering above me. I had an urge to push them both back a little so I could breathe more easily – they were taking up my air.

"So, are we going to see more of you back in Blàs?" I asked Jim.

"You might well do. I have the application for funding for a feasibility study to see whether it would be better to have a permanent feature at the dun or a bigger exhibition in the hall. But you will know all about that, I suppose."

Before Scott could respond, Stag appeared and thrust two cups of fizzy apple lemonade under Scott's and Jim's noses.

"Buy our apple juice. We need to get me skull back, and all money is going to pay for that. Aren't you the one who has my skull?" Stag frowned at Jim.

"Not me. I'm the good guy. I'm the one who will help see if you will get the money to pay for exhibiting the skull." Jim smiled down at Stag.

"It's my skull. You can haf this juice half-price then as long as we get the money. You haf to pay proper price, Scott."

"Here," said Jim, thrusting a five-pound note at Stag. "Put the change toward your fund."

"Wow, fanks." Stag's smile lit up his face, so like his twin at that moment.

"Here's my contribution, Stag." Scott handed over £10. "This lemonade better be good."

I smiled at Jim and Scott before making my escape. Honestly, men could be so predictable sometimes. At least Stag was getting the benefit of their competitive side. We could do with a few more escapades like that to help our fundraising, but I'd rather not be present next time it happened.

All the rumours were true. Inbhirasgaidh was indeed getting more than its fair share of the tourist trade thanks to *The Darkest Depths*, but some visitors were still making their way to Blàs. The following market day in the village, we were doing brisk business. The twins' lemonade had been selling well considering the time of the year. They were delighted to see the amount of money they were raising. Jill still looked reasonably sane, considering she was the one supervising them most weekends during market hours.

"Stag is a born salesman. He was charming the passers-by, making up for his sister's silence. She's still smiling but not saying a word, not a squeak to anyone. It doesn't seem to worry her or her brother that he's doing the speaking for them both."

I watched the twins head home, holding hands with their money box tucked inside their bag. A huge box sat at Jill's feet containing their empty bottles and jugs.

"Here, I'll give you a hand with that box." Scott had appeared at our side. He leant down and picked up the huge box. "Was it a success then, the market?"

"Yes, it was. Thanks, Scott. Most of us locals appear to have sold well. We will be starting the run-up to the Christmas buying season soon. I've already gained a few more commissions myself. I'll need to get some more stock done though. That's what I would normally be doing at this time of the year, but these weekly markets are taking all my stock and my time. Just put that box down there, please; Rap will be along to pick it up later. Drink anyone?"

"Not for me, thanks. I'm hoping to have a word with Stroma actually. Have you got a minute? We could walk while we talk if you need to dash off?"

I hadn't seen anyone since the previous market as I had been working full-time, including most evenings, trying to keep up with the commitments of my waged job. I have been doing quality assurance assessments on Gaelic pre-school groups both locally and up north. My evenings had been spent discussing my findings with the staff and their committees. At the same time I was setting up a Gaelic immersion course due to run in Blàs. GLADS had decided to focus on the autumn season since our summer and winter courses were so successful. A few tourists still flirted around the area enjoying the bonnie colours and smells of autumn. My boss had decided that we should tap into both the tourist and local population for a combined short two-day course. So no ceilidh or heavy drinking sessions were to be encouraged. I think he had forgotten who was teaching the course. Auntie Lottie would do her own thing no doubt.

Scott strode along at my side.

"I'm worried about Ellen. I feel she is bottling up her grief. She's really pushing herself and involved in too much. She's never in."

I laughed out loud.

"I don't think it's funny, Stroma. I thought you could help."

"Firstly, Scott, Ellen has always run everything here. If there is something needed doing, everybody asks her. She has always been that person. She only ever broke that rule when she knew you were coming, so she could free up some time to be with you. Even then, she normally still had something going on. You are just taking it badly that she's so busy all the time. Secondly, it wouldn't be a bad way for her to choose to deal with her grief, and if that's what it is, well, good luck to her. And finally, she listens to no one, so good luck to you if you think you can stop her."

"You know, Stroma, with you two being so close, I really thought you might want to help. I can't believe you are being so glib." Scott stormed off. Well, what did he think I could do? The only person who could ever tell Ellen to slow down was Helen, and she was no longer here. So much for all that anticipation I'd had for Scott's return. I had been daydreaming about how things could develop between us, but so far, all that had developed was my knowledge that he was already in a relationship. *How old was this existing relationship anyway?* I wondered. And had it been existing when we were having our occasional flings during his stays here. On top of it all, he now thought I was heartless. I found myself contemplating checking on Ellen, just in case.

I left my pondering there, but it kept creeping back to haunt me throughout the rest of the day. By evening, I had arranged a wee get-together, with Mary, Auntie Lottie and Maureen as backup. If Ellen really was storing up her grief, we needed to know so that we could allow her a way of unloading, to at least one of us.

First, though, I had to get the two-day course up and running. We were already almost full. Auntie Lottie's growing reputation was pulling in new students. It was freely admitted within Gaelic circles that she was the most successful language tutor in the Highlands.

GLADS, who paid my wages, considered themselves lucky that she chose to work with us. It was her students who tended to either come back for more or go on to access full-time language courses. Many of her past pupils were fluent, or well on their way there. All inspired by her rather unique method of delivery.

Still, Auntie Lottie running a course on her own patch had

me a tad worried. There was no way she was going to tone it down for the sake of local propriety, and I was scared we would end up disgracing ourselves, in one way or another. Working on your own patch was never easy. One slip, and I would never hear the end of it. I had organised, checked and rechecked everything. I fussed and pleaded with Auntie Lottie for her lesson plans. "Oh for goodness sake, Stroma, relax. What could possibly go wrong? We have done hundreds of these courses."

"I know, Auntie Lottie, but not here, not in Blàs, where everyone we know can see us."

"What are you worried about? Everyone here loves you, and you know that every student I have ever taught has loved my courses."

That was true, but normally, her courses involved alcohol and visits to unusual places and adult jokes, and well, just Auntie Lottie being incorrigible in general. I could only hope she was going to behave herself, at least up to a point.

The market was once more being held in Inbhirasgaidh. It would have to survive without me and a few other regulars who were attending our course. It rained, thankfully. Everyone who had registered for our first local taste of a Gaelic weekend turned up. If the blue sky and sunny weather had stuck around, I knew we would have lost a few to the outdoors.

As it was, the dig was rained or, more correctly, muddied off. All the archaeology students had decamped to the hall, where it was warm and dry. Hot coffee or tea, and homemade cakes, courtesy of Ellen, were handed around. Much to my surprise, Swallow and Lark had taken a day off from the market to attend along with their dad, Ralph.

Unusually, it was him who had undergone a permanent name change since his wedding. Jill had only ever called him Ralph, and since their nuptials, this had rubbed off on the rest of the community. Even Ralph himself never referred to himself as Rap anymore.

"Well, most of you have the Gaelic, so we want to at least learn some of the language. I need to know when you lot are calling us names." Ralph had smiled good-naturedly when he appeared at my door, children in tow.

Unfortunately, I could not offer the twins a place on the course. They were too young, but they were now being taught through the medium of Gaelic at the primary school anyway. Swallow and Lark had been too old to join the Gaelic stream at the school, but Ralph reckoned rightly they would acquire some of the language through playing with the local children. Attending the course would give them a boost though. However, we needed them to enjoy the course, as it would be awful if they were to be put off speaking the language, so Auntie Lottie had come to the rescue with the suggestion that Old Tam take them for some of the time. It was proposed that they could help out on the croft belonging to one of his cousins, who also had good Gaelic, rather than stay in the class. We put this to Ralph who immediately endorsed the idea.

"That would be great. Then they can't be showing me up in class. I mean, we have all picked up the swear words, but their understanding of the language, in general, is way better than mine already. So, I'm all for it, if Old Tam is happy with it."

After an initial introduction to the course, Swallow and Lark were sent on their way. A handful of survival phrases had been firmly drilled into them for use where necessary.

"*Ciamar a chanas tu sin sa Ghàidhlig*/How do you say that in Gaelic?"

"*Chan eil mi a' tuigsinn*/I don't understand."

And finally, "*Tha mi ag iarraidh…*/I want…" Helpful if you need a drink, toilet or anything else important like chocolate. Auntie Lottie had firmly ordered that no language other than Gaelic was to pass their lips.

"And I mean *no* other language, Tam, that includes your

Dundonian one, and any of the other colourful varieties you can come up with. They are only bairns, kindly remember that."

Old Tam was heard muttering as he left with his charges "*Uil, thusa nas eòlaiche air droch chànan na mise co-dhiu*/Well, you're more familiar with bad language than me anyway."

Old Tam had been one of the lucky ones of his generation. His parents had seen the value in their mix of culture and languages. His father had spoken to him only and always in Gaelic and his mother had never lost her Dundonian accent. Growing up, Old Tam's accent had then mixed in with the local accent, giving him a unique way of speaking. While many of Old Tam's peers had been actively discouraged from speaking anything but English, he had grown up rich in all his languages and traditions.

Auntie Lottie tutted as she settled her class. All my fears disappeared as the day eased into its normal routine peppered with much laughter, innuendos and the breaking of natural shyness. Adults, in general, are way more uptight about making mistakes than bairns. Children appear much more at ease learning a language and have no hang-ups about sounding 'wrong'. Therefore, the bairns learn quicker and without so much embarrassment.

Auntie Lottie was amazing at zoning out all cultural restrictions, and she broke down many inhibitions early in the class. By lunchtime, real progress had been made. The scent of homemade soup had led to another lesson about soup, taste, temperature and asking for salt, bread and all sorts of other things.

I had been up to check on Old Tam and the children. All seemed to be enjoying themselves. Old Tam was almost happy. Only his role as the Chief of the Highlands Games came anywhere near to producing the same level of enjoyment he was having delivering the course to the youngsters. Here he was again, among the sheep and the things he loved. Passing on his knowledge and his father's tongue to two children who revelled in the experience. Swallow and Lark were clarted in mud, though fortunately, they were wearing oversized boiler suits and grubby wellies. It was difficult to tell who was enjoying it the most.

Back at the hall, I jumped, not because the hatch had opened so suddenly for the distribution of the bowls of soup that were now being handed out, but because Scott was there. I hadn't seen him since he had stomped off. How was I going to act cool when I knew my face flushed bright red? Anger started to take over the embarrassment. *Just who did he think he was, accusing me of not caring?* I probably knew his aunt better than he did. Although, I *was* feeling a bit guilty that our organised little chat with Mary and Maureen hadn't taken place.

Scott sidled up to me.

"Peace offering?" He handed me a bowl of hot lentil soup. "Look, I was maybe a bit out of order the other day. I'm just concerned, that's all. She's up at all hours of the night. I keep waking up to smells of cooking. The fridge is full of meals she is preparing during the night. Although, you couldn't tell in the morning, as the kitchen is gleaming. And she is out most evenings. Is there nothing you can do?"

"Ooh, well, maybe that is a bit unusual, even for Ellen. Look, I'll talk to Mary and Maureen again, see if we can't get her along for a chat. Actually, Auntie Lottie could maybe help, if I can get her away from Paul for long enough. The friendship between your aunt and Auntie Lottie has got even tighter now that Auntie Lottie is back here permanently."

"Well, I'm off with Paul, Ralph, Old Tam and Shep, of course, for a day fishing on Wednesday… any chance of doing it then?"

"I'm sure that can be arranged. So you are definitely here for a while yet then?"

"As a matter of fact, yes. It doesn't matter where I work from as long as I have the internet. We could be seeing a lot more of each other. Aah, must dash, there goes Grace lifting all the boxes from Ellen again."

I watched him stride off, a faint smile on my lips. I tilted my head as he hoisted the boxes up – from my angle, things were definitely beginning to look a lot better.

Mac the Shake had died. He was the local pharmacist, hence the name derived from his need to shake together liquids for certain medications. It had come as a surprise to the community, as most deaths do. The timing of such tragedies is never good, but for Auntie Lottie and myself, his untimely death had particularly unfortunate repercussions.

"What do you mean his funeral is on Saturday? Whose idea was that? Why Saturday?" Auntie Lottie was throwing these questions at Maureen who had come to inform us of the occasion.

"Well, his family chose the time and the day of the funeral. They wanted to give relatives living away the chance to attend, so a Saturday it is. Sorry, am I missing something here? Was poor Mac the Shake's death not convenient for you then?" Maureen looked my way for support. Death was a serious event, especially when the deceased was a local born and bred. Nothing was permitted to stand in the way of a proper send-off. The whole community would be involved. No doubt, Peter the Pipes was already polishing up his bagpipes.

"Well?" Maureen looked from Auntie Lottie to me again; she had sensed the undertone in the room. "What is it then?"

"It's Alice's wedding the same day in Inverness," I supplied.

Maureen started to laugh. "Oh, you have to be joking. You've been looking forward to that for ages." She laughed again. "So what are you going to do? You can't go to both… or can you?"

"I hadn't thought of that. What time is the funeral then?" Auntie Lottie looked at Maureen who supplied us with all the details.

Mac the Shake's service was to be held in the morning. Once out of the church, the mourners would follow behind his coffin as it travelled along on the old hand-pulled cart. Hundreds of locals over the generations had taken their last journey in this way. The mourners would make their slow progress toward the deceased's final resting place. Every able person would take a step forward, grip the cart handles and walk a few paces until the next person stepped in. Others would line the way to the graveyard, filing in behind the cart as it made its way.

Maureen confirmed that, after the graveyard service, a wake would be held in the pub, which would go on for most of the day. She didn't have to add, "and probably for most of the night as well" – we all knew that. Auntie Lottie and I were trying to plan how we could attend at least some of it then disappear without causing offence or appearing callous.

"Look, Auntie Lottie, I have to go the service at least. He was so kind to me and Iona when we lost our parents. I should really go to the wake too, but I'm sure there will be so many there by then, that I won't be missed."

"The wedding is not until the afternoon. We have to be there before the bride, obviously, but we could still make it if we get our timing right. I could slip away when we're halfway down to the graveyard and get the car. We'll pack it on Friday night, with our wedding clothes and overnight things. You could speak to his widow and family as you leave the graveside. Give them your condolences then hightail it away. I could meet you just around the corner from there, nobody will notice, much, hopefully. We just have to get our timing right, that's all. And hope there are no hold-ups on the roads."

It all sounded feasible, but I was unsure how much I would want to go to a wedding, right after a funeral. We had been so looking forward to Alice's wedding. Her fourth husband was the instructor from her Salsa class. They had been dancing their way toward the aisle for the past two years. Alice was ninety-six and like an older version of Auntie Lottie. Full of fun and life, although, she was a firm believer in marriage which is where she differed from Auntie Lottie.

Paul, despite his best efforts, still hadn't managed to get Auntie Lottie down the aisle, even though she openly said he was the love of her life. Alice, however, had already outlived three of her husbands. Eduardo, her soon-to-be fourth husband, was a few years younger than herself. They should have been married a year before, but Eduardo had fallen ill. Now that he was back to full health, a small ceremony had been arranged, followed by nibbles, and of course, a Latin-style dance.

Friends, neighbours and their entire dance class were all invited. Auntie Lottie and I were the only ones attending from Blàs. We had already booked into a small hotel, so we could dance our way through the night till morning, if we wanted. Only now, there was the small matter of a local funeral to get through first.

The day dawned dry and clear. More the sort of weather you would order in for a wedding than a funeral. I had always felt it was mean to have a bonnie, hot, sun-filled day when you were putting someone to rest. It hardly reflected the emotions of the people involved in these events. Stormy, dark grey skies, rain-swept and cold, like it had been at Angus' funeral, would better mirror the turbulent feelings of the bereaved. Then again, that would hardly have been fair to Alice. She was looking forward to her day, hoping for a crisp white frost with cobalt-blue skies and blazing sunshine.

I'd put on a colourful snug-fitting top, totally suitable for the wedding, but not so much for a traditional dark-clothed funeral. No one would see my inappropriate dress though, as I had covered it up with a dark jacket. The rest of my wedding outfit was hanging up in Auntie Lottie's car, ready for a change on the way through to Inverness.

Auntie Lottie had been far more selective in what she had on. She was wearing a beautiful dress with a clever cut. It moved with her and would look amazing when she was dancing at the wedding. In deep purple, it wouldn't look out of place at either occasion. Her neck jewellery, she hid under a large purple and blue shawl, one of Jill's beautiful creations. She could have pulled off the role of a very sophisticated, smartly dressed woman attending a sad occasion, if it wasn't for her swishing walk which she just couldn't contain.

Her hair, of course, she couldn't refrain from embellishing. It was swept up in an elaborate style and pinned in place with a very large sparkling diamanté accessory. Auntie Lottie's make-up was also a bit on the obvious side, more like, 'Wha-hay where's the party? I'm ready and I'm coming,' than, 'Oh dear, I may cry, better hang back on the mascara, I don't want to look like a panda.'

"Don't look at me like that, Stroma. You can't expect me to organise my hair in the car now, can you?" Auntie Lottie patted her amazing crown. "I'll just need to refresh my make-up when we get to Inverness, and I will be ready. Since I'm driving, I need to be ready before we leave. I won't be able to change in the car like you."

In truth, I wasn't sure I *would* manage to change in her car – there wasn't a lot of room. I was mentally kicking myself for not putting more thought into what I could have worn to both events. The thought of having to wear my 'death clothes' to a wedding didn't appeal to me. Instead, I wanted to shed it all well before I got there. A shower in between would have been welcome, if only I could have fitted it in.

§

The minister must have ramped the heating up. That or the sheer amount of people inside had raised the temperature. It was no good, I would have to at least unbutton my jacket. Others had already taken off coats, scarves and gloves.

"Are ye nae tae hot in thon coat?" Old Tam had leant forward from the pew behind. "Here lass, stand ye up, an eh'll tak yer jacket off fae ye." He started to pull my jacket down from the back, so I had no option but to let it drop. "Oh meh, lass, weel, ye wull definitely be a bitty cooler noo."

Whispers rose into the rafters, mainly from those around me who had seen the full wedding effect of my unfortunate funeral attire. It was not that low-cut a blouse, but it felt like I was almost topless in the face of the reaction it got. I found myself pulling it up to try and cover myself a bit more which only drew more attention.

"Nice top. I hear you are off to a wedding after this," Scott whispered at my side. I glanced in his direction. "Maureen told me. I could have accompanied you as your plus one if you had asked. I'm told I'm a good mover."

Oh my God, was he flirting with me in a church, and at a funeral of all things. Then again, heightened emotions and all that were supposed to make people say the most improper things at funerals.

"Em, that didn't come out exactly the way I meant it." I could see the red infusing up his neck into his face.

"Well, actually," I whispered back, "I am Auntie Lottie's plus one. She asked me before she was with Paul. And he is quite happy for me to go instead of him. So you see, I couldn't have asked you. Even if I wanted to."

"Ah." Scott leant back in the pew, a slight smile on his face, which given the occasion, I thought perhaps a little indelicate, but then again, I had a nice fuzzy feeling inside, so I was just as bad. A loud sniff from the front pews brought me back to the business in hand. *Concentrate, concentrate,* my brain urged whenever our legs met as we both stood up, sat down, bowed her heads, clasped our arms, sighed and basked in forgotten memories swirling around Mac the Shake and his life among us. By the end of the service, I was glad to escape the atmosphere of the church. I watched the coffin being positioned on the cart as a cold wind froze my core. I quickly pulled my jacket over my wedding top and fell in beside Auntie Lottie and the other mourners. We marched slowly toward the graveyard, each step keeping time with Peter the Pipes' slow, sorrowful melody.

"Now remember, Stroma, I'll be waiting in the getaway car, just over there. We won't have much time to get to Alice's, so best foot forward once you are out of there." Auntie Lottie ducked down a lane to head back for her car.

Others also left the cortège, either unable to face the graveside service, too infirm to attend or content they had paid their sufficient respects in church. Maureen trundled up beside me, followed by Scott. We walked either side of Maureen's wheelchair in companionable silence, thoughts of how Mac the Shake had touched all our lives flowing around us. The walk gifted us time to focus on our personal journeys with him through his life.

Ellen was missing. She couldn't face another funeral so soon after losing Helen. She and Mary had paid their respects the night before when they had visited the widow. I knew Mary wouldn't leave Ellen's side much today. They intended to spend the day together, baking and going over Development Trust business.

Thankfully, before it was my turn to grab hold of the cart handle, we reached our destination. The main male relatives to Mac the Shake stepped forward again and drew the cart into the cemetery. A short service took place; it was cold and bleak.

As planned, I had the chance to say my piece to the family of the bereaved at the gates. His widow hugged me once, and her eyes filled with tears as she said, "Now off with you. You have a life to live, get away from the smell of death while you can. Go on now." Someone had obviously told her about my double-booking. She was giving me her blessing to go, but somehow that made it feel even worse. I was debating how to tell Auntie Lottie that I had changed my mind and couldn't face a wedding after all when she flew up in her car and screeched to a halt, raising a cloud of dust. All eyes blinked away dusty tears. *Not much chance of disappearing quietly now then.*

"Sorry, Stroma, I thought I was late. I couldn't find my car keys then remembered they were in my other coat, the one that I packed for the wedding. Hop in then."

I could feel a hundred eyes staring as I climbed into the car. I pictured myself nonchalantly walking away, making out this getaway plan was nothing to do with me, but I immediately dismissed the idea when visions of Auntie Lottie shouting out the car window, "Stroma, Stroma, where are you going? We have a wedding to get to," flooded my mind.

"Well, did you see the look on Effie's face? She knows where we are going and isn't happy, but that is more to do with not getting an invitation than because we aren't going to the wake. It will only be filled with all the worthies and frequent fliers who attend all these events anyway. So I am not bothered one jot. Paul will be there to represent us, and no doubt he will be there till the end anyway. Now, come on, get out of those clothes and into your glad rags."

We roared off with my arms shooting out in all directions while I attempted to strip off my funeral jacket. We must have looked a strange sight, as I attempted to metamorphose from a darkly dressed funeral attendee into a colourful wedding guest. The space in the car was so cramped it was near impossible to change out of my trousers never mind into a skirt. I almost knocked Auntie Lottie's eye out as I pushed my arm into my wedding jacket. When Auntie Lottie took the corners, I was slung about trying to put on tights. By the time I was redressed, I felt I had completed a high-energy workout, and was all hot and flustered. My make-up would have to wait until we got to Inverness.

"That's better. I'm so glad you are out of those clothes. That's us truly on our way to the wedding." Auntie Lottie switched on some music. We only had about fifteen minutes left of our journey, but she was right. As I had wrestled off and on with my clothes, I had disrobed the melancholy that had surrounded me. I was ready to celebrate life again. A Latin-dance-style wedding, with a lively 96-year-old bride was just what was needed.

25

News of a death is often followed by the announcement of a birth. Never to do things by half, Blàs soon had the pleasure of welcoming not one but two new arrivals. One, it has to be said, was planned for. The other was a bit of a surprise to everyone. Thank goodness, you would suppose, we had a resident midwife in the village.

The phone call came in the middle of the night.

"Can you come over, Stroma? Only, Paul is on a call out and I can't settle. Poor Whisky is padding around like a fat sausage. I'm afraid she may burst."

"Don't you think you would be better calling the vet?"

"No, no, Paul says she is fine, but I'm not. My poor wee doggie. Why did I think having puppies was such a good idea? Stroma, you have to come over."

It was 2.30 a.m. Like human babies, it appeared that puppies liked to be born in the early hours. I shivered into some warm, comfy clothes and made my way to Auntie Lottie's house. At that time in the morning, there weren't many lights to be seen.

Apart from the ones shining out of Rose Cottage that is, but that wasn't unusual. Since the cave-in at the dun, both Stag and Fawn requested that some lights be kept on at all times. They shone like tiny beacons, as I made my way across the village.

Light temporarily blinded me when the door opened. Auntie Lottie grabbed my arm and hauled me inside.

"Hurry, hurry, they're coming. Oh, my poor Whisky. I don't think I can watch. You will have to tell me how she is doing. I can't go in there again, I just can't." Nothing much worried Auntie Lottie. She was one of the first to try anything without a second thought. She had, it appeared, finally found something that knocked down all her defences: her dog in labour.

She shoved me into the warm room that she had previously used as a snug. The lighting had been lowered, and a newly built whelping bed lay up against one wall. Inside it, there were old newspapers that Whisky had shredded. On top of this stood Whisky. Her head was down, and she was busy licking something.

"Oh my, Whisky, look at you. Clever girl," I whispered, creeping nearer to sit on one of the chairs a safe distance from her 'den'. I could see a tiny movement and hear a small squeak as the little puppy moved around looking for food and comfort. Whisky settled down, and the puppy latched on.

"Auntie Lottie, come and see. You must come in and see this. Whisky has had a puppy already. See, it's doing fine. Look, she's suckling the wee thing."

Auntie Lottie walked slowly into the room and collapsed into the other chair.

"Oh my. Will you look at that, a baby. Well, aren't you the clever one, my pet?" Auntie Lottie held a scrunched-up tissue to her eyes. "Oh, Stroma, thank you so much for coming. Paul said there was nothing to worry about, but I just couldn't sit here on my own and watch her suffer." With that Whisky started padding around her den again. "It's no good, I can't watch. Stay with her please, Stroma." And before I could reply, Auntie Lottie left the room. The same scenario was played out four more times during the night, until exhausted, Auntie Lottie finally settled down. Whisky, on the other hand, was the perfect new mother. She cleaned each puppy, fed them, then got up to do it all over again. By 6.30 a.m. it was finally all over. Whisky had given birth to her last puppy.

"Oh look, Stroma, five! We have five puppies, that's almost a record. They normally have such small litters. The Caledonian Dandie Dinmont Terrier Club will be so happy when I tell them how well she has done. And her a rescue to boot. I wonder how many I can persuade Paul to keep?"

"Well, I think you may have two females and three males there. But it is hard to be sure this early. If I'm right, both the females appear to be mustards, although it is difficult to tell. I think all the boys are peppers. And if you don't mind, I'm off—" Before I could finish there was a loud banging on the door.

"It's meh, it's meh, Tam, ye hiv tae come please, ye hiv tae, thar's somit wrang wi Morag." Old Tam hobbled into the room white as a sheet. "It's Morag, thar's somit affy no weel wi' eer. She's no been feelin eersel these twa days past. I heird eer up, an the peur wee lassie is on eer kitchen flair, noo lookin weel at ah. I chapped on Ellen's dair on the wuy ower, an she is wi Morag the noo. Eh sawed yer light on, n cam ower. Please, ye hiv tae help eer."

"Shouldn't you phone for an ambulance, Tam? If things are that bad, they may send for the copter," I said, as I ran out the door. Auntie Lottie reluctantly left her new mum and puppies behind.

Fresh air banished any tiredness we felt as we hurried toward Morag's house, all thoughts of a nice breakfast before heading to my bed dashed. We met Shep hobbling along, obviously trying to catch up with Old Tam, who was right behind us. I glanced back to see Shep turn around and start to hobble his way back toward Old Tam and Morag's house. I rushed into the house and headed straight for the kitchen.

Ellen was gently trying to coax Morag to stand up.

"Come on now, lass, this is no place to lay. Let's get you into bed now. Are you sure we shouldn't call the medics?"

"No, no, yes, yes… oh God, Ellen, I think it's the baby. It's too early, we're not due yet." I could hear the fear in Morag's voice. "I thought I ate something that hadn't agreed with me. I kept getting cramps, but I didn't think I could possibly be in labour. I'm way too early."

"Oh, hen…" Old Tam started.

"Oh my God, oh, oh, I can feel movement, please no, I think baby is coming, right… coming right now. Ellen, I can't make it stop… Please, Ellen, help me… Not yet, please, baby, not yet." Morag panted in between tears. "Please, baby, stop, wait… please."

I was trying to work out how many weeks early she was, but my brain was incapable of working out the simplest sum at that point.

"Tam, Tam, phone for help. Tam! Quick as you can," Ellen barked.

Old Tam immediately pulled out his phone, "Oh aye, right ye are, lass. Eh, wull jist gae throu the ben."

There was a stunned silence when he left the kitchen, the implications of what was happening right before our eyes becoming clear. Morag started panting heavily again, just as Old Tam returned to the kitchen. "Right, Tam, out. Lottie, towels. Stroma, help me get her pants off."

"Ach, ach—" Old Tam was ushered out of the room just as Shep finally made it back to his side. The door was firmly closed on both of them.

Ellen and I had disposed of Morag's pants and had placed towels under her. Ellen's head was poking up between Morag's legs.

"Right, Morag, there's a good girl, can you just push a little? I can see the baby's head already. Right, pant… and again… that's right; you are doing fine." And for the second time within a few hours, I saw the birth of a new mum.

Morag herself then supervised where and how to cut the cord. Old Tam was called back in to hold his new great-grand-son, while we cleared up the general mess.

"Eh cood o helped eer, eh cood hiv, ye ken. Eh've delivered tha many sheeps. Ach, wull ye noo look at em. Jisit gey a deek o thon hair."

The on-call midwife was next to arrive, along with the local doctor. A few minutes later, the air ambulance crew walked in and whisked Morag and the new baby off to the Special Care Baby Unit at Raigmore Hospital in Inverness. That only left one other person who could possibly come through the door next.

The backdoor flew open, and Maureen trundled in.

"What have I missed then? I heard the air ambulance. Right glad I am to see you there, Tam. I was worried you had taken ill."

"Noo meh, lass, Eh'm as fit as a fiddle."

"Lottie, surely you are not over here telling them all about your new puppies so early. Yes, of course I know all about them. Four, isn't it?"

"Five, as a matter of fact, Maureen. I was just about to head back. You can come and see them if you want?"

"Well, I don't mind if I do but—"

"Or," continued Auntie Lottie, "you could congratulate Old Tam here on becoming a great-grandad."

"Oh, that's lovely news. I'll spread the word, Tam. I was on my way to Mary's, so that's two lovely bits of news to share with her. So, who are the new parents? She is bound to ask."

"Oh, that'll be Morag and Neil," supplied Auntie Lottie, a big smile on her face as she filled in our local town crier on all the doings of the night.

"Morag? Well I never. Is she not a bit early? Is everything okay?"

We assured Maureen that, although the baby had needed some extra help, so far, he was doing well. Maureen looked as relieved as the rest of us. "What a turn-up. Our very own midwife giving birth to a baby on the kitchen floor, and her not realising she was in labour. She'll have a job living that down. Though I expect, to start with, most people will say nothing… at least until they see her pushing the pram around, then they will know all is right with them both. The pair of them will be in Raigmore for a wee while yet, no doubt. Everyone will send them their best wishes, I'm sure. With the wee one being so early, she won't have much ready for him either. I'll spread the word. I'm sure the other young mothers will soon supply them with loads of bits and pieces. Mary will need to get on with that cardi she was knitting for him. Well, I better get on and see these puppies. I've a busy morning ahead."

Of that, there was no doubt. Maureen headed off with Auntie Lottie. She would be off to dispatch the news around the community after that while the rest of us, including the new mums no doubt, tried to get a few hours extra sleep.

26

"How do we improve on nature's work then?" Mary asked at the last encounter between the Development Trust and Jim. Mary's point was valid, but we had been over all this before. Neither one of them would budge on the issue. "The woods have been there for generations. They have kept themselves going all that time and regrown without interference every spring. There is a natural balance; we don't want to damage that."

"Part of the grant states that you have to re-establish the parts of the woods that have been damaged or neglected over the years." Jim sighed. "You really have no option. The Trust agreed to these conditions when it accepted the grant money."

"Tsh, it is not neglected. Many creatures live and thrive in these areas you say are neglected. It is from there that the new growth and balance come from." Mary had not taken to the notion that we now had to abide by another organisation's rules regarding what we could do with Coilltean Sìthiche.

"I understand that. I was a qualified Woodland Conservation Officer before this. I am trained to look out for and research what happens with different habitats, and how they affect our local wildlife, however big or small. I am only trying to help you understand these things too. It's part of my job. You have to spend the money in certain ways, Mary."

Poor Jim had been here so many times before with her. He actually did sympathise with her issues. Mary's eyes were sparkling dangerously. Normally, Ellen would have stepped in, but she was talking to Giulietta and hadn't noticed the change in atmosphere.

"I suppose all these new paths that you've proposed, the ones that will rip through our woods, are also an improvement then?" Mary's voice quivered with rage, and here was the real reason she was so against Jim's suggestion. A condition of the grant was that we made more paths. They were to be developed to allow for people with impaired walking to access the woods. Mary had no problem with the idea of allowing better access. After all, hadn't she in her younger days helped carry, push, dig and haul Maureen's wheelchair backward and forward along tiny root-covered tracks throughout the woods. She was all for helping others gain access to the woods. It was just that she didn't want big, wide, cement-covered walkways taking her away from being right next to the trees and bushes. "As for being trained, there isn't a certificate that tells you what is right and wrong with nature. All you have to do is observe it and treat it with respect to see what works and what doesn't. Slashing through our woodland with more big paths is not a good thing for nature. Isn't that right, Maureen?"

"Well, Mary, I totally agree with you. So I've been doing some research myself." Maureen pulled out a stash of paper. "Here, we can use wood as long as it is maintained well. Or hoggin, that is a mixture of gravel, sand, cinders, or clay. Well, they are all natural, aren't they? I was thinking that you, me and Lottie could go and measure some of the path routes, and then get quotes from people. I'm sure some of the paths are already wide enough for my wheelchair. We don't even need to make them *all* that wide. Though, I think we should probably have a decent wide path leading to the dun and back. Just look at how the paths around the dun are getting all mushed up with the number of people working there and just going along to visit. If we don't do this now, Mary, all our little trails may be lost anyway. What do you say? I haven't been into the woods for a while – it would be nice to see if we could do something without harming what we have."

Jim looked gratefully toward Maureen before he turned to address Mary again. "I would like to come along if that is okay. You are right, Mary, in that we don't want to lose the character of the woods. We could still keep that if we are careful about which paths we choose to widen and which we can leave the same, but we do need to plan for the wear and tear. The traffic on the paths is going to increase, and we don't want to lose any more flora or disturb more animals than we have to." This was not the first time he had asked to accompany Mary to the woods, but Mary had continually refused to acknowledge his offer.

Ellen was now deliberately ignoring what was going on. I suspected she had probably had a word beforehand with both Jim and Maureen. My suspicions were confirmed when Ellen gave a small nod of her head that would have been difficult to intercept if you weren't already looking out for it.

"You don't understand. None of you understand." Mary slowly raised herself up from her chair, her eyes glistening. "I'm leaving now." And with that she was gone.

Into the silence that followed, I whispered, "I'll go." I hastened after Mary into the night.

"Will she be okay, do you think?"

I hadn't realised that Scott had followed me out.

"I don't honestly know. She is not normally so emotional. I can't ever remember her walking out on a discussion about… well, anything. There is something else at the back of this, I'm sure."

"Well, if you don't mind, I will tag along. I promise to sit quietly and listen."

We entered Mary's house just as she was taking off her coat.

"I'll put the kettle on then, will I?" she said, recovered slightly from her earlier outburst.

"Mary, what's wrong? There is more to this than paths. I know you and Angus loved the woods. Does this have something to do with him?"

She started to open her mouth, but before anything came out, a thumping could be heard at her back door which flew open, and in came Maureen.

"Well, that was a fine to-do. I left them all there discussing our 'Grow your Own Woods Day'. I'm not needed for that. Gosh, I'm that parched, Mary, glad to see the kettle is already on. Right, my lovely, are you going to finally tell us what this is all about?"

The best and worst thing about Maureen was her directness. At times, you just wanted to ignore her and hope she would go away, but sometimes, her approach was just what was needed. This was one such occasion. Despite Maureen's bluntness and their difference in years, she and Mary had a strong, unbreakable bond. They had both helped each other in so many different ways over the years.

I helped Mary put the tea out, and we sat in her warm kitchen as she brought out an old bottle. Small glasses were filled with a spirit that we knew would warm our souls.

"Come on now, Mary, what is it? I know you would like it if I could access the woods easier, so there's something else going on here. What is it?"

"It's Angus. It's Angus' patch that will be ruined."

"What do you mean by Angus' patch, Mary? Do you mean the Druid Tree? The path is going around it. It wouldn't be harmed. Nobody would want to lose or have that bonnie tree ruined now, would they?"

The Druid Tree was a magnificent oak that dominated all around it. It didn't matter how many times you saw it, it caught your attention every time in the way it rose and towered over the other trees and flora near at hand. Children over the decades had claimed and hidden in its branches and leaves. Youngsters had danced and run around its broad trunk, and adults had enjoyed its shelter and colourful autumn canopy for generations. The oak still called to many in the community in its many different ways.

"No, no, of course, it is not the Druid Tree – that's safe. That's the problem. I've looked at all these proposed paths, and they will have to go straight through my Angus' trees, straight through, so that they will avoid the Druid Tree, and the rowans, and the hawthorns, and nobody, nobody will want to take *them* down, not with all they mean."

Scott was looking blank at this point.

"The rowans and hawthorns are the fairy folk's trees. None of the older members of the community would be happy if we were to cut any down." I whispered to him. He looked at me, incredulous, shrugged his shoulders and carried on listening. I considered just how odd this must all sound to someone who wasn't brought up with this mixture of ancient traditions and beliefs. To us, our customs mingled seamlessly with the modern world. Technology, and what it can now do, is almost as magical in its own way. We accept that into our lives, so why not our old traditions too?

"I don't understand, Mary. You've never said anything about Angus having a tree in the forest. If it's not the Druid Tree, which one is it?"

Mary took a sip from her glass. "He promised his dad and his dad before that. It is what made them all so good at story-telling, that promise. Angus believed that what they promised made him as great and honoured as any storyteller in the community."

"What promise and to whom? Maybe I should get Lottie to do whatever Angus did too, seeing as she seems to be taking over that role. I thought I knew most of the important stories around here. Though, I don't recall one about Angus and his family making promises to trees, or anybody else, for the gift of storytelling and local history. I think you need to start at the beginning, Mary."

"I agree. Looks like we have arrived just at the right time." Ellen had appeared at the door with Giulietta and Auntie Lottie. After placing some cakes on the table for everyone, they sat down. Mary then explained why she was so reluctant to endorse the widening and laying of paths in the woods.

Most locals knew at least a little of the culture that surrounded the local trees and woods of the area. We all knew, for example, that rowans were traditionally grown at the back door to ward off evil, and that hawthorns were grown at the front. Many Highlanders knew that hawthorn, rowan, aspen and elder all had strong connections and beliefs related to the *sìthichean* or fairy folk. Whether you believed in the stories or not was beside the point – they were a part of tradition. Many areas still bore the names associated with the old Gaelic names they had been given.

The elder tree was held in much respect and, in some cases, fear. They could only grow in rich, fertile soil, so weren't found in abundance throughout the Highlands. This made them even more valuable for what it told us about where their roots had been established. In the woods, in Blàs and other parts of Easter Ross, the ground was rich enough to grow this magical tree. A few grew not far from the giant oak, or Druid Tree as it was known.

Elder trees were renowned for helping musicians who choose to make their pipes from the wood. The sound these instruments produced was reported to be beyond any other, and the skill of their musicians' untouchable. But what people didn't know so well was that if you slept under an elder on midsummer, when it was believed that the fairy king and queen would pass, they would bestow on you a gift that would enhance your enjoyment of life. In Angus and his forebears' case, this meant the gift of storytelling and the ability to recollect the history of the people who had dwelt in Blàs down through the centuries.

Angus, as a child, had accompanied his father to the elder grove. Angus Mòr had explained to his son the tradition of placing food under the trees to pay homage to the fairy folk. Angus then returned the next Midsummer Eve to again place food. Only then, he also slept under the chosen elder. Angus firmly believed he had received the gift of storytelling for his devotion. He returned many times to the elders and made sure that, for any that had died, another would have already started to grow in its place.

"So, you see," said Mary, "I can't let Angus down. I can't let the trees be removed to widen the path, even though we couldn't pass that tradition down to someone of our own."

"Well, of course, you can't let those trees be destroyed, Mary, and we won't let that happen either. Will we, Ellen?" Auntie Lottie said. "In fact, Maureen and I are going this very night to leave some food there, and we'll sleep the next midsummer right under them. Since I seem to have fallen heir to the storytelling, and Maureen here has taken over the history of our people, it's the right thing to do. What do you say, Maureen, you up for a little trip to the woods? Paul is puppy-sitting, so we can go straight from here? Oh, look, nobody has touched Ellen's big cake yet, so we can take that?"

"Well, I'm game if you are, Lottie. Stroma and Scott can come along too in case we get into trouble. What do you say, Ellen?"

Ellen looked around at each of us. "You're all grown adults, so who am I to argue, but I think you should wait until morning. It's not really the time of year to go off gallivanting into the woods this late."

"Ach away, we will be fine. Come on, Maureen. Mary you can come too and be sure we find the right elders."

As we trooped outside, Scott leant into me "What was in that drink? Even I'm feeling a bit woozy, or are they just all a bit mad hereabouts? Were things like this happening when I was here over the summers too, do you think?"

"Probably, though I don't see anything unusual in this so far, so you can take it this is quite normal. From memory, it never seems to matter when you go to the woods, there is always someone from the older generation there. Don't you remember?"

"Actually, yes, you are right. Angus and Mary were always about, even Old Tam."

❧

We had reached the woods. Maureen and Mary switched on their torches. Luckily, we had a super moon, so we didn't need much artificial light. Auntie Lottie, Maureen and Mary's voices floated back to us, as we tripped our way inside. Owls hooted and swooped overhead, and small animals could be heard sniffing about the undergrowth. The woods never felt sinister, even at night. In the soft, luminous glow, there was a surreal and magical atmosphere surrounding our little group while we made our way merrily toward the Druid Tree. From there, we would take our bearings to locate the elder grove. The only interruptions to the sounds of nature were the bumping of Maureen's wheelchair as it struggled through the tracks and the occasional 'Oh' and 'Oops, sorry, didn't see your foot there' from the women in front.

"Wow," Scott whispered nearby. The Druid Tree was silhouetted against the night sky. It appeared even bigger in the dark. Three figures could be made out underneath, talking softly and giggling like schoolgirls.

"What-ho, Scott. You afraid of banging into three old women in the woods?" Maureen laughed.

"Speak for yourself, Maureen. I am not old," Great Auntie Lottie stated so loudly that her voice seemed to echo through the branches of the giant oak.

"This way." Mary shone the torch, and we all followed.

"Don't you think that they are all a bit old to be doing this sort of thing?" Scott asked.

"Well, feel free to ask them that, but I wouldn't like to think of the answer you might get. They are happy, and everybody needs a little adventure now and again. I'm surprised your aunt didn't come along."

"Are you trying to say that Aunt Ellen is as mad as this lot?"

"Oh, Scott, she can be a lot worse when she wants to be." I let him ponder that for a while.

"Where have they gone?" All the torch lights had disappeared. There was no sign of the three others, though we heard lots of noise coming from the bushes in front.

"Will you just put that back?"

"Ouch, that branch… What are you doing?"

"My hair's caught, I can't move. Stroma, where are you?"

"Coming, we are coming. Could someone shine the torch, please? We can't see you." And there they were, cramped together under what I presumed was an elder tree. It wasn't as tall as I had expected nor was it in the least bit extraordinary looking. A small tree with three women stuck within its branches. Auntie Lottie's hair was entangled. "How on earth did you manage that?"

"Well, Mary asked me to lay the cake down underneath here, and when I stood up, my hair got caught."

"And my damn wheelchair is caught in this rut. I can't move," Maureen added.

"And where is Mary?"

"Ach, I'm fine, dear. I've just been making sure that this is the right elder tree as there are a few here. Angus did say it didn't matter which one, as they can be damaged in a storm, though there is always another one that will grow up in its place. But yes, I think this is the right one. Bit muddy though… oops." Mary grabbed hold of a branch to steady herself, which promptly broke. Luckily, we managed to grab her before she fell backward into the mud.

Maureen was not so lucky. Her wheelchair was stuck fast in the soft, spongy ground. Regardless of how hard we pushed or pulled, the chair was not going to move. Scott and I were able to keep fairly warm from the effort, but the temperature was dropping. More in desperation than belief, Scott asked me once more to push. Maureen's wheelchair moved a fraction. Not forward, but to the left. Enough to swing me off balance. I landed face-first in sticky, smelly mud. I crawled up onto my knees, while the mud did its best to keep me within its grip. The gloopy substance clung to my clothes and flesh like thick glue. I dripped smelly gunge from everywhere. It seemed that I heard laughter, but then I became aware, as I struggled to my feet, that Auntie Lottie was shouting at Maureen. Why, I had no idea.

"Are you okay, Stroma?" Scott asked, keeping a safe distance from my mess.

I grunted and affirmative and tuned into Auntie Lottie's voice.

"Right, that's it sorted. We don't want any more mishaps. Paul is on his way. It wasn't a very good signal, but thank goodness that Maureen brought her phone with her."

Ah, so she hadn't been shouting at Maureen then, just yelling into the phone.

"Never leave home without it these days," Maureen supplied "and I can save wee notes on it too. Very handy if I forget any little pieces of news I've heard."

"I don't think there's any chance of that happening to you, dear," Mary sighed. "Stroma, there is some long grass over there, dear; you may be able to rub some of that mud off you."

"Look, oh, look up there through the trees." Auntie Lottie pointed.

Not a fairy to be seen, but shimmering lights of many colours raining down from the sky. Green, blue and red sparkled and lit up the heavens. An owl ghosted above us as it silently accompanied the spectacle. A low growl broke the enchantment that nature had spread over us, and we turned to see twin pinpricks of light that grew brighter as they headed toward us.

Paul of the Sheds had arrived complete with a tow rope. He threw a towel in my direction as he and Scott lifted Maureen onto the quad bike then pulled out her mud-encased wheelchair.

"I'll need to take this back, clean it up and make sure it is all in working order. Okay, hold tight to me now, and I'll take you home."

"Oh, I'm looking forward to this. I haven't been on one of these for years. Bye, ladies."

And off they went. We had done what we set out to do. The cake had been left under the elders to pay homage to any fairy folk that may be around. We turned and made our weary way home.

They all kept their distance from me as I smelt and squelched my way ahead. The best thing that came out of our encounter that night was that Mary saw the need for the new paths first-hand and became more willing to work toward a solution. As to the cake, well someone had a good feast. By morning, there wasn't a sign of it anywhere.

27

Thankfully, we hadn't had too much frost. The woods were damp, cold and smelt of wet, decaying leaves. Since our little adventure in the night, the weather had become relatively dry, so it wasn't quite so muddy underfoot. Our latest combined event for Coilltean Sìthiche was scheduled to take place that day. We had thought long and hard about when we should do this one. If we had waited until late spring, we could still be under snow… or in the middle of a heatwave. The weather is very reliable in Scotland, in that it can be relied upon to be totally unpredictable. Not for us the thunderstorms that Floridians can set their watches by. No, here we can go from heatwave during the day to freezing conditions at night, and this can happen at any time from October to June.

October that year had not brought the frosts we were so used to. The blue skies and cold had not materialised, replaced by grey, wet, windy days. Our eyes had been glued to weather reports for weeks, as we had slipped slowly toward our November event. Not that it made much difference; it's not like we would have cancelled due to the weather. If we did that every time it rained, snowed or blew a gale, we would never have any outdoor events. Preparation was the key to moving forward. Organisers and participants were expected to arrive with not only the right food and drink but also the appropriate clothing. At any time of the year, that consisted of a warm jacket, scarf and hat, sun cream, and a brolly – to both shelter under and to protect any cooking fires from going out due to any deluge. Fleeces or warm blankets were a must, whether for sitting on in good weather or hiding under in cold weather.

There was to be no new-fangled barbeque for this event. No, it was back to campfires and tales, singing and celebration. We just had a day's work ahead of us before the fun could begin.

After Mary had finally told us what had been worrying her, a plan had been hatched which included a revisit to the planned routes for the widened paths. Maureen had coordinated with both Mary and Jim, and a plan had emerged that suited everyone while taking the agreed theme into account. There had been much debate between me and Mary about what theme would best reflect not only our community but also the many tales we had about the woods.

"Well, I know the Smith children would love it if we had a fairy theme. We could use trees like elder, rowan and oak. The twins would love that."

"I think Fawn would love that, but I'm sure Stag would much rather have a hanging tree or something that would include that skull he keeps going on about."

They weren't the only children in the village, and it was Karen who came up with the best idea in the end.

"The eighteen letters of the Gaelic alphabet are based on trees. Each tree name reflects one of the letters. As an example, A for *ailm*, which is elm, fir or pine, B for *beith*, the birch and so on. Our big oak is the fourth letter, the D of *dair*. We already have quite a few of the alphabet trees. We could plant any we don't have. They have something like it in Salen, but we've got nothing like that around here. I've just been doing some work on it with the children. It brings our traditions and language together, and we could have displays explaining that."

It was a great idea, and one, given my job was Gaelic Development, I should have thought of. The trees were also associated with their own myths relating to Celtic folklore and fairy tales.

Jim and Mary offered to go around and identify which trees we already had that represented the Gaelic alphabet, and take note of any that we didn't have. In the end, it was decided to add a loop to a yet uncultivated part of the woods that would include each letter. Trees, like the big oak or *dair*, would have their own board explaining the relevant beliefs held by many different folks throughout history.

There was a disused quarry adjacent to the woods that we had also inherited which had been gradually re-establishing itself over the previous few years. This was to be left to do its own thing. A call had been put out in the area, asking for old photographs of when the quarry had been in use, and pictures of it as it started to re-seed and change from a gravel, barren-looking waste ground to a birch, whin and gorse-yellow paradise.

"You know, I think Helen did a photography project on the quarry years ago. I'm not sure how long back it went, or when she last took pictures, but I'm pretty sure she said she was recording how it was changing. She'd even given it a title: Rewilding. Leave it with me. I will have to go through some of her photos. It may take time, but if I am right, you can have them for your exhibition space. She would have loved to think they would be included." Ellen was right. It would be a great way to commemorate Helen and her photos in a permanent display. We would still need the community's help if we were to carry on recording the quarry over time. Once more, Karen came up trumps.

"The children at the school could do that over the years. It would be a great way to tie them in with past pupils, and also it will teach them how nature comes back. I love it," she said. "We can do so much which fits in with the curriculum with this project. It saves us coming up with something new all the time. Can you imagine coming back in twenty years, and looking at the quarry and seeing how much it will have changed just with the flora? Our camera club at the school is always looking for things to photograph – this will all fit in perfectly."

Crowds of children and adults littered the ground where the loop was being established. This was where our 'Grow Your Own Woods' event was taking place. Businesses, locals and ex-Blàsians now living all over the world had been asked to sponsor trees for our trail. We had a range of them waiting to be planted. A forestry ranger and a woodsman had come along to help us identify each sapling and make sure we were planting them not only in the right order but also in the right conditions. Fawn, Jill and Mary had acquired some young rowan, hawthorn, aspen and ash, as they all had the strongest connections to fairy folklore.

More elders with their equally strong connections were to be planted in the loop, even though Mary's elders were to be left in peace. Fawn had given this combination of plants their very own category – the fairy trees. Maybe not the most scientific of names, but she understood, on some level, that plants needed put into groups. The rest of the trees chosen all had connections to Celtic and druid culture. More work would be done around this as our project developed over the years.

"I'm helping to plant *nuin* – that's ash, you know. They were used in making coffins. Imagine that? Coffins. We could cut this one down when it is big enough and put my skull in it."

"Thank you, Stag. I think you have shared that little bit of information enough, don't you?" Karen turned around and shooed him away. "Honestly, I have had some of the more sensitive children in tears after they heard him repeat that. I am just waiting for some of the parents to corner me today and complain. Nothing so far, but it is just a matter of time, I'm sure. But hey, at least we've got a good turnout."

She was right. Lots of people had come and were busy digging and planting along the loop. Ellen and Giulietta were coming down later with hot soup and sandwiches. We only had a few hours to plant, as the nights descended early in November.

Auntie Lottie and Maureen were booked to put on another storytelling event in the woods that evening. A thank you to all who had taken part. Positioning of the lighting and fires was being discussed as the day went on. The original gathering area had been moved to nearer the start of the woods in a clearing just past the dun. We would have to be careful with our footing that night, though, as all the paths had been mushed up with all the activity. By four o'clock, most of the tree planting session had been finished. People headed home to wash the mud off their boots before they came back again to enjoy the free storytelling and refreshments.

Stars sparkled, but the moon was nowhere to be seen as warmly clad figures headed back to the woods. It was eerie watching all these dark figures heading into the shadows. This was the time of the Reed Moon, according to an old Celtic calendar. Maybe not the best time to be telling stories of old that may scare the children. I hoped that Maureen and Auntie Lottie would tone it down a bit, just in case any children got swirled up in the atmospheric evening. Tall torches lined the path toward the dun. I was pondering on a new name for the Gathering Place or *Àite Cruinneachadh*. Should we change it to *Àite Sgeulach* (story place) or *Cearcall nam Ban-Sìthe* (fairy circle) – Fawn would love that. The new area would have semi-circular raised mounds covered in grass, where audiences could sit and watch what was taking place. Families and others could hold their picnics there or just sit and listen to the woods. It would be well used, that was for sure.

In the dark, you couldn't see all the planting that had gone on during the day, but you could smell the earthy damp ground in the air.

"Boo!" Scott had come up beside me. "You don't mind if I join you, do you? Only Ellen is going to be sitting with someone else, and I don't want to get in the way."

"Well, as long as you don't mind children. Karen and Grace are keeping me a space near them."

We followed the smoke and shadows down to the new area. It was still under development, but I could easily see how it would all look once it was finished. Three circles set slightly back from one another enclosed the area. The grass had not yet grown over the mounds, but the overall effect could be seen in the flickering light coming from the large fire pit. Hay bales had been placed on the mounds to cover the bare earth so the audience would at least be kept dry. Since the previous storytelling, Auntie Lottie and Maureen had made a tent from lots of colourful fabrics. The colourful shelter now stood erected off to one side. Maureen was seated beside the fire awaiting everyone to quieten down. She flicked her hand toward the fire, and it crackled, rising a few feet higher. Everybody's attention switched to her.

"Our tales tonight are a wee bit different from our usual fare," she began. "Our *Seanchaidh* will be out shortly. She is going to tell you stories about all the trees you have been planting today. Some are magical, some carry a sinister warning being of a more druidic and Celtic nature. To those of you who have rowan trees at your back door, you have nothing to fear. To those of you with hawthorn at the front, even less. To those of you with neither, I have heard, if you leave a nice, wee, honey-coloured dram out tonight that will provide the same luck and protection." A shout could be heard from behind her. "Oh yes, and a piece of chocolate too." The adults in the audience laughed.

"Ach well, I'm sure the Smiths will still have some of that golden liquid you are talking about, Maureen. You do mean apple juice, aye?" came a voice, rising over the laughter.

"Aye, very funny, Moth. You're living up to your name tonight," Maureen quipped. Moth had been given his name due to the way he acted when asked to pay for anything. Nobody was sure if this was because he flustered and fluttered about in agitation, or whether the rumours were true and moths really had flown out of his wallet on the few occasions he had opened it. Whatever the original truth, he stayed true to his nickname. I was not alone in having no idea what his given birth name was. Although, if he had been of this generation, it would have been perfectly possible that his birth name really was Moth.

As the laughter rang around, another flare of the flames from the fire heralded the appearance of our *Seanchaidh*, or as she was better to know to the community, Auntie Lottie. It was obvious that Maureen and Auntie Lottie had been working on their skills together since the last session. Maureen was more involved in the delivery this time, and gone was Auntie Lottie's barefoot delivery. In its place, she had donned strong ankle boots – far more suitable for storytelling in the woods at this time of year. However, her clothes remained just as dramatic and had been chosen to swirl and circle around her body as she swooped and swayed. Her arms reached out and implored the audience to listen to what she said. They stretched up to the dark sky and threw down the beliefs of the past at the listeners' feet. We were spellbound by her telling. A perfect successor had been found for Angus. So different from his rhyming deliveries, Auntie Lottie had found her own more dramatic style to carry forward our deeds and beliefs of old. Maureen knew all the secrets and tales, but there was no getting away from it – Auntie Lottie knew how to deliver them. What a formidable pair they made.

"What a woman, just look at her, my Lottie." Paul was sitting on the top mound right above me. He was mesmerised. Before much longer, I reckoned, he would be pressing Auntie Lottie to set the date again. As it turned out, I wasn't wrong about that.

28

St Andrew's Day came and went with the usual torchlight procession to the hall followed by a ceilidh. This was the last community event that would not be tinged with the Christmas sparkle. The last event in Blàs before the tinsel-infused month of December. No one was digging up at the dun now, and all the television people were long-gone. Even the tourists had generally headed home for a wee rest before the pre-season got its grip on them again.

Three markets were to be held before Christmas – two in Inbhirasgaidh and one in Blàs itself. All three would be liberally sprinkled with Christmas dust and good cheer. The stalls would reflect the festive theme; we even had a Christmas pudding one booked in. Giulietta had been busy making novelty-shaped treats, and her delicious hot chocolate had been given a decidedly seasonal flavour with cinnamon on top. The Smiths' lemonade stall was focusing on red and green drinks, with the addition of sugar mice which Jill had helped them make. On the cake stall, mincemeat pies and rich fruit cakes took the place of Victoria sponges and scones. Seasonal cards and calendars played a more prominent role than the usual handmade birthday cards.

School pupils were selling Christmas decorations from their woodland stall. Made from collected pinecones and branches, they were painted silver and gold. Warm hats, gloves and mittens replaced thin, delicate home-knits. Hot, thick soup and stovies (a mixture of cooked-down, hot butter potatoes and corn beef) were more in demand than sandwiches, although tea, coffee and cakes were still doing a good trade. Not surprisingly, apples were very much available in many forms, including chutneys, jams and, of course, various alcoholic versions. A hot, sweet, spiced 'Christmas' apple juice could also be sampled. There was no disguising the December theme at all three of our markets.

Your first breath on entering any one of the halls was a festive assault on your mind filled with the unmistakeable scents of Christmas. Fragrant air, sweet and rich, clouded the room and flowed through your senses to mix with memories of bygone celebrations. Both in Blàs and Inbhirasgaidh, people crowded into the market halls, desperate to become part of the festivities and drink in the atmosphere.

Grace and her wee boy Cavan were making the most of the stalls in Blàs. His large, brown eyes were huge as he looked around at all the goodies within his reach. He was an enchanting child whose smile could charm even the hardest of hearts. Paul of the Sheds had been smitten since the first sight of his grandson, with Auntie Lottie not far behind.

Thankfully, Cavan's birth had been a lot easier to attend than any of Karen's labours. Karen turned into a living nightmare as soon as she went into labour. Grace, on the other, had sailed through labour in a laid-back manner. She had suggested a nice long walk together. We had wandered around the village and countryside, stopping occasionally for her to catch her breath. I had been avoiding bringing up any mention of Marcos, the absent father-to-be. It was Grace herself who finally spoke of him.

"I'm definitely over him. I had a lucky escape." Holding on to her tummy, she drew in a deep breath and let it out again. "His new wife will never be able to trust him. I don't want that for me, or my baby."

"Does he know about the baby, Grace?" I asked gently.

"No, and he never will, if I can help it. He betrayed me, and our baby. How he could think it was acceptable to woo me when he already had plans to marry, and not tell me… ooh… ooh." Grace rubbed her tummy a few times before we continued. "I still can't believe he thought I would stay with him after he got married, that I'd be his mistress. Ooph." We stopped our conversation there while she continued to pant. When we reached her flat Grace went for a bath, and I rang Karen.

"Grace is in labour. She's having a bath. Could you bring the car around, so we can be ready to go when she's done?" I asked Karen.

"On my way. Will be right over."

Karen arrived about two minutes later.

"Right, where is she? We'd better get going. Baby waits for no one."

"No, I think that is you, Karen. You and your babies wait for no one. Honestly, Grace is so calm and serene. I didn't know it could be like this."

"Well, she's not there yet, so just wait and see. Anyway, it's not a competition to see who can bite their lip the longest. Have you checked on her since she went in the tub?"

"Er, no. I thought I would leave her in peace. It's probably the last chance she'll get."

"You're probably right. I'm off to check up on her anyway."

"I could hear her heavy breathing and sighing, but she's been very quiet compared to some I know."

"Well, how far apart were the contractions? God, we don't

want her giving birth in the back of my car on the way to hospital."

"Not sure really. She reckons she may have started these practice ones yesterday morning, but by this morning, she knew they were real. Let's see. She had one as we passed the shop, and we talked to Old Tam until it passed. Then she had another one as we passed the pub, but it wasn't as long, so I don't think that counts. Then she had one before we got back here, and then another one before she climbed into the bath, then I don't know. What? What's wrong?"

"God, Stroma, how many births have you been forced to attend? And you *still* can't tell when someone is in full labour. It's only minutes between those places, and if she had started properly, and they weren't practice contractions, she could be having the baby right now."

"Oh ha, ha, if that was the case, then she would be screaming, or swearing, or turning into monster mum like you do when you're in labour."

"Not everyone is the same. Honestly, I'm off to check up on her. You maybe see if her bag is ready."

"It's Grace. It has been packed for weeks, and is right there beside the door, see."

I heard Karen knock on the bathroom door and head in. Two seconds later, she came out.

"Right, find out who's the midwife on call. We need her now, like right now. The number's on the fridge door. Come on, Stroma, move. I'm helping Grace into her bedroom. Grab some towels as soon as you can and follow me. Hurry up, come on."

And so Grace gave birth in her little flat. No yelling, not much effort on her part it appeared, and just in time for the new grandad to appear with something nice he caught for her tea while he was out fishing. The on-call midwife swept into the flat, exuding warmth and efficiency, then immediately took charge. Not that Grace appeared out of control at any time.

Karen was sobbing with joy as this was the first birth she had been at where she wasn't the one in labour, and I was relieved that all I had to do was wait, sigh and fall in love with yet another baby. That was very easy to do. Cavan was born with a head of curly hair and a charm that oozed from him with his first breath.

All that had been eighteen months ago. Cavan's excitement at the market made Grace light up with happiness. He wasn't the only reason for that happiness though. Our project officer Jim accompanied the little family from stall to stall. His arm was gently placed on her back as he helped to guide them along. Picking Cavan up and putting him on his shoulders made a clear declaration that they were together. Well, I hadn't seen *that* coming. I hadn't even known they were aware of each other. Trust Grace to have kept that quiet!

29

It stood before me as it had done for others throughout the millennium. Unfeeling, dark, despite the fine snow that filtered down. Somehow, the delicate snowflakes just made it look even more ominous.

"Come on, Stroma. If we don't get a move on, I won't get much of a chance to catch up with Nora. I'm so looking forward to seeing her." Despite living in the village for well over a year, Auntie Lottie was still finding friends she hadn't 'seen for a while' dotted around the Highlands.

"And I don't want to be staying out here after dark when I have the puppies at home. I can't leave them with Paul for too long. He still thinks they are not-dog-enough dogs, just because they are so small and lovable. Did I tell you, he's threatening to get a bigger dog if I keep one of the pups?" She had, loads of time. I knew she was trying to lever me into taking one of them. She wanted to know where they were all going to be, and for them to go to people she knew. Trouble was, most people around Blàs who wanted a dog already had one. For myself, I quite liked the lack of responsibility, but I knew I was beginning to weaken.

I raised my head to look at the mountain pass ahead and cursed myself for agreeing to come. It wasn't because it was so near Christmas, or that there was anything wrong with the group that had requested the training session. They were nice, and generally entertaining company. The real reason for my reluctance was the road I had to travel to get there.

There were no trains, few buses and miles of single-track roads. None of which would normally cause me the slightest bit of worry. I usually loved travelling around the Highlands. But between home and my destination of Applecross stood Bealach nam Bò or Bealach na Bà, depending on which side of the scholar's debate you sat on – did you think it should be 'Pass of the cows' or 'Pass of the cattle'… the argument was about something like that anyway. Bealach na Bà was once a drover's road. They took their cattle along it to markets in the south. Apart from splashing some tar on it, the route hadn't been improved that much since those droving days. Okay, they had blasted through a few areas, but still, the road clings precariously to the side of the mountains leaving no room for error.

It isn't even classified as a proper road. It doesn't have an M at the start to indicate motorway, nor an A to suggest a main road or even a B to let drivers know it's a minor road. Nope, the Bealach is filed under C for 'are you certain you want to drive this?' It is the C1087 to be precise. Not that many could have told you that. It was only ever referred to by one of its titles.

After turning off the A road, you jump straight to this C road, completely bypassing all the Bs. That in itself should be warning enough for any unsuspecting driver. There then follows a series of warning boards that scream danger and inform lorries, caravans and motorhomes that the road is unsuitable for the likes of them, so they should turn back. Too late. Once you are committed to the road, there is no room to turn back. I often wondered if some official with a dark sense of humour knew this full well but got a kick out of frightening some poor, unsuspecting souls. By the third warning sign which practically screams 'for goodness sake what are you playing at, TURN

AROUND NOW!', that official must have been bent double with evil laughter.

"I could always drive, you know, but I don't really like these narrow roads," Auntie Lottie offered. I wondered, not for the first time, which would be worse. I decided I was the safest bet. What if she freaked out at the narrowest bit? I would be hysterical by then and probably grab the wheel, and we would both be over the cliff. Off sideways, slipping backward, losing power, or just plain falling off the C1087 was one of my greatest fears. This stretch of road filled my nightmares whenever I felt stressed about anything.

"Stroma, there's a car coming."

"Yes," I growled back. "I can see it. I'm not blind. I can see that stupid, bloody car heading straight for us; why is it even driving on this road?" *Breathe, breathe, slip into the passing place, you can do this.* The car waited opposite the passing place. The nice driver had waited for me to come abreast of him. We squeezed past each other, almost coming to a halt. I sighed as we made it past each other and tried to relax a bit. We continued to climb upward, unfortunately, so did my heart rate. I was panting like a woman giving birth. Sweat was dripping down my face and my shirt was stuck to my back. Even Auntie Lottie had gone quiet. Not because she had nothing to say, but because she sensed I had turned into a crazy woman.

Just as my hands threatened to slip off the steering wheel, we came upon it. The double switchback bend, followed closely by a sharp corner, an overhanging cliff, and no visibility whatsoever of anything that might be coming in the opposite direction. It made the Berridale Braes in Caithness look like a toddler's walk.

Then, just above the booming of my eardrums, I heard Auntie Lottie gleefully exclaim, "I've always thought there isn't much chance of letting anyone else through at this bit if you were to meet another car coming the other way."

She was right, and I was not going to stop for any other driver even if they were coming straight for me. There was no space for passing and a sheer drop loomed to the side of us. A big slice had been taken out of the mountain to allow for one car, and that car was mine. Decision made, I was stopping for nothing. We were not going to be the ones who plunged off the cliff to our deaths. My car was going to be the one that got to the top, and if necessary, it would batter anything coming in the opposite direction out of the way.

Tears had started to form in my eyes. Where was the summit? Had it moved? We should have reached it by now; I couldn't go on. Then suddenly we burst onto the top of the world. The view was amazing, if we could have seen it properly through the snow, that is. My shoulders started to drop from around my ears, and my breathing returned to normal. Really, what a fuss I had made. Then I remembered, I would have to do it all over again on the way home.

"Your Auntie Lottie is visiting Nora MacLean that was, I'm hearing."

Local women who had married were rarely referred to by their married names. It left no one in doubt which family they had originated from. The addition of 'that was' clarified they were now known by another surname which ironically wasn't often mentioned. "They'll be swapping some wild stories, no doubt! She has a good heart does your Lottie, but mind, a bit of a wild streak in her my dad always said. A bit older than me, but I remember her coming over here on her summer holidays when she was a girl. She helped out an old relative that lived here. Herself and Nora were as thick as thieves then."

I was having a well-earned cup of tea with some of the committee who had organised the training day.

Most of the parents had headed home afterward, but the older members who had made the snacks had stayed on. I knew Auntie Lottie had connections to this side of Ross-shire, but I didn't often get the chance to hear stories about that, especially ones about her youth.

"They didn't like being told what they were allowed to do. Especially if it was something the boys were allowed to do, and they weren't on account of them being girls. Was like a red rag to a bull, so it was. It was all very well having women's lib and all that, but when it came to competition between the girls and the boys, it was always understood the boys would win."

That didn't surprise me in the least. Auntie Lottie never liked being told she couldn't do something, even now. My tea-making friend continued. "The MacDonald boys had been boasting about how much stronger, fitter and faster they were than anyone in the village, which they were, to an extent. But Nora and Lottie weren't prepared to listen to them all summer, so they challenged them to a dare. Two teams made of John and Donald MacDonald, the other being Nora and your Lottie. They had agreed to walk up Sgurr a' Chaorachain at the Bealach, place a stone on the cairn, and come back. The MacDonalds were sure the girls would 'chicken out' but they didn't. There was some excitement around the village then among us youngsters. Only the adults then heard about it and weren't happy. The last part of that walk is more like a climb, very steep it is. Anyway, Neil, Nora's twin, suggested instead that they just walk up the Bealach from Applecross, camp the night, then walk back down. Leaving out the Sgurr completely. First to reach the campsite would be the winners. As long as Neil went along, it was agreed. I think the adults thought the girls' reputations were safe camping out, as long as Nora's twin brother was there.

"In the end, all the teenagers went along to make sure there was no cheating, or at least that was the excuse given. I was the youngest, not quite a teen, but since my two siblings were and they were going along, I got to go too. Anyway, the day arrived, and we all set off. Unbeknown to the adults though, there was a cousin of the MacDonald's who had a car waiting for the teams, just out of sight. He gave them a lift up to the Bealach to the starting point of where the walk to Sgurr a' Chaorachain started. Some of us younger ones carried on walking up the Bealach together along the road, in case anyone was looking out for us. All the teenagers were involved one way or another." That also didn't surprise me. Like Mary and Ellen, Auntie Lottie had that knack for encouraging people to take part in schemes.

"It was midsummer's eve so lots of light. We had a great time singing and talking our way up. Everyone was in high spirits. Once the two teams reached the start to Sgurr a' Chaorachain, they set up camp so it was all ready and waiting for us when we arrived. It was our job to make sure that food would be ready for when they got back. I tell you, I wouldn't have walked it. The road was enough for me. Never did like heights myself. Sgurr a' Chaorachain is way too steep at the top, and at night too, even if it was almost daylight at that time of the year. We had a grand old time at the camp. Never even entered our minds how dangerous it was. In the end, no one won as they all had to help each other on the really steep bit of the climb. They got back just before sunset. It was amazing watching the sun go down and then come back up again so soon, and we felt we were right on top of the world. The fact that Nora and Lottie had done the climb put a stop to any more ribbing from the boys. We thought it was probably because they were scared the girls would suggest something even more dangerous next time, and so on until one of them got hurt. The adults didn't have a clue they had gone up the Sgurr till a good few years later."

We left not long after. Auntie Lottie was waiting with Nora and her husband John MacDonald. Climbing the mountain wasn't just the end of the competition between the boys and the girls, it had also been the beginning of a lifelong love affair between Nora, John and the mountains. Both were still keen hillwalkers.

I turned the car toward Bealach na Bà and home. If four

teenagers could climb Sgurr a' Chaorachain for a dare, I was sure I could drive that road home without having a heart attack.

"Are you ready then to tackle your mountain, Stroma?" Auntie Lottie asked.

"Don't you mean yours, Auntie Lottie?"

"Ah, you been listening to gossip then?" She smiled. "Right, let's get on the road."

30

Frost sparkled in the weak sun. Not quite a white festive season but the quiet, laid-back feeling of the holiday was in the air. So unlike the summer months when things could feel frenetic with all the tourists swamping our wee village. Wintertime, and especially the festive season, brought on that strange dreamlike quality of being somewhere special for a while.

As usual, our students and young people had made the extra effort to come home, happy to be with family at this time of year. The term was almost finished for the younger ones. Karen had taken the school choir around the village. Members of the older generation who couldn't get out had flung open their windows and doors to let the children's voices drift in.

I was on my way up to the hall where the last combined event before the holidays was being held. The primary school was giving a concert. Secondary school pupils had stayed home that morning to man charity stalls around the hall. They had been busy making goods to sell. Many of these stallholders would also provide some entertainment in the form of music later on.

A steady queue of parents would arrive during the afternoon

to pick up their offspring and head home to start their own celebrations. This was one time the Development Trust didn't ask for
or sell wares; it was a time for us to support other deserving
causes. That didn't mean we weren't involved though. Ellen,
Mary and Maureen were going to be running the stall providing
hot drinks, Christmas cake and mincemeat pies.

"Now, make sure you're there," Karen had commanded. "We
have a special announcement that may give Ralph and Jill some
peace over the season."

I very rarely missed this yearly event, but sometimes work
did get in the way. Mostly though, things did settle down
enough during the winter season to allow me some to time to be
sociable. Picking up Iona was another task that occasionally
meant I missed a year. Although, given my sister's usual late
arrival home, this was a rarity.

Iona wasn't expecting to arrive in Inverness until at least tea-
time. The concert would be well finished by then, and if I did get
held up, well, she would have to wait for me for a change.

I was looking forward to a quiet Christmas. Paul and Auntie
Lottie were spending Christmas with Grace and Cavan. Scott
had gone back home to see his parents, so Iona and I were
having our Christmas dinner with Mary and Ellen. It would be
hard on Ellen this first Christmas without Helen. Fussing over
Iona and me would help her get through the day. Mary would
fill us with more stories of her youth as we saw out the day
together. I was already looking forward to the twenty-fifth. First
though, was the concert, some charity stalls, and anything else
that could add to the overall Christmas atmosphere.

"Have you any idea what this announcement is about?" I asked
Jill as I handed her a cup of hot chocolate.

"Not at all. Karen sent out an e-mail saying it would benefit us all. So here I am. The twins are so excited, they can barely contain themselves. I thought it was about Bodach na Nollaig coming, but I'm not so sure now."

Right on time, the children from the *sgoil araich* and *cròileagan* sang their little hearts out with a rendition of Father Christmas – the Gaelic version, of course, as befits any Gaelic pre-school group.

"And now," said Karen, sprouting a red, flashing reindeer headband, "we have a special announcement. I am sure all you parents, but especially Stag's parents, will be happy and somewhat relieved to hear… Stag, if you are ready?"

Stag and Fawn stood up. "Remind I found a skull," he began.

I heard Jill groan, "Not again."

"Well, we got a letter here from some people that have been looking after it. It says here that we can have a copy of it back and display it in the exhibition centre when it opens, but they are keeping my skull. They are going to put a face on it and send it up to us to see."

"Yuck," was heard from the audience.

It didn't sound like a very Christmassy thing to me, but then again, I hadn't had Stag continually moan about it for months.

"Oh, thank goodness. I had a horrible feeling they were going to give it back. Who wants somebody's head laying about the place? Well, apart from Stag, that is," whispered Jill.

"So because they are keeping what I found. They have given the school a book on bones, a skeleton and head – not proper ones like, but made-up ones for us to use – and they 'ave also given me a book with stickers and some other fhings to do with bones and pencils and the like. So I'm okay about them keeping my skull now. My teacher wanted me to fank them and let you all know what was happening. Fawn's treasure is being checked to see if it is worth some money, and if it is, that could be put toward the new centre. They think it might be some special stone, isn't that right, Miss? Fhat what they says here?" Karen nodded encouragement for Stag to continue. "So me sister, she also got stuff on artilogie which is digging in dirt and finding treasures. Oh, and the school got stuff too. Is that it, Miss, can we sit down now? I want to show me dad and Jill our presents."

Karen stood up and thanked them both before saying. "To clarify for everyone. We know Stag is very excited to hear about his skull, however, it looks likely that Fawn's find is of even more value. It is believed she could have found a rare Scottish sapphire. Not many of them exist, and none have been known to have been found outside of Lewis in the Outer Hebrides, until now, possibly. A lovely piece of news to leave with you all as we look forward to celebrating the festive season. All that is left to me now is to wish everyone *Nollaig Chridheil*." To sighs of 'ooh' and 'aah', Karen turned back to her pupils and made sure all went back to their parents, grandparents, or carers before she came over to us.

"Well," I said, "hearing about the skull may not have been the best Christmas message I've ever heard. I thought this was supposed to be a celebration of birth, not death." I grinned.

"I know, but given that Stag has been driving the entire population of Blàs mad with his continual mentioning of that skull, I thought we all deserved to know. Hopefully, we can all get a little Christmas peace from it. But what about the possibility of having a Scottish sapphire in our midst. How exciting is that?"

"I agree. If true, it's amazing. I hope it turns out to be a rare gem, but I still reckon you've given Jill, at least, the best Christmas present with the announcement about the skull. They can now enjoy a great Christmas without dead bodies and headless men taking up all their conversations. Look at Stag – he is looking a lot happier." And he did.

❧

Iona had finally made it home along with two extras. One hailed from New Zealand and couldn't afford to go back home for

Christmas. Her other companion was from Spain and needed to return for working an early shift on the twenty-seventh, so didn't have time for a festive journey home... although they probably could have got to Spain quicker than to Blàs, depending on the weather and roads.

They arrived, ate, then went off to the pub for a catch-up with friends. I had the distinct impression that they had all been celebrating a little beforehand. Iona invited me to join them, but I had agreed to meet up at Grace's house and have a wee dram before helping her to wrap some last-minute presents.

"Thanks anyway, but I think I will keep Grace company. She is enjoying being a mum, but I think sometimes she misses the freedom she once had."

Like many a child on Christmas Eve, Cavan was refusing to sleep. Grace had put him in his cot, but he was having none of it. She attempted to soothe him while I went into her kitchen. I was labelling the last of her presents when I suddenly heard a racket outside.

"Oh look, Cavan, look! Stroma, you have to come and see this. Stroma, come on." I left my completed work on the table and walked through to the living room. A cold blast met me as Grace stood at the open window. "Will you just look at that?" Grace said. "Now I know why you insisted."

Years before, Grace, Karen, and I had decided to go Christmas carolling around the houses to raise money for some charity or other. After we had finished, we all agreed to go home and meet up later for pre-Christmas drinks. Grace never made it home but headed straight for the pub. By the time we met up again, she was very merry. So happy that she decided to do a spot of solo carol singing for the village. To the strains of Slade's Merry Christmas, she staggered her way around the houses singing at all the younger children's doors. It became a yearly ritual, heralding in Christmas as sure as any festive bells. Grace would arrive home from whatever part of the world she happened to be in that year, jump in my car, switch on Slade, and belt out their song as I drove past all the houses in Blàs. It only ended once Grace had Cavan, but children still talked about her Christmas Eve serenading with longing.

§

I peered out at the slowly falling snow as it changed to pink in the coloured Christmas lights. I could hear the strains of that classic Christmas song. Looking down, I saw, covered in a thin layer of soft snow, five figures wrapped up and huddled together.

"This is for you, Grace," yelled a familiar voice. "For all the Christmas Eves you did it for us. My friends here wanted to join in one of our traditions." She pointed over and her two visiting companions bowed to us. "Of course, more of us locals wanted to get in on the act." The additional two figures waved their gloved hands in our direction. "Okay, ready everyone."

And out came the mixed words and accents from the singers below with their perhaps not quite word-perfect version of Slade's 'Merry Christmas'. Cavan smiled and clapped his hands as the singers fought their way through the song. Once they had finished, Grace yelled down,

"Oh thanks, thank you all. Cavan loved that. I can see now why you were disappointed when I stopped. He would have missed out on that. Merry Christmas, Iona and everyone else. Thank you. Merry Christmas."

Grace closed the window, the light catching the extra water that now reflected there. "She's a special person your sister, you know."

"Yep, she learnt from the best," I replied.

"But do me a favour for next year, would you? Could you

teach her the right words? I don't think 'look to the future now and wiggle your bum' is in the original version."

We both burst out laughing and wished the now sleeping Cavan a good night and a very Merry Christmas before I headed home to celebrate with my very own rather merry carollers.

S torms, lashing rain, and semi-darkness heralded in the new year. That was nothing new. According to our national bard Robert Burns, he had been born in a storm in January. Despite trying not to have too many travel commitments during the month, I found myself up on the north-west coast of Sutherland again, or more precisely Dùthaich Mhic Aoidh.

GLADS was considering running short Gaelic workshops based on the one we had held in Blàs – so more a taster session than a full-blooded course. We still had pent-up demand for the second and third stages of our Gaelic language course, but they would have to wait for now. We wanted to improve on the numbers of people who had a least a basic level of the language. We hoped that, by providing a crèche, we might succeed. It had the bonus that those children attending the crèche would pick up some Gaelic too by learning through play, action songs, stories, and puppets. Fun through the medium of Gaelic was one of our main goals.

This was not a new concept for GLADS. We were hoping to take our normal programme one step further and offer this family-friendly set-up to the many separate communities that made up Dùthaich Mhic Aoidh. With a small population of about two thousand spread throughout the whole district, it was difficult for each settlement to justify holding its own course. This often led to classes being too short on numbers to go ahead – the result of the timetable being made up by someone who didn't have a clue how to grow the use of the language.

It would go something like this. We need twelve people if the class is going to run. In Inverness, Dundee or any other highly populated area that is no problem. But in rural areas, it simply can't work. Nor does it take account of who is learning the language. For example, in a city, maybe eight of that twelve could be made up of retired people or people whose children have left home, so no possibility of passing the language on to another generation. Whereas in rural areas, you may only have six students, but they could all be parents learning together with their children. Their children could then go forward to be educated through the medium of Gaelic. In the end, the smaller class in the rural area would produce more Gaelic speakers over a longer period.

Unfortunately, this just didn't seem to penetrate the thought process of those who held the purse strings. Never mind how often it was explained – numbers, numbers, numbers were all they thought about. Long-term planning and quality had no place in their mindset.

GLADS was trying to get around this conundrum by including tourists in short, rural courses. They hoped to hit the acceptable numbers that would allow the classes to go ahead and build on the Gaelic speakers in the area. These courses also offered the holidaymakers the opportunity to meet local families and be introduced to the language and culture of the area.

The idea was similar to the way some tourists would spend a few hours at, say, a whisky tasting session. Only without the whisky. For the morning and afternoon sessions, at least. Evening sessions… well, who knew? They were almost always bound to end up in a ceilidh anyway. Locals and tourists alike could opt for any or all of the sessions. It meant the tutors, like

Auntie Lottie, would have to be flexible to the various expectations of their pupils, but I knew she and the other Gaelic facilitators were more than capable of making sure everyone had a good time. Students would take away fond memories laced with a few helpful phrases.

It had been proposed that we would start in Scourie and follow the road up to Kinlochbervie, then north to Durness, Tongue, Bettyhill, then Strathy and Melvich. The following week would take in areas that were once well-populated but had been virtually cleared of people during the dark days of the Highland Clearances.

Between the mid-eighteenth and mid-nineteenth centuries, landlords under the guise of improving the land forced their tenants out of their homes. Sheep were a much more profitable 'crop' than crofters. Many Highlanders found themselves forced to take ship to a new life across the Atlantic. Often, it was their descendants, eventually returned, who made up a large proportion of the tourists we welcomed to the area. People who came back to their roots to trace the culture and language of their Highland forbearers.

We had been asked to provide some of our sessions at the RSPB centre at Forsinard. Other sessions were to be held at former hunting lodges no longer used so exclusively for rich holidaymakers. The owners were keen for us to provide courses that would be of interest to their clients and were open to locals attending the language classes in exchange. The cultural evening sessions, however, would remain the domain of their clients. All four districts that made up Dùthaich Mhic Aoidh: Kylestorme, Forsinard, Dalvina, and Crask would have some form of Gaelic language offering as part of the planned programme.

We would provide our roaming course over three weeks in the summer which seemed an awful long way away when driving through the wet, stormy January weather. The initial work and meetings needed to get everything set up, however, had to take place at the beginning of the year to ensure everything would be properly organised by the time the warmer months came around.

Thankfully, the local communities were on board and were keen to make the most of the opportunity to develop their Gaelic skills. Many of the native speakers had died out, but the local learners were adamant that we offer them Gaelic in their particular Sutherland accent.

I arrived home to Blàs late one afternoon, after a three-day trip of meetings with various committees and funding bodies. It was thundering down with rain. I was tired, cold and wet. I put a light to the fire and went into the kitchen. Before the kettle had had time to boil, in stormed Auntie Lottie with cake in hand. I automatically forgave her intrusion there and then.

"That bloody man." She vented, as she grabbed a towel to dry Whisky and her pup Malt. This was the dog she had kept in the forlorn hope that I would change my mind and take her. *Oh no, here we go again,* I thought as mum and pup shook themselves off and went to find somewhere warm and dry to rest.

"Paul. I'll give him Paul of the Sheds. Well, he can just stay in one of his sheds along with that monster. I'll have tea, thanks."

"What's he done to send you here in this state? Surely, he hasn't asked you to set the date again – that's not what's wrong, is it?"

"Yes, I mean, no, I mean…" Auntie Lottie was becoming more and more flustered.

"Come on, Auntie Lottie, it's not a difficult question. What happened?" I handed her a cup of tea and a slice of cake, and we wandered over to settle down next to the fire and the dogs.

"He gave me an ultimatum. He said if I kept one of the pups, he would get himself a dog. A big dog, not a little mite like mine. He said that one small dog in the household was enough. He couldn't be expected to walk something so little – it made him look daft, said he needed a proper dog. How can he say that about my precious Dandies? They may be small, but they are big characters, they make you smile just looking at them." She was right. If Disney were to pick a real-life breed, it would be a Dandie. Large top-knot, big eyes and lovely big black nose with long ears that flapped out like Dumbo when they ran – they were difficult to resist. I had already picked up Malt without realising and now had a soggy dog happily sleeping on my knee.

"Well, I can kind of see his point. You do have two dogs to his none. Why can't he have a dog anyway?" I asked.

"Well, for one, he never wanted a dog until I got one. Two, I'm only looking after Malt until you come to your senses and take her off my hands, and three… well, three, he is just being stubborn because I only really have one dog – you shouldn't even count a puppy as wee as Malt – and four, yes, four, he has only gone and got one like he said he would. Big, smelly brute it is too. I haven't got a look in sideways since it came. All because I said we should wait a bit."

"Aah, well he has waited for quite a while now; you can't blame him for being impatient to marry you. Some women would bite your hand off to be in your position."

"I know, well we both know of at least one who would, but what woman is going to name the day when he put it the way he did, honestly?"

"What did he say? Is that why you said no? You didn't like the way he asked you to name the date?"

"Don't say it like that, that makes me seem fussy. But really, Stroma, would you say 'yes, of course, why don't we get married a week tomorrow' if the love of your life puts it like this?" Auntie Lottie put on a low growl trying to mimic Paul of the Sheds voice. "'I think it is about time we set the date for our wedding, no point in waiting any longer. I mean, lass, it's not that we aren't used to each other's bad points by now, and you are not getting any younger either. Let me be clear before you start running up excuses,' he said, 'if you don't name the day,

I'm going out and getting myself a dog that will love me and won't be scared to stay with me in my own house forever. So, Lottie, what's it to be? Do I get you… or a dog?' I mean, it hardly stands up there as the most romantic proposal of the year, does it? What woman is going to bow down to that macho attitude? And what does he mean? I'm not getting any younger – bloody cheek of the man. 'Away and get a dog then,' I said. In jest, I will admit, but off he stomped and slammed the door. Next thing I see is him with a big hairy brute of a dog."

"I was only away for three days; how did he get hold of one so quickly?"

"I have no idea, and I am not asking him. Who does he think he is giving me an ultimatum like that? It's not the 1950s you know. Women don't need men; we can be free and independent and, and… What if I change? What if I turn dull and boring? Then he would grow to hate me anyway. I'm never going to be the type to have his dinner on the table or iron his clothes or… but I already miss him, and he is just being so stubborn."

"Auntie Lottie, listen to yourself: you want to be with him. He well knows, well, we all know, you are never, and I mean never, going to be a boring person. Anyway, getting married doesn't turn you into a boring person. I'd hardly say Karen is boring or Mary is or ever was boring. Paul knows what you are like; he wouldn't want you to change. You will not lose your independence either, you have your own money, your own home and your own tutoring job. Paul has no problem looking after the house – he has done it all his life. Believe me, if all he wanted was a glorified housewife, he could have had his pick, but he picked you because, well, because you are you, just a little quirky around the edges." That was a big understatement. Auntie Lottie was a one-off, and more than a little quirky in her ways, but I didn't want to upset her too much. "You should go home and have a good think about what you want. It's not fair to keep Paul dangling. If you have no intention of marrying him, you need to tell him, okay?"

"I'll think about it. *Oidhche mhath*, Stroma. I'll see you in the morning, and don't forget to at least give that puppy some water."

And off she went. I hadn't even realised I still had a hold of Malt until she mentioned it.

"Well, little one, it seems you are having a sleepover with me tonight."

Malt made a small squeak and settled into my neck. One night, that was all she was staying for, just one night, then she was going right back home again to Auntie Lottie's house.

Three days later as I was heading back from the village shop, I met Old Tam and Shep wobbling along. It still shocked me seeing Old Tam in the latest all-weather gear. He was almost unrecognisable with his thick hood up. He hadn't quite been able to leave his cap behind though, the edge of which stuck out slightly from his hood. A layer of cold, wet sleet lay along the top of Shep's matching waterproof jacket.

"Ye should nae hiv thon peur wee soul oot on a day like this. Jist look at eer, peur wee thing. She's drookit." He bent down and ruffled Malt's head.

"Well, she needed out, and I needed some food. She's got a hairy coat; she'll be fine."

"She's only a puppy mind, nae got a great muckle coat likh Shep here tae keep eem warm. Did ye see if thar were ony o thon rolls fae thon bakery still left?"

"Aye, I did, but you'd better hurry. I saw Jock heading in their direction."

"Morning, Stroma, how's the wee pup doing then, now she's with you." Paul of the Sheds ambled over with a large, hairy, tan and fawn dog. Malt was straining at the lead to get closer to make friends. "Meet Dylan."

A large, black nose pushed into my hands. Dylan's shaggy

coat was rather wiry, but his tail never stopped wagging as he said his hellos to me and Malt.

"I'm not keeping her, Paul. I've just not returned her to Auntie Lottie yet. Ah, Dylan. He's lovely and friendly. Do you know what mix he is?"

Paul of the Sheds smiled "Oh lass, wait a minute, this here is a real-life pedigree, purebred."

"Really, he looks a little, well, dishevelled to me for a thoroughbred."

"Aye, well looks can be deceiving as we all know. This long-haired, rather daft brute is an otterhound. Like your wee lass there, quite rare. They have great noses, you know. I've been thinking of training a dog for rescue. They have great scenting abilities, so I could use one of their kind, would save having to wait on DJ if he is already out. We could have done with something like him when we lost the children. Mind you, you have to start training them young."

"Malt is not mine, Paul, I keep telling you." Dylan had leant against my legs for a cuddle, and I could feel myself being pushed over. "Well, Mr Otterhound, you may not be the most handsome dog I've ever seen, but you are very engaging. Malt seems to like you anyway." Malt was jumping up at the large dog who was taking no notice of her whatsoever; he was more interested in getting his long, floppy ears rubbed.

"Will you keep Dylan if… sorry, *when* I take Malt back?"

"Well, Stroma," Paul said, winking at me. "Not everything is as it may seem. Come on, Dylan, old boy, time to get you back and towel-dried."

I watched the pair of them head away. Dylan moseying along at Paul's side. I had to say his otterhound looked more in keeping with his build than the Dandie did. Given how full of energy Paul of the Sheds always was, Dylan suited him much better. There was more to this than it appeared though. Something was tickling the back of my mind, but I just couldn't put my finger on it. I was sure it would come to me eventually.

The sleet had stopped, but the sky was still heavy and grey. Time to get myself and Malt back inside now that I had something better than cooked chicken to give her. I had to get her back to Auntie Lottie soon. Then I remembered how nice it felt having her little body nestle into my legs during the night. I would have to be strong – she needed to go back home where she belonged. *Home is where the heart is,* whispered a voice I was finding it difficult to ignore.

3 2

An urgent meeting was called. Mary was busy handing out her interpretation of wee nips to those who attended. A crisis meeting it may have been, but the invitation had only gone out to a select few.

"Stewart Munro has been in touch. We will have to move quickly." Maureen swirled her drink before gulping it down. She stared at my blank face. "Really, Stroma, you know Stewart – he often comes over from Inverness… well, maybe not quite so often these days. It's his knees you know."

No, I didn't know, and frankly, I didn't care about Stewart Munro's knees or anyone else's if it came to that. Anyway, who was this Stewart Munro, and what sway did he have with the community that required this hush-hush emergency meeting.

"I see I am going to have to enlighten you, Stroma. Well, Stewart is my mother's second cousin twice removed. No, wait, it could be three times removed, husband. Yes, I'm fairly sure that is the connection. He is a relative anyway, and as it happens, a good friend. Actually, Lottie here had the hots for him when we were in high school."

"I most certainly did not," Auntie Lottie countered, blushing. "Well, maybe a bit. He was a fine-looking young lad. Quite a bit older than us, so it was never to be. He's probably ancient-looking now, isn't he, Maureen?"

"Well, I wouldn't necessarily say that exactly—"

Before she could continue Ellen broke in. "Could we keep to the point please, ladies? Maureen, please tell us what Stewart said."

"Oh yes, well, apparently the UHI has finished with the skull. A lot quicker than we expected. Since it is too old to have any known relatives hereabouts—"

"Oh, lass eh widnae put doon yer knowledge o th folks here aboots. Giv'n time eh'm sure ye wid be able tae find some for em," Old Tam interrupted.

Maureen smiled. "Thank you, Tam. Anyway, after their ethical committee meeting, which Stewart sits on as one of his many roles, they have decided to bury it in a casket in the Old High Church graveyard in Inverness. What with all its history and that... I mean, imagine, they say St Columba preached on that wee mound the church sits on in AD 565."

"I dinnae care whar ee preached or hoo auld thon church is. Thon skull needs tae come hame, bak here." Old Tam was not happy.

"It's okay, Tam, don't get yourself all worked up. That's why we are here – to work out a plan on how to retrieve the skull and bring it back." Mary patted Old Tam on his hand. "Here now, have another wee nip, it will help. There are some of us here that have experience of repatriation of a sort, aren't there, Stroma?" All eyes swivelled towards me.

I knew it, I just knew she wouldn't be able to keep quiet about our little adventure a few years ago. Angus and Mary had talked me into being their getaway driver. All because a relative who had spent most of his life abroad had wanted to be buried alongside his mother after he died. Unfortunately, for him the graveyard had been closed to new burials. Apparently, it was unable to cope with a few little ashes. The full truth was a bit uglier than that. The deceased had fallen out with the family who would have been able to give the permission needed to allow this burial to go ahead, but their bitterness with the deceased had continued past his death.

Angus and Mary had previously promised they would bury their relative, with or without the required permission, beside his long-dead mother. Only they had become a bit infirm and weren't able to carry out the daring deed by themselves. That was where I had come in. I had spent a very cold and wet night scrambling around with the geriatric pair in the old graveyard, looking for the right grave to place the remains in. I still had nightmares, imagining hands coming up to grab my ankles as I dug down. It was a night best forgotten.

"Isn't it the Old High Church where they shot the Jacobite prisoners after Culloden?" I interjected in the hope of distracting them.

"Oh, yes," replied Maureen, warming to her subject. "There are two gravestones, nine paces apart. The weaker prisoners who couldn't stand were sat up against one of them. Poor souls were led out blindfolded, you know. Anyway, a soldier rested his musket on the other gravestone for a better aim. You can still see the groove in it. One by one, all the Jacobite prisoners were shot, right there. Awful times it was."

"Maureen, please," Ellen pleaded, "get to the point."

"Well, we need to rescue the skull before they bury it," she finished.

"Oh, come on, you can't be serious. Can we not just appeal and ask that they bury it here, where it was found? What's the reason they've given for not doing that anyway?" I looked over to Ellen.

"According to what Stewart said, the committee decided that, since the dig at the dun was ongoing, together with developing the woods, for a few years yet, a final, settled resting place should be found. Hence the Old High Church."

That I could understand; we still had a lot of work to do in the woods, but I was sure we could have found a quiet, undisturbed spot.

"Apparently, they are going to put up a plaque to say where it was found along with other details relating to it. They have offered to update the information when we get the exhibition centre open. They suggested having a replica of the skull in the new centre, alongside an explanation of where the skull was reburied."

"They jist dinnae understand, weeh need it back. God knows wha wull happen if weeh cannae get it buried here." Old Tam was shaking his head.

"Now, now, Tam, don't fret yourself. We have a plan that even my Angus would have been proud of. They can bury a skull if they want to, only it won't be ours. Right, Ellen, let's get the final details sorted out."

Before we left for Inverness, Jill had a word with me.

"It will be a way of getting some closure on this whole affair. Stag seems to have finally accepted that he can't get it back but is keen to accompany Ellen and Mary to Inverness. We will be waiting for him here."

I was very ill at ease involving Stag and Fawn, but as Mary had pointed out, we couldn't carry out our plan without them. The twins, on the other hand, were highly excited about the whole thing.

Now we were in Inverness, and it was the night before the planned internment. Old Tam and Maureen had elected to stay behind in Blàs and await the return of Mary and Ellen with the twins. I tried not to glance at Stag's backpack. He would be giving up his precious replica for this and would receive nothing in return. Well, apart from the knowledge of what had really taken place.

A small ceremony was being performed in the Old High Church that night, before a small outdoor one planned for the morning when the casket was laid to rest. Academics from the UHI stood together with the Lord Provost and two other councillors. A minister chatted with them. The caretaker stood solemnly at the back, head bowed. Twenty minutes later, we were all out on the street. We said our goodbyes to the twins, Mary and Ellen.

"I would rather come with you, Stroma, but I feel I should go home with Fawn and make sure she's alright. It will be nice to have a wee drive back to Blàs with Ellen. Now, you will take care, and let us know first-thing in the morning how it all went?"

I reassured Mary I would. They turned away, disappearing into the city crowds. It was strange to be entering the city centre after the relative quiet of the church.

"Lottie, so lovely to see you. You haven't changed a bit." It was the caretaker.

"I could say the same of you, Stewart, age doesn't appear to have touched you much." Auntie Lottie twinkled.

"Oh, lass, if only that were true. These knees of mine aren't what they used to be. Now, are you hungry? I thought we might have a wee bite to eat and something to give us some Dutch courage before we head, excuse the pun, back here to do the business."

"Oh well, if it's Dutch courage you are after then Mary has supplied us with a good bottle of some of Angus' sweet spirits."

"Come on then, girls, let's be off."

For the next three hours, we ate, drank and laughed. Stewart informed us he was in the process of retiring and would be heading back to Blàs once his house sold. I listened as both he and Auntie Lottie caught up on the years they had been apart. If it wasn't for what lay ahead of us, it would have been a most enjoyable evening.

"Okay, time to go grab your coats and torches. We need to be off."

There was no one around when we arrived back at the locked gates. It was so cold we could see our breath in the dark. We crept quickly inside.

"Oh, there's not much light in here once you are away from the roadside is there?"

"Shh lass, someone will hear." We could hear Stewart unlock the church door. The sound of the key turning was way louder than Auntie Lottie's voice.

Darkness enclosed us as we walked inside the building. I felt I had taken a step back in time. The atmosphere was strange and dreamlike. Stewart switched on a torch. It had a small, narrow beam.

"Ah, here it is. Good boy, he left it just as we discussed." Stewart lifted Stag's backpack. "Come on, ladies, we've a swap to make."

We tripped forward, further into the church. Dark shadows danced on the walls and drifted away. A sharp pain exploded in my arm.

"Ouch," my voice filled the rafters and echoed off the walls. "Gees, Auntie Lottie, let go, you're nipping me."

"Sorry, so sorry, I thought I felt something brush my leg. It may have just been my coat. Sorry." I had forgotten how jumpy she could be in the dark. Although, to be honest, I think perhaps it was the quiet that really freaked her out.

The hairs on the back of my neck rose as a loud creaking came from in front.

"Alas, poor Yorick! I knew him well." Stewart held the skull up.

"Less of the Shakespearean quotes, Stewart; can we just get on with it?" Auntie Lottie interjected,

"Ah, my friend, we are going to take you back to where you belong. I just have to wrap you up in this. That's right, okay in the bag we go with you." Stewart continued talking to the skulls as he switched one for the other. "Okay, my beauty, we have a nice home for you too. I wonder what they will think if they ever reopen your box to find not an ancient skull but a modern replica. Although by that time you may be ancient yourself."

"I think perhaps that man has spent a little too long on his own, or with his nose in his books," whispered Auntie Lottie in my ear.

"Right let's zip you up and get out of here. Come on, ladies, gently does it now, we don't want to be caught with the skull in hand."

"At least he has stopped quoting *Hamlet*," Auntie Lottie whispered, as she made for the door.

The gate clunked closed again.

"Ah, Stewart, I wondered if it was you." A tall policeman towered above us.

Blood rushed to my face; I could hear it thunder through my ears. I was taking short breaths and trying not to be sick at the same time. What were we going to do? I had thought this skull was supposed to stop bad things from happening.

"Oh my, is that you, Ruairidh Macleoid? It is, isn't it? Well I never, just look at you. How are you doing? I haven't seen you since, well, since… was it Rob the Dog and Jane's wedding?" Auntie Lottie had gone from the quiet robber to her normal animated self.

"Lottie, Lottie, my, look at you. What are you doing here? I heard you were living it up in a city down south."

"Ach, you know what it is like. The Highlands call you back eventually. I'm at home in Blàs now for good," replied Auntie Lottie.

"Is that right now. Well, well, so what exactly are you doing here right now like?" Ruairidh's jovial tone has been replaced by a firmer one.

"Ach, that was me, Ruairidh, you were right. I left my backpack here at the church earlier. I was just escorting the ladies here back to their hotel and thought I would drop in and pick it up on the way past."

"Ah right then. Only someone reported they heard a shout coming from somewhere near the church. I thought I would investigate, just in case there was some sort of damage being done. You haven't heard anything unusual, have you?"

"No, nothing. We have been too busy blethering to hear anyone else. We had a lot of catching up to do."

"Aye well, I dare say I understand that. Only I know this one's reputation, and if anything unusual or daft was going on, if I remember rightly, Lottie here was never far away." Ruairidh looked sternly across at Auntie Lottie who beamed a wide smile at him. The street light caught a faint twitch of Ruairidh's lips before he looked back at Stewart. There was a momentary deep, brooding silence. I held my breath.

"Okay, I'll say goodnight to you all then and just put it down to a passing drunk maybe. I take it everything it securely looked up for the night, Stewart?"

"Aye, it is that. *Oidhche mhath*, Ruairidh."

"*Oidhche mhath*, Stewart, ladies," and off Ruairidh strolled, eating up the ground with his long strides.

The following morning, well wrapped up, Auntie Lottie and I watched as the casket bearing the replica skull was lowered into its final resting place. Stewart stood solemnly by. Surprisingly, Ruairidh was also there, a puzzled look on his face. He knew we had been up to something, I felt sure. But he thankfully couldn't work out what.

That same afternoon back in Blàs, we watched as Old Tam placed the real skull in a beautiful ash box that Paul of the Sheds had found in the back of one of his buildings. The box was then placed in a bigger steel one along with documents describing the finding of the skull and its safe return to the village. No names were mentioned. These would find their way into the village legends.

We all trooped into the forest where, despite the whole event supposedly being a tightly kept secret, many of the community lined the route. Peter the Pipes played a lament as we lowered the box. Maureen said a few words and thanked everyone for their effort in returning the skull to its rightful place.

Once the box was covered over, a young yew tree was planted on top. Folklore would have us believe the ancient druids regarded the tree as sacred. It was believed the yew would help lead a soul to eternal life in the spiritual world, while its branches remained forever green.

"Stroma, Stroma, have you heard anything yet?" It was Stag, followed by Fawn, followed by Gillie Dubh. Gillie Dubh, another of Whisky's pups, had worked wonders since Auntie Lottie had arrived, pup in arms, at their house one night. The puppy had been Fawn's constant companion ever since. Jill's presence and the pup had combined to have a profound effect on Fawn after the trauma of the cave-in. Her self-imposed mute-like state had shifted. She squealed in delight as Malt and Gillie Dubh sprung at each other then crouched down and tumbled as they greeted each other in glee.

Thankfully, Stag had been outnumbered by his siblings when it came to naming their pup. Unsurprisingly, he had suggested Skull as an appropriate name for him. He was not delighted with the thought of naming their dog after a Scottish Fairy. However, Jill had explained to him that a Gillie Dubh was generally friendly to children, but a bit wild. Better than that, at least as far as Stag was concerned, it was also where the army got the name for their camouflage ghillie suit, as a Gillie Dubh was reported to be great at hiding in moss and leaves where no one could see him.

Gillie Dubh, unlike his sibling, was a handsome dark pepper Dandie. Fawn had both Malt, who had never quite made it back to Auntie Lottie's, and her pup sitting eagerly awaiting their expected treat. I knew what Stag was asking about, and he wouldn't be happy with the answer, but he would have to learn that things went at their own pace. A difficult lesson for any person, never mind how old.

"Sorry, Stag, but with everything else going on, I'm afraid getting the funding for the exhibition will take time. We have to get the paths completed in the woods before we even start on the exhibition room."

"But I'll be all grown up by then."

"Look, I was speaking to your teacher, and she is arranging a visit near the end of term to Edinburgh where you can see all sorts of ancient finds in the museum. Inverness Museum is coming to help with your project on ancient civilisation as well. You never know, maybe the UHI will allow you to go on their dig. I know it is frustrating, but it takes a lot of time and effort to get this sort of thing up and running properly."

Since the burial of the skull, Stag had shifted his attention to commemorating it within the exhibition centre.

"I was running a computer game the other day where ancient tribes battle against each other. You can make villages and find out lots of interesting things as well. I could come along and set it up in the school for you to check out if you want?" Scott's voice rolled over my shoulder. I didn't even know he was back.

Stag's face lit up. "Yes, that would be way better than learning about them fairies and what they ate and boring fings like that. Come on, Fawn, I want to tell Gordie and the others we are going to see battles."

Gillie Dubh took one last look at his sister and tottered off after his pack.

"You're back then?" Obvious, I knew, but I couldn't think what else to say. This was the first time I had seen Scott since before Christmas.

"Yes, and for good. My flat is sold, furniture is in storage and Aunt Ellen is happy to put me up until I can find something more permanent here."

"Oh, you hoping to buy here then?"

"Well, we will see how things turn out. I'll start renting first and see if anything develops from there. I can't stay with Aunt Ellen indefinitely. She has her own life. I had been kind of hoping maybe your Auntie Lottie would have finally moved in with Paul of the Sheds so I could have looked into renting her place, but Ellen says nothing is moving fast there."

"Long story involving dogs, and proposals and, well, just Auntie Lottie really. You hungry, do you want some lunch?"

"Aye, that would be nice. It will give us time to catch up. Speaking of dogs, I see you have acquired one yourself." Scott bent down and rubbed Malt's ears.

"Well, actually it was Malt I was offering lunch to, but why don't you head along with us to the hall? They've got some nice soup on, and I need to talk to some of the hall committee who I will probably find there anyway."

It was warm and smelt inviting as we opened the external doors. Thankfully, most of the businesses in the area had taken on our suggestion of following the Borders example and were happily catering for our hairy four-legged friends. Old Tam and Shep were sitting beside Jock who had his collies sleeping quietly under the table. Ellen was on duty, dishing out soup. Mary, Maureen and Auntie Lottie, Whisky at her feet, were deep in conversation at another table. Malt decided that was where we were going. She stretched and pulled us toward Auntie Lottie and, ultimately, Whisky. Scott offered to pick up our soup and sandwiches while I joined my friends.

"I never see him nowadays. I mean, I'm a dog lover myself as you know, but he is always out and about with that hound. As for physical contact, well, I'm a demonstrative woman myself, and here I am at my stage in life playing second fiddle to a damn dog," Auntie Lottie complained.

"Well dear, far be it for me to judge, but you have kept that poor man of yours dangling like a fly caught in your web. It is hardly surprising he has found something else to love," Mary said.

Auntie Lottie huffed. "I suggested we all go out for a walk the other day. Only we couldn't even have a conversation. Every time I opened my mouth, he would say something to Dylan. If I took his hand, two seconds later he would be throwing a ball for the dog. As to cuddling up on the couch, I can't get near him. Dylan is there first. If I wasn't a dog lover myself, I would boot that hound out."

"I kept telling her maybe he's just enjoying having a dog about. The novelty will wear off soon," Maureen said as she patted Blether who sat firmly on her knee.

"Well, excuse me for pointing it out," said Auntie Lottie, "but it hasn't exactly worked for you now, has it? That puppy should be on the floor with the rest of the dogs."

"Not at all, Lottie. Blether here is a very discerning wee lady. She can't be down on the floor with the rest of them. She needs her mummy's cuddles, don't you now, my wee precious, you don't like getting your wee paws wet or dirty, do you?" Blether snuggled further into Maureen, her large pink bow getting squashed in the process. Auntie Lottie raised her eyes to the ceiling.

"Now we have two of them totally besotted. I probably should be thankful Paul didn't take on one of Whisky's pups. I would have been disregarded totally."

"At least you will have him all to yourself at bedtime," Mary interjected with a gleam in her eye.

"Don't get her started, Mary," Maureen mumbled into Blether's coat.

"Bedtime," shrieked Auntie Lottie, just as Scott arrived with our tray. Silence blanketed the room. "Bedtime, don't get me started about that."

"Maybe I should go, and let you ladies talk?" suggested a rather nervous-looking Scott.

"Not at all, Scott. You come and sit down beside me. We were just finding out how Lottie was feeling toward Paul's new dog." What was Mary up to with that sparkle and mischievous little smile? Why would she willingly allow Auntie Lottie to crank up her anger again? I could tell Mary had an agenda, I just wasn't sure what it was.

"Paul's got a dog. Not another one of your pups then, Lottie, is it? It seems a fair number have never left the village," Scott said in all innocence.

"Well, why should they have gone anywhere else? They are all loved well here, although some seemed to be more spoilt than loved." She sniffed in Maureen's direction, who appeared not to take any offence at the suggestion, rather she carried on feeding Blether from her plate.

"I'll have you know, unlike like some big brutes, my dogs do not smell or make loud noises."

Well, that wasn't true. I'd had Malt only a short time, and already her bark was much louder than you'd expect for such a little dog. Not a yap, but a full-fledged low bark, and as to her snoring, well, let's just say the volume on the telly sometimes had to go up a notch or two.

"Nor do they take up so much of the bed that you can't get your legs down. I'm having to sleep with my knees to my chin. I've woken up in the night thinking Paul has his arm around me, to find it's that bloody hound come between us with his paw. And that's not the worst of it. Not by far. This morning… disgusting it was, disgusting. I was sure Dylan had got off the bed during the night. There I was enjoying a nice wee cuddle. I turned around expecting to see Paul, and that great mutt slurped all the way down my face with his tongue."

Barely suppressed laughter chortled around the table. Auntie Lottie scowled. Before she could say anything, Maureen intervened. "Lottie, I really don't want to know about your love life if you don't mind." Only we knew she would be filing away this little piece of information for later use.

"I would have had no problem if it had been Paul showing me some intimacy. But no, it was that bloody dog. Licked my face from forehead to chin with his doggy breath and slobber. Not a nice way to be woken up, I can tell you. I've seen what goes in that dog's mouth."

Hilarity and groans of 'yuck' erupted among the group.

"Well, really," Auntie Lottie said, picking up Whisky's lead and standing up, "I can see I'm not getting much sympathy from any of you. I always expected to play second fiddle to that boat of his. It is as good as any mistress at keeping his attention. I never expected I'd lose his affection to a hairy four-legged male. I'll see you at four, Mary, goodbye." She pulled her dignity around like a shroud and marched off, Whisky jogging in her wake.

Our giggling finally got free rein.

"Oh my," Maureen said, "that was an awful way to wake up."

"Do you think it is the dog or just disappointment that it wasn't Paul?" Mary twinkled.

"Mary, I would be shocked at you, if I didn't already know what you were like." Maureen laughed. "What are you meeting her for later anyway? Haven't you had enough of her on her high horse?" Maureen could not quite let go of any chance to gather further information.

"Ach, we're just having a wee chat, that's all. We had arranged it before we all met up here by chance. I'd ask you to come along, Maureen, but I know you are visiting the Maclean's to talk about their naming ceremony at that time, and I wouldn't want to interfere with that, being as it's so important and all. The rest of you will all be working I expect, so it will be just me and Lottie."

This was all said in her soft, lilting voice. It left none of us in any doubt, however, that we were definitely not invited. It confirmed my suspicions that Mary was engaged in something that none of us here was privy to, at least not right then. But I was sure we would find out soon enough, and I was right.

3 4

There was a big sky by the time I got back home. I stood mesmerised as I shut the car door and watched the Northern Lights glitter and wave in the heavens above. Stars shone through the colourful display as the night sky danced above. A gentle tug pulled me sidewise. Malt didn't rate the aurora borealis, much preferring her supper and a nice cosy place to sleep. My little companion was slowly taking the place of Auntie Lottie who I hadn't seen since that day in the hall.

Few language courses were run between January and February. I was still busy, however, with other priorities taking precedence. My presence was still required in many of the small communities around the area. Never mind how much technology was available, nothing took the place of a real face-to-face meeting. In many situations, it was the unofficial chat at the beginning and end of meetings that often provided the real reason the group was finding things difficult.

Although I missed Auntie Lottie's cheerful chat on these journeys around the area, not having her comments constantly invading my thoughts was a relief in many ways. Malt's company allowed me to appreciate the peace and quiet that a dog's companionship could bring. To a certain degree though,

Malt could be more work. Auntie Lottie could normally be trusted to wait until we hit civilisation before she needed to find a toilet. Malt, on the other hand, required the car to stop immediately once she started whining.

Untreated snow and ice covered the lay-bys and country paths, leaving it nearly impossible to walk. We slipped and slid our way over the surface. Me carefully, Malt without a care once she had relieved herself. It had felt strange at first, stopping and getting out of the car between one village and the next. I normally would have carried on till I reached my nearest destination. However, as long as I was wrapped up, I had come to enjoy these little stops. The locals in each area, after fussing over Malt, were pleased to be able to share their knowledge of the most pleasurable walks to take your dog on. I'd even found some for myself. All these places I had passed for years and promised myself I would come back to and never had had now been checked out and thoroughly sniffed over by Malt. She had added another element to my enjoyment of the Highlands.

"Stroma, thank goodness you are back. I saw your car lights. Get the kettle on. We need to talk." Auntie Lottie bent down to Malt. "Who's a good girl then, where have you been today? Did you miss your Auntie Lottie then? Whisky has been missing you too, haven't you, girl?"

"Auntie Lottie, you nearly gave me a heart attack. What are you doing sneaking around at this time of night in the dark?"

"Firstly, I do not sneak. Secondly, it may be dark – it is February after all – but it is not late. Thirdly, I could do with a hot chocolate, or maybe a wee malt whisky. No, no, not you, you daft pair. Maybe naming you like that wasn't so clever. Should we change your names to Dram and Buie maybe?" Auntie Lottie gently pushed the little dogs away from her legs as we walked inside.

"Ah, that's better," she said as she settled into the chair with her chosen drink.

"Okay, what is it that couldn't wait till morning?"

"It's Maureen. She needs our help, but she won't ask, silly besom that she is."

"Why? What's wrong?" This was a bit of a shock; Maureen rarely needed our help – she was very independent. I couldn't recall the last time she had asked us for any.

As if Auntie Lottie had been reading my mind she added, "It's her pride, you know, won't ask for anyone's help. You know what she is like. Lives by that proverb 'a worry shared is a worry halved', by spreading everyone else's troubles around, but nothing about herself. Oh no, you never hear about her private life. But we are all about to now, and she is scared, very scared about what to do about it."

"Okay, so what can we do? I take it she hasn't asked for your help either?"

"Well, not exactly, but she is going to need it. The poor woman is going demented. I've spoken to Ellen and Mary, and obviously, Paul knows."

Given the recent dealing with Auntie Lottie about Paul, that wasn't at all obvious to me. "And now you know too."

"Know what? You haven't told me anything, but it can't be that bad, surely."

"Well, you'll hear about it tomorrow anyway, so here goes. It's Eric, Maureen's husband, he is alive and, what's more, coming to visit her tomorrow."

According to legend, rumour or local modern history, depending on how you want to view it, Maureen and Eric had been a couple since the dawn of time. In reality, it was their parents who had had a deep friendship. They were constantly in each other's houses from the day their children were born, two days apart.

Eric and Maureen were more thrown together by the circumstance of their parent's close relationship. Eventually, the families made a joint decision. They moved away to Spain for a better life and sunshine when Eric and Maureen were fourteen.

Maureen found herself cast adrift from her close childhood friends – Ellen, Auntie Lottie, and my mum. Eric, who had always been a quiet soul, had found it equally difficult. They clung together as their parents enjoyed their new life which, according to Maureen, consisted mainly of partying every night. By the time she was sixteen, she and Eric had married and set up home with their parents' blessings. Or rather, as Maureen would later admit, with her parents' blessing and his mother weeping at the altar.

Maureen and Eric lived a relatively happy life for a few years, but as they grew up, they also grew apart. They could sense it themselves, and then Maureen's dad died as the result of a work accident. This was followed quickly by her mother going off with Eric's father. They'd been having an affair for years, it turned out. The pair disappeared together to start again in South Africa. Thus leaving Eric's mother blaming Maureen and her family for all her troubles.

Rumours and gossip were rife in the British community where they lived, putting more pressure on Eric and Maureen's marriage. When Eric's mother decided to up sticks again, Maureen had had enough. By mutual consent, she and Eric separated. He left shortly afterward with his mother to pastures new. Maureen herself, disillusioned with love and Spain, decided to return to her roots: Blàs. She longed for the comfort and security she had felt as a child and the warmth and love of the friendships of her youth.

"It just happened; it wasn't intentional." She further explained to me the following day in Mary's kitchen. "Only when people asked what had happened to us all, I found it difficult and said I'd rather not talk about it. I was fed up of being discussed and pointed at when I was in Spain. Our parents were not exactly the shy and retiring sort, everybody seemed to know them and what they got up to, even the locals. I wasn't thinking straight by the time I got home.

"When someone said they had heard about an accident, I said it was true, thinking of my dad, and before I knew it, everyone believed that it was Eric who had died in this accident. People assumed that was why I was so upset and unable to talk about it. You know how rumours start here, and how often people get the wrong end of what's happening."

I bit down hard on my lip to stop myself saying 'that would mostly be because it was you who started the rumours' but stopped myself. It was hard enough for Maureen to have to dredge all this up from her past.

"As time went on, I got mentally stronger, but I couldn't change what people believed. I couldn't risk being cast aside again if anyone found out. It just got easier and easier to believe that no one would ever know. It's one of the reasons I try and get all the news out as soon as possible. If I get it wrong, then someone can put it right quickly. Nothing is buried. No one is suffering, haunted by their past, just waiting for someone to find out and realise what a fraud they are. And now this – years later, things like this happen. Your ex-presumed-dead-husband decides he wants to show his children where he was brought up." Maureen looked across at me. "Oh, I'm so sorry, Stroma, your mum would be so disappointed in me too."

I looked across at Maureen's face as silent tears trickled down her cheeks. Blether, sensing her mistress' distress, stared lovingly at Maureen's face with her big, soft brown eyes, and gently sniffed at her tears. Maureen hugged her close. Only she could have come up with such skewed logic, but we all knew Maureen's way of thinking was unique, to say the least.

"Ach away with you, Maureen. My mum would never have been disappointed in you; she would have told you she loved you, that you were one of her best friends but were as daft as a brush punishing yourself with worry all these years. Then she would have laughed her socks off at how daft you had been, hugged you, wiped your eyes and handed you a dram. Much like Mary is doing now."

"I never laughed, lass," Mary said as she handed Maureen a tissue and a dram.

"Yes, you are right, Mary, but mum would have. She laughed at everything."

"Aye, she did that, right enough," Ellen interjected.

"What with you losing Helen, I don't know what you must think of me?" Maureen said.

Ellen reached across and held Maureen's hand. "I lost one of my soulmates, this past year. I don't want to lose someone else I love. I don't agree with you about not telling us before this, and I can't say I can defend what you have done, but I can, knowing you and who you are, understand how you got yourself into this situation. In the end, life is too short as I know to my cost. You were young, in pain. I think you have suffered enough over this, Maureen. We all need to lay this to rest."

"And what exactly do you have in mind for that, Ellen?" Auntie Lottie, as always, picked up on any hint Ellen laid down of a plan on the brew. "And seeing as Eric is due in about three hours, I don't think that gives us very long."

Ellen's answer to saving face for Maureen, and dispelling any initial shock in the community, was to come up with our own version of Eric's resurrection. Old Tam was the first to be told. If there were going to be any awkward questions, they would come from him. Only they didn't. He had either forgotten the presumption that Maureen's husband was dead or hadn't been aware that it was what everyone had assumed anyway.

There would be some who would be very doubtful if we managed to pull off our little plan, but no one would be able to prove one way or other whether Maureen had said that her husband had died. In reality, it had to be said that Maureen had never uttered the words, "My husband died." So, in a way, we were only righting a mis-held belief. It would only be the older members of the population who had any idea that Maureen had ever even had a husband anyway. Anyone under the age of about thirty-six wouldn't have known or cared much about Maureen or her husband, deceased or not. Once Eric left, everything would quieten down again.

The plan was fairly simple – well, we didn't have time for anything more complicated. Ellen was to waylay Old Tam at the shop when he went for his lunchtime snoop at the daily newspapers. As soon as she left Ellen's house, Auntie Lottie would begin to casually mention around the village how nice it was that Eric, Maureen's ex-husband, was coming for a catch-up along with his family, to show them where he was brought up. When some shocked locals exclaimed, "But she said he was dead," or, "Aye, but he died years ago," Auntie Lottie would fake surprise and say no, you must have misunderstood, it was Maureen's dad that had died. Maureen had come back home after she and Eric divorced, and they had stayed in contact ever since.

I had to position myself in such a way that I could pretend that I was just passing. Then Auntie Lottie would hail me. "Here, Stroma, did you hear that Maureen's ex-husband is coming for a visit?" To which I was to reply, "Oh, that's nice, Mum liked him. She used to say it was so sad when Maureen and he decided to split up in Spain." Or, "I expect he will see big changes since he left," anything, as long as it made it look like I knew he had been alive all this time. That way any shock or disbelief would be squashed before it even got a chance to take hold. The important thing was to make sure that this was heard by the right – or wrong – people, depending on your feelings on the matter.

After a few initial strange looks, people appeared to accept that perhaps their assumptions regarding Maureen's husband had been mistaken. Ellen even overheard Betty MacDonald claim to Patricia MacFlynn, "Of course I knew Eric was alive. Haven't they kept in contact all these years? Everybody who knows them well knows that."

By the time Eric, his wife and two sons appeared, people were greeting him on the street or waving and smiling at him from a distance.

"It is so nice to see you again, Eric, and of course meet your family. Such a lovely surprise," Mary said, as she greeted them when they came into the hall for refreshments.

"Not half as much of a surprise as it was for Maureen," Auntie Lottie whispered in my ear, and of that she was right.

Blue sky, cool sunshine and the tentative shoots of apple blossom. Spring had sprung at last. The taste of new beginnings and anticipation flavoured the atmosphere. It wasn't just the early bright weather that was putting that spring in Auntie Lottie's step. She and Paul of the Sheds had finally reconciled their differences, and the date for their wedding was looming. The pitter-patter of otterhound puppy paws was expected, and both Paul and Auntie Lottie were delighted.

"I'm that glad he has taken that brute back to where he belongs. Although, I will miss Dylan. This way I can get used to having a bigger dog around in stages, as he grows up," she informed me as we met up outside the shop.

I was on my way to Mary's after picking her up some essential shopping – wine gums which she deemed one of her tastier sins. I could think of some sweets that were way more potent, but Giulietta was back home visiting family, and so her wares were not to be had. By the time I arrived back, Mary already had the kettle on waiting for me.

"I'd invited Grace as well, but she is working today. Ach, everybody is working it would seem, so you and me can have a cosy wee chat." I was tempted to tell her I was working too, and this break meant I wouldn't be finishing until late that evening, but I knew that reality would be lost on her as it was with most people.

I was a bit apprehensive – 'a cosy wee chat' with Mary could often result in a major prod into my personal life with a cunning, but often misplaced, action plan quickly formulating in her mind. She scrutinised me carefully as she handed me my tea. I had obviously passed some test as she smiled and twinkled at me, nodding her head.

She couldn't know; I mean, how could she? Then the tell-tale red flush crept up my neck onto my face. *Bugger.*

"You are looking well, Stroma, I'll say that for you. Well and happy, lass." She grinned sweetly. I squirmed in my seat, but I need not have worried. She had others in her sights, thankfully. "You will have heard that Paul and Lottie are finally tying the knot. What a fuss that woman has made. That poor man, kept him treading on hot coals, so she did. She just needed a wee push to get her down that aisle. It has worked out fine now, wouldn't you say? I am right looking forward to their wedding. I take it Iona will make it at the last minute, as usual?"

That was one of Mary's trademarks. She wouldn't directly say, unless asked, that she had been meddling, or rather, as she put it, 'lending a helping hand' or, as in some cases, 'a gentle boot up the backside'. But she liked it to be known that she had been the instigator in resolving any 'wee hitches' along the road to people's happiness.

I took a few minutes and reviewed what she had said. After a slurp of my tea, I put together the hints she had dropped and asked what I hoped was the right question.

"So, Mary, I don't suppose you know what changed Auntie Lottie's mind, do you? Only the last time we talked, I wasn't even sure they were going to stay together. In fact, until Eric turned up, I got the distinct impression from Auntie Lottie that

Paul of the Sheds' passions had been moved firmly onto that big dog of his. What happened to it, by the way? One minute it was here, then I go away for a few days and come back to find it missing, and the big romance is back on. Don't suppose you know anything about what happened, do you?"

Unsurprisingly, she did.

It transpired that Dylan the dog was not a lost dog or even a dog that had been looking for a permanent home. Paul's great friendly beast of a hound already had a very nice home, thank you very much, and was more than happy to get back to it, as was his owner, Andrew, to have him back. Andrew had broken his leg and had been unable to walk Dylan until it was properly healed.

Mary knew about Andrew, unsurprisingly, from Maureen who knew a friend of a relative of… well, through her usual channels. Paul had been keeping in touch with the Otterhound Association, as he was keen to get a puppy he could train. It was at that point in the story that I remembered what had tickled me before. Paul had said he wanted to train an otterhound to track missing people using scent, but you had to start that when they were young. Dylan was old. I distinctly remembered Paul referring to him as an old man, but I hadn't picked up on it at the time. Maybe he had been trying to include me in his little scheme.

Anyway, between the Otterhound Association and Maureen's contacts, Paul was approved as a foster carer for Dylan while Andrew recuperated. This allowed Paul of the Sheds time to see if he did indeed like the size and nature of such an endangered breed. Meanwhile, his name was put forward to a breeder as a possible owner of any pups that might become available. Mary's role in all this had been to advise both Maureen and Paul on how to handle the situation with Lottie.

Maureen was to keep quiet about the whole thing, which could not have been easy, but she, like Mary, was anxious to see her friends happy and settled.

Paul was to simply love the dog. "Well, more than just love, Dylan. Spoil him, and he would have needed it too, having to leave his own home for a virtual stranger's at his age. I told Paul he had to put all of his attention, especially when Lottie was about, on the dog. Take him for loads of walks, scratch his belly and ears, and allow him access to his couch and bed, that sort of thing. I knew Lottie wouldn't fight for Paul if his attentions wandered to another woman. She would have simply decided that, if he didn't want her, then she didn't want him. It would have hurt her, but she would never fight another woman for a man's affections, but a dog, well, that was a different matter. Especially when she has one of her own now and understands the power they have over your heart. You are like shadows, aren't you?" She bent down and placed Malt on her lap. "You creep into our hearts, seep into our blood and our very souls, and we can't remove you. Only you get caught too, as you are inside us, we are just as much a part of you. Isn't that right, little lady?" As Mary fed Malt a bit of biscuit, her brown, solemn eyes bored into Mary's. It was a little embarrassing to watch such blatant use of the 'I love only you forever' routine from Malt. Mary chuckled, well used to this form of manipulation from her years of working with children. "Anyway," she continued, "it seems to have worked. Lottie soon realised that she didn't want to be replaced by a dog or anyone else. With Paul not so anxious to trail around after your aunt, or indeed bow to her every wish, Lottie eventually changed her ways. She always was a bit of a flighty one. Paul was so scared she would bolt if he stood his ground. But I knew she wasn't going to do that. Anyone could see how she felt. They just had to redress the balance between them, to equal it up so to speak.

"So, when is our darling Iona going to appear for this wedding? I understand you are both going to be bridesmaids."

And just like that, due to a combination of Mary's meddling, large dogs and resurrected husbands, Auntie Lottie had finally decided that the time was right for her wedding.

36

"What do you mean exactly? That you lost your phone in a chemical toilet? No, no, forget that, I don't think I want to know." After all, it wasn't exactingly the first time Iona had broken, misplaced, forgotten, sat on, drowned, melted, or anything else it was possible to do to a phone. She thankfully refused to buy anything but a cheap mobile due to her mistreatment of them. If there was a phone equivalent to the SSPCA she would have been charged with gross cruelty to phones dozens of times. "Well, whose phone have you got now?" Of course, it was a friend, or more correctly a friend of a friend, also a Highlander, who was returning north.

She had boarded the train, a day late of course, with him and had invited him to the wedding as a thank you for letting her use his phone. Thankfully, knowing Iona, Auntie Lottie had already allowed for one or two extras. "You know, just in case she comes home with a crowd of friends. When will she stop bringing home all these randoms she meets? Honestly, what a girl." Auntie Lottie was of the firm belief that Iona brought all these strangers home with her so she would have a good excuse to leave again. "She has a fear deep-down that you will force her to stay, daft wee thing."

"I love my sister dearly, but could you imagine if she stayed here? She would be awful. Champing to get away, thinking I was trying to keep her here when nothing could be further from the truth. Although, I have to admit, it would be nice if she stayed a bit closer. Inverness would be just fine. She'd have her freedom to live her life, and so would I."

Iona was brilliant, funny, lovable and hard-working. All her virtues were combined with a quirky, offbeat nature. She blew hot and cold, and although I wouldn't change her for the world, she was hard work to live with for long. Her timekeeping was like that of many who worked around the seasons rather than around a nine-to-five-five-day week: awful.

I was thankful she was at least on the train. I could only hope that she didn't get waylaid in Inverness on the way home. We still had two days before the wedding. I had her bridesmaid dress here. She had finally succumbed to shopping for it after Auntie Lottie had stepped in and offered to go down to Edinburgh and accompany her around the shops. Two days after Auntie Lottie has spoken with her, Iona phoned me from a changing room. Phone angled, she presented her choice.

"Look, it's long, the right colour, and it fits."

"Iona, I think it has to fill more than just the right colour and size. Do you like it? Does it feel comfortable?" I was glad I wasn't with her. Her attempts at clothes shopping were legendary. Apart from Auntie Lottie, no one who knew her ever offered to accompany her. Helping at a safe distance was always preferable.

She swirled around the cubicle and posed a few times. "It's not bad, even though I say it myself. It doesn't make me look too girly. I was worried Auntie Lottie would insist on something flowery, or pink, or worse – frills."

"Even Auntie Lottie wouldn't go as far as frills, Iona. So what do you think? I like it on you. The colour suits and it hangs nicely."

"I agree. It is not as awful as I thought it would be. So, should I take it, do you think? You're sure it looks okay?"

"It looks lovely on you. How does it feel compared to the others you have tried?" There was a slight pause.

"Well, it is definitely my favourite to date. Yes, definitely. I'll get it."

"Iona, exactly how many dresses have you looked at, or even tried on?" I knew her so well. "Oh my God that is your first one, isn't it? You can't just grab it because you can't be bothered trying on anything else." I stopped when I saw her expression. "Or maybe you can, if you look that good in it."

She smiled into the phone "You know, Stroma, you're not bad as sisters go. And you have a lot better taste than me. I know it's my first dress, but I do like it. I'm not buying it just because it is the first one I tried on. Trust me, I don't think I'll find anything else I'll like so much."

And that was it. Iona had chosen her dress. I was in Inverness the next day and picked up an identical one in my size and her size too. It wasn't outside the realms of possibility that she would leave her dress behind in her flat.

Despite my concerns, Iona turned up later that day, less the Highlander she had met on the train. "Ach, he was meeting some of his family right off the train, and my other friends in Ness were either busy or not wanting to come out on a worknight. So, I just came straight here." She dumped her backpack, grabbed a shower, some food, then we both headed over to Auntie Lottie's. Mary, Ellen and Maureen were already there. Morag, Karen, and Grace were expected later. Giulietta, who was fast becoming a permanent member of our circle was coming with them. Rather than the rowdy and dirty modern blackenings, Auntie Lottie had voiced her opinion that she thought the more old-fashioned type, where the women of the village got together and generally had a woman's night in, was more her kind of thing. Someone so proud of her hair was not about to allow it to get spattered with gunge and muck of the awful smelling kind. Instead, an evening of fragrant indulgence was planned. Our hair *was* covered, but in deep-conditioning oils, our finger and toes nails were washed, varnished and polished. We were pampered and cosseted. Snacks and drinks accompanied laughter, songs and stories. Iona, who in normal circumstances avoided anything resembling this sort of event, threw herself into the evening, delighting everyone with her comments and reminiscences. If she had chosen to stay in Blàs, there was no doubt she could have taken over the mantle of the community storyteller, but that would never happen. Iona would only ever grace us with her brief, rainbow-coloured visits. Like a butterfly dancing in, stealing the eye and igniting a spark of wonder before vanishing again for a time.

We left Auntie Lottie, full of laughter, food and a great sense of wellbeing. Everyone agreed that if they were to be brides, they would go back to this old-fashioned form of the blackening. As Auntie Lottie said, "I'd much rather my hair was smelling and looking this good by the end of the night than dripping in fish guts while I'm trying not to throw up." But then, where Auntie Lottie was concerned, her hair was her crowning glory. Now, all we had to do was get her down the aisle.

Wafts of sweet, heady scent flowed and flavoured each breath the congregation took as sunshine yellow surrounded the clearing now referred to as Cnocanach. It reflected, as many Gaelic words did, the shape of an area. In this case, the hilly semi-circles had been created out of the earth. Their existence was an open invitation to sit and relax. Its description wasn't the only reason for the name choice, however, mostly it was because the village children loved the sound of the word.

Prickly gorse at the height of its season added to the joyous atmosphere below. Pale yellow primroses mixed with late snowdrops, and croci added splashes of purple and white. Cherry blossom fluttered down, natural confetti showering friends and family as they listened to a clarsach player's enchanting melody. The pure sound evoked impressions of water drops on a pond.

Paul of the Sheds stood with his excited puppy at his feet, and a huge smile on his face as Auntie Lottie walked toward him. His bride was elegant in a midnight dress and soft tartan shawl. Yet another one of Jill's creations, its tartan colours mixing that of the two families who would be joined together through this marriage. Iona and I had similar shawls to keep out the slight chill that could be felt this early in the year. Grace was smiling, encouraging her son Cavan forward into her arms, as Whisky, adorned in a blue bow around her neck, trotted proudly at his side. Thankfully, the paths, at least as far as Cnocanach were finished, so no wellies had been needed on the day. Instead, most guests wore smart boots and low heels.

Maureen's voice fought with that of the spring birdsong, as she led the service and the happy couple in their vow-taking. It was the piper who finally won the battle of who could create the loudest melody. Then we fell in behind him and withdrew from the woods to head back to the hall.

The theme of the woods, so important in our lives over the year, continued into the hall where branches of cherry trees, festooned with pink and white blossom, hung from the ceiling. Leaves and pinecones, pots of daffodils, and spring flowers added to the springtime feel. Bare seedlings that would eventually be planted within the forest covered tables and edged the floors. Villagers, old and new, swarmed into the hall like bees returning to their hive.

The Smiths were there, handing out the last remaining bottles of bubbly apple wine instead of the usual champagne. Fawn followed Swallow swooping around the hall chasing after their brothers, causing shouts and laughter to echo in the rafters above. Jill smiled and patted her rounding belly. Another brother or sister would be joining them soon.

Ellen, Giulietta and Scott all stood together sipping their sparkling drinks.

I sighed, wondering what the night would bring as the band took their place.

The conversation abruptly stopped when the piper announced the arrival of the newly married couple in the traditional way. Paul and Auntie Lottie danced their way into the hall. Their guests flocked forward to wish them well.

After the speeches, Maureen announced, "Let the celebrations begin."

I found Mary behind a crowd of admirers and friends holding court.

"Well, Stroma, come over and sit with me a while. My legs need a wee rest before the dancing proper." Her well-wishers took the hint and dispersed among the crowd who now focused on the spread of food available to all.

"Wasn't that a nice wedding? It does my heart good to see those two finally married. What a time we have had, don't you think? And finally, we have my Angus' storytelling legacy covered with these two." Mary nodded in Maureen and Auntie Lottie's direction, where the pair were laughing together at something. "Totally different from my Angus, but I'm sure he would be honoured to see that these two have carried forward his love of the trade. I'm so glad not too many decided to miss this wedding for that special on the TV tonight either." I didn't have the heart to tell her that most of the people here who had been employed as extras on a special of *In the Darkest Depths* would be recording or downloading the programme to watch another day. "And so nice to see Ellen smiling again. That chocolatier is quite a find. I'll not tell you how many of her chocolates I've consumed tonight." Mary's eyes sparkled. "So, my dear Stroma, what will be our next adventure, do you think?"

"Well, I'm hoping we can take it easy for a while. I seem to be spending all my spare time fundraising or applying for grants. I would be happy to have a wee rest from it all, I'm thinking."

"Oh, no dear, that is what helps to keep us a community, looking forward and helping each other. But you are right, there is more to life than just that." She paused and looked around. "Oh, there's Scott, looking for a dance, I believe. Don't keep him waiting too long. I don't want to have to intervene with you two as well." Mary had no qualms or embarrassment about that, I knew. "Life is so exciting sometimes, don't you agree? We never know what is just around the corner as my Angus used to say. Well, lass, I can't wait to see what develops over the next wee while. Now off you go. Scott won't wait forever, at least not without a little help." Mary laughed and took hold of a hand extended to her for a dance.

Off she went, her twinkling eyes and toes taking her around the dance floor. She was totally incorrigible and greatly loved. But she was right, it would be exciting to see what the next year brought. Paul and Lottie swept by with eyes only for each other as I accepted Scott's hand, at least for duration of the next dance.

Recipe Mela Blàs

This recipe was inspired by the chocolate Mela Blàs in the story
and created by the wonderful Highland Thistle Chocolates of
Tain.
Please check the ingredients list for anything you may be allergic
to before you try it.
If you would like to try any others in their range, you will find
them here:
highlandthistlechocolates.co.uk

APPLE AND CINNAMON TRUFFLES

110ml water
75g unrefined golden sugar
400g dark chocolate
120g dark drinking chocolate powder for covering or crushed
nuts of choice
100g freeze-dried diced or apple flakes.
1 cinnamon stick
10g cinnamon powder

1. Place 110ml of water into the pan along with the sugar, cinnamon, and 75g of the diced and flaked apple. Bring to a gentle simmer and do <u>not allow to boil</u> as this will burn and taint the mixture.

2. Chop the chocolate into small pieces ready for adding to the mixture.

3. Pour the simmered syrup over the chocolate slowly, making sure to cover as much of the chocolate as you can.

4. Leave to stand for one minute...! Then start mixing the chocolate, ensuring the syrup is blended into the chocolate, make sure also you take the chocolate mix from around the side of the bowl.

5. Once the chocolate is melted, use a hand whisk to mix vigorously to produce a lovely creamy mixture. You can use a stick blender if preferred.

6. Allow the mixture to cool and transfer into a bowl lined with cling film. Cover the mixture to ensure no air can crust the surface of the mixture. Leave in the fridge for three hours or until firm enough to form into balls or squares.

7. Cut the firmed mixture into small pieces, around 14g – use a set of scales to ensure size consistency.

8. Using the tips of your fingers only, roll the mixture to get the shape you require. Once you have shaped the truffle mixture, now comes the fun part of decorating with either chocolate powder or chopped diced apple, crushed nuts, or even just chocolate sprinkles.

9. The remaining diced or flaked apple now needs to be finely diced to cover the truffles.

10. Place the finely diced apple into a bowl and then roll each ball between your fingers for a few seconds to allow slight melting, then, place in a bowl to coat, rolling the truffles around in the mixture.

11. It may take time to gain the technique, but it will come with practice. Quality control means those not up to standard can be eaten by you...!

BLACKENINGS

Blackenings still take place in Scotland today, although they are not nearly as common as they once were. When at college, I was thrilled to hear an old recording of an Alness woman speaking Gaelic. This was noteworthy for two reasons: it was recorded in the 1950s and so was the first time I had heard the old Easter Ross Gaelic accent. Sadly, that has since died out. However, we have a new one spoken by the many young speakers we have today. Secondly, the woman was speaking about cleaning the feet of the bride before her wedding the following day. I had no idea then that one day that glimpse into an old tradition would eventually find itself into one of my stories. It did leave me thinking that the old ceremony sounds quite nice. I wonder, if more women knew about it, would they would prefer it rather than being pelted with smelly muck. But at least the tradition still survives in some form. Typical Scots that we are, we have, however, managed to turn it upside down, so instead of it being a way of getting spruced up, we have turned it into getting completely slimed down.

TREES, APPLES AND SCOTTISH
SAPPHIRES

Although my mum was a great forager, my knowledge is not nearly as good as hers. I find it difficult enough to spot the difference between one piece of a jigsaw and another, never mind two mushrooms that look alike. Berries to seaweed, she could choose, and we would eat (this has also inspired the theme for my third Blàs book which will follow this one). Not being able to trust my identification skills, I mostly turned to the internet to find the information for *Roots in the Soil*.

Not so for the information on the rowan tree. It has its place in many cultures and is also known as the Quicken Tree, Delight of the Eye and Lady of the Mountain. An Irish myth tells us that the first woman came from the rowan tree. It is also known by some as the Wizard. Perhaps this comes from the belief that druids used rowan branches on funeral pyres. Most tales agree that the rowan, in one way or another, has some connection to the fairy folk, whether for them to dance around or as a gateway between their world and the human world. Rowan were also often grown in graveyards to protect the dead from evil spirits. Even today, many people have rowans planted outside the front of their houses in Scotland to ward off evil spirits and illness, while at the back door, a hawthorn is believed to do the same.

My own neighbour has a lovely rowan tree arch as you walk in their front gate. Rowan, meaning little redhead, is also used as either a girl's or a boy's name. I am sure there are many other beliefs out there associated with this bonnie tree.

Apart from what I learnt growing up, these are the main websites I used to gather interesting facts and cultural references related to trees and foraging:

treesforlife.org.uk

woodlandtrust.org.uk

For making apple juice and cider, I checked out this site:

almostoffgrid-co.uk

There are eighteen letters in the Scottish Gaelic alphabet, each represented by a tree. A Gaelic Alphabet woodland walk already exists in Lochaber. More information on this can be found here:

forestryandland.gov.uk

wildlochaber.com

Scottish Sapphires do exist, but they are extremely rare and have only be found at one location on Lewis so far. They are deep blue without any treatment being required to bring out the colour, unlike sapphires from other countries. Once more, it would be nice to own one!

DOGS

I couldn't, in all honesty, leave out the dogs that accompany me on my many forest walks. Firstly, the rare and totally incorrigible Dandie Dinmont terrier, already immortalised in Sir Walter Scott's novel *Guy Mannering*, the breed also has a whisky and its own tartan. It is lovable, cute and friendly with typical terrier characteristics. Just seeing one makes you smile. If you want to lose yourself on the internet, take a look at the sources listed below, but beware, you will leave them craving a Dandie, and as they are so small, it is easy to consider more than one.

caledoniandandies.com

Also on Facebook, under: Caledonian Dandie Dinmont Terrier Club

As for the otterhound, these are equally as rare. Back in the day, they were used for hunting one of my favourite animals which I won't hold them to blame for. Thankfully, that practice has stopped, but as a result of no longer having a defined job, the breed fell out of fashion. However, their 'sniffing' abilities can be used in many other more productive and helpful areas. One of the best ways to put them to good use though is just as a big, lovable, friendly family dog. True, they love being out chasing, but like many big dogs, they are equally as happy at home, lazing on the couch. I had hoped to own one of my own by now, but they are so difficult to come by. Who knows, maybe one day!

otterhoundclub.co.uk

Also on Facebook, under: Otterhound Club UK

ACKNOWLEDGMENTS

Thanks as always to my editor Fran Lebowitz who gave thoughtful and insightful advice. This story developed into a much more cohesive work of fiction thanks to your input.

Thank you Kat Harvey of Athena Copy once more for your edit, proofreading and comments. To Annemieke Leverenz for producing another cover I love. The addition of the Dandie was so well received

My gratitude and thanks to Highland Thistle Chocolates of Tain for their generosity and help in developing the special chocolate and for your lovely tasting sessions.

I can never complete a book without thanking the Gaelic Books Council and Lisa Story of Leabhraichean Beaga. If they hadn't believed in my Gaelic writing, I would never have taken that leap into English. Thank you all for the confidence you bestowed in me and still do.

Thanks also go to my Eden Court writing buddies, in particular Barbara Henderson for keeping us all together and in touch online. I look forward to being able to meet up once again. I felt your encouragement all the way. Also, my friends in the Society of Authors, Scotland, in particular Mac Logan and Jane

Mackenzie who developed into true writing friends. A special thanks for Jane's lovely quote.

To my sisters, Mandy and Sam, for their love, help and advice, and my mum for her friendship and never-ending support. The dedication at the beginning is to my late aunt: a teacher, an educator and an amazingly strong woman. If she hadn't picked up on my dyslexia and dyspraxia so early, I may never have been able to write anything.

To every one of my readers who has bought any of my books and especially those of you who have taken the time to review them, thank you.

Finally, and always, thank you to my family who has shared the whole working from home experience with me over this last year. For their cups of tea, Kyle for your help with IT, Lucy for your words of encouragement, and Tori for believing I could master some sort of social media. Malcolm, first an apology for the controlled chaos that is my desk, and second a thank you for never once questioning my right to the comfiest work chair. You all continue to be my inspiration.

ABOUT THE AUTHOR

CC Hutton lives and works in the Highlands of Scotland. She spent many years as a Gaelic Development Officer working around the spectacular North Highlands. It inspired her to write her first Blàs of the Highlands book. This is her second in the Blàs series. She writes Gaelic Children's books under the name Ceitidh Hutton. *Grumpa agus an Latha Fuaimneach,* won best young children's book of the year 2019 at the Royal National Mod. She was short-listed in the 2020 Gaelic Literacy Awards for an unpublished story. She is registered with the Scottish Book Trust Live Literacy Programme and is the secretary of the Society of Authors, Scotland as well as a member of ALLI

When not writing, she can be found drinking tea, walking dogs, and taking part in book events, workshops and school visits. She still promotes Gaelic when she can. She can be contacted on her website at cchuttonwriter.com or her Facebook page:

Facebook.com/cchuttonwriter

Lightning Source UK Ltd.
Milton Keynes UK
UKHW011534120921
390445UK00003B/88